LIKE A PUFF OF SMOKE . . .

Sally and Monte and Louis were less than ten miles out of Fort Smith when they saw a wagon coming toward them in the distance.

Sally spurred her horse into a full gallop and raced toward the man in the wagon. As she pulled the horse to a stop, she noticed the man was holding a Winchester Yellow Boy cradled in his arms, the hammer cocked.

She grinned. "Are you Marshal Tilghman?"

He glanced over her shoulder at Monte, and Louis, who were just arriving, and moved the rifle a bit so it covered all three.

"Yeah."

She inclined her head at the rifle. "Are you expecting trouble, Marshal?"

"Expectin' it or not, it usually seems to find me. Who are you an' what can I do for you?"

"My name is Sally Jensen, and I was told you were bringing my husband to Fort Smith to stand trial for murder."

Tilghman nodded and seemed to relax just a bit. "I was."

"What do you mean, was?" Sally asked, moving her horse a little to the side so she could see in the back of the cage. "Isn't Smoke with you?"

"No, ma'am," Tilghman answered shortly.

"Well, where is he?"

"On his way back to Fort Worth, I 'spect."

"Marshal," Sally said, her exasperation clearly showing in her voice. "Would you please tell me what's going on? What about my husband?"

"I'm fixin' to tell you the damnedest story you ever heard, ma'am," the marshal said, grinning as he glanced sideways at her.

Sally shook her head. "Marshal, if you knew Smoke like I do, you'd know nothing you can say about him will surprise me."

JUSTICE OF THE MOUNTAIN MAN

William W. Johnstone

Pinnacle Books
Kensington Publishing Corp.

http://www.pinnaclebooks.com

PINNACLE BOOKS are published by

Kensington Publishing Corp.
850 Third Avenue
New York, NY 10022

Pinnacle and the P logo Reg. U.S. Pat. & TM Off.

First Printing: November, 2000
10 9 8 7 6 5 4 3 2 1

Printed in the United States of America

One

Smoke Jensen buttoned up his buckskin shirt and walked into the kitchen where his wife, Sally, was bent over putting biscuits in the oven. He stepped up behind her and hugged her.

"You shouldn't do that to a man fixing to leave town for a few weeks," he said, his voice husky with desire.

Sally grinned as she leaned back against him. "Why, do what, Mr. Jensen, sir?"

He gave her an extra squeeze. "You know what, you tease."

She turned, placing her arms around his neck. "Do you really have to go, Smoke? Our herd is doing fine without those bulls you want to get."

He poured himself a cup of coffee and sat at the kitchen table, eyeing her with one eyebrow raised. "Sweetheart, it was your idea in the first place to cross our shorthorns with the Santa Gertrudis from Texas. You having second thoughts now?"

She shook her head as she poured herself a cup and sat across the table from him. "Yes, it *was* my idea, but I just hate the idea of you traveling all that way right now, just after that mess with Jim Slaughter was cleared up."*

---

*Heart of the Mountain Man

He grinned. "You think the old man's too old for the trip?"

She shook her head, eyeing the scar on his neck from the bullet wound he'd received in the shootout in Big Rock. "No, but you're just now getting over being shot, and knowing you, it might just happen again on your trip."

"Now what makes you say that? After all, I'll have Cal and Pearlie with me to keep me out of trouble."

"A lot of good that'll do. When the three of you go off on a trip together, it always seems to lead to gunplay."

"But, Sally, we really need those bulls. I know the herd is all right as it is, but if we get some of those Santa Gertrudis bulls from Richard King on the King Ranch down in Texas, it'll almost double the amount of meat on our shorthorn crosses, and make them more resistant to both drought and cold weather."

Sally finished her coffee, got up from the table, and broke three eggs into a cast-iron skillet and began to scramble them, looking over her shoulder at Smoke as she worked. "I know it'll be better, but I hate to see you go that far to get them."

"It won't be so bad. Cal and Pearlie and I'll take the train to Fort Worth and buy some horses there to ride the rest of the way. Heck, most of the trip'll be fun."

She smirked. "Yeah, I know your idea of fun. You and the boys will play poker all the way down there and you'll win their wages for the next year, and then turn around and give them back."

Smoke grinned. "You're probably right, but it will be a lesson they need to learn. Don't play cards with money you can't afford to lose."

She laughed and handed him his plate of scrambled eggs and bacon. "Here, tinhorn," she said, "start on these while I get your biscuits out of the oven."

Smoke noticed a plate of dough on the counter formed

into the shape of bear sign, Sally's famous doughnuts. "What's that I see on the counter?" he asked.

Sally laughed. "You don't think you're going to get Pearlie and Cal out of town without an ample supply of bear sign to take along, do you?"

"Hell, to take enough to last Pearlie until he gets back, we'll have to pack a steamer trunk full!"

A knock came at the door and Cal and Pearlie walked in. Pearlie, a tall, lanky, cowboy with mustache and sun-wrinkled face and sparkling sky-blue eyes, tipped his hat back. "Did I hear something about bear sign?"

Sally held her hand up. "Uh-uh, Pearlie. You stay away from that dough at least until it's baked!"

Pearlie nodded and sat next to Smoke, leaning over as he smelled Smoke's breakfast. "Hmmm, that sure smells good, Miss Sally."

She shook her head. "You and Cal get yourselves some coffee while I scramble up another batch of hen's eggs and bacon."

Almost before the words were out of her mouth, Pearlie, a noted food-hound, had his hat off and was straddling a chair at the table. Cal, younger and a tad more polite, said, "Thank you, Miss Sally," before he removed his hat and took a seat.

As the boys dug into the food, Smoke leaned back and thought about how they'd both come to work for him and Sally, and how they'd since become almost part of the family . . .

Calvin Woods, going on nineteen years old now, had been just fourteen when Smoke and Sally took him in as a hired hand. It was during the spring branding, and Sally was on her way back from Big Rock to the Sugarloaf.

The buckboard was piled high with supplies because branding hundreds of calves makes for hungry punchers.

As Sally slowed the team to make a bend in the trail, a rail-thin young man stepped from the bushes at the side of the road with a pistol in his hand.

"Hold it right there, miss."

Applying the brake with her right foot, Sally slipped her hand under a pile of gingham cloth on the seat. She grasped the handle of her short-barreled Colt .44 and eared back the hammer, letting the sound of the horses' hooves and the squealing of the brake pad on the wheel mask the sound. "What can I do for you, young man?" she asked, her voice firm and without fear. She knew she could draw and drill the young highwayman before he could raise his pistol to fire.

"Well, uh, you can throw some of those beans and a cut of that fatback over here, and maybe a portion of that Arbuckle's coffee too."

Sally's eyebrows raised. "Don't you want my money?"

The boy frowned and shook his head. "Why, no, ma'am. I ain't no thief, I'm just hungry."

"And if I don't give you my food, are you going to shoot me with that big Navy Colt?"

He hesitated a moment, then grinned ruefully. "No, ma'am, I guess not." He twirled the pistol around his finger and slipped it into his belt, turned, and began to walk down the road toward Big Rock.

Sally watched the youngster amble off, noting his tattered shirt, dirty pants with holes in the knees and torn pockets, and boots that looked as if they had been salvaged from a garbage dump. "Young man," she called, "come back here, please."

He turned, a smirk on his face, spreading his hands. "Look, lady, you don't have to worry. I don't even have any bullets." With a lightning-fast move he drew the gun from his pants, aimed away from Sally, and pulled the trigger. There was a click but no explosion as the hammer fell on an empty cylinder.

Sally smiled. "Oh, I'm not worried." In a movement every bit as fast as his, she whipped her .44 out and fired, clipping a pine cone from a branch, causing it to fall and bounce off his head.

The boy's knees buckled and he ducked, saying, "Jimminy Christmas!"

Mimicking him, Sally twirled her Colt and stuck it in the waistband of her britches. "What's your name, boy?"

The boy blushed and looked down at his feet. "Calvin, ma'am, Calvin Woods."

She leaned forward, elbows on knees, and stared into the boy's eyes. "Calvin, no one has to go hungry in this country, not if they're willing to work."

He looked up at her through narrowed eyes, as if he found life a little different than she'd described it.

"If you're willing to put in an honest day's work, I'll see that you get an honest day's pay, and all the food you can eat."

Calvin stood a little straighter, shoulders back and head held high. "Ma'am, I've got to be straight with you. I ain't no experienced cowhand. I come from a hardscrabble farm and we only had us one milk cow and a couple of goats and chickens, and lots of dirt that weren't worth nothing for growin' things. My ma and pa and me never had nothin', but we never begged and we never stooped to takin' handouts."

Sally thought, *I like this boy. Proud, and not willing to take charity if he can help it.* "Calvin, if you're willing to work, and don't mind getting your hands dirty and your muscles sore, I've got some hands that'll have you punching beeves like you were born to it in no time at all."

A smile lit up his face, making him seem even younger

than his years. "Even if I don't have no saddle, nor a horse to put it on?"

She laughed out loud. "Yes. We've got plenty of ponies and saddles." She glanced down at his raggedy boots. "We can probably even round up some boots and spurs that'll fit you."

He walked over and jumped in the back of the buckboard. "Ma'am, I don't know who you are, but you just hired you the hardest workin' hand you've ever seen."

Back at the Sugarloaf, she sent him in to Cookie and told him to eat his fill. When Smoke and the other punchers rode into the cabin yard at the end of the day, she introduced Calvin around. As Cal was shaking hands with the men, Smoke looked over at her and winked. He knew she could never resist a stray dog or cat, and her heart was as large as the Big Lonesome itself.

Smoke walked up to Cal and cleared his throat. "Son, I hear you drew down on my wife."

Cal gulped. "Yessir, Mr. Jensen. I did." He squared his shoulders and looked Smoke in the eye, not flinching, though he was obviously frightened of the tall man with the incredibly wide shoulders standing before him.

Smoke smiled and clapped the boy on the back. "Just wanted you to know you stared death in the eye, boy. Not many galoots are still walking upright who ever pulled a gun on Sally. She's a better shot than any man I've ever seen except me, and sometimes I wonder about me."

The boy laughed with relief as Smoke turned and called out, "Pearlie, get your lazy butt over here."

A tall, lanky cowboy ambled over to Smoke and Cal, munching on a biscuit stuffed with roast beef. His face was lined with wrinkles and tanned a dark brown from hours under the sun, but his eyes were sky-blue and twinkled with good-natured humor.

"Yessir, Boss," he mumbled around a mouthful of food.

Smoke put his hand on Pearlie's shoulder. "Cal, this here chow-hound is Pearlie. He eats more'n any two hands, and he's never been known to do a lick of work he could get out of, but he knows beeves and horses as well as any puncher I have. I want you to follow him around and let him teach you what you need to know."

Cal nodded. "Yes, sir, Mr. Smoke."

"Now let me see that iron you have in your pants."

Cal pulled the ancient Navy Colt and handed it to Smoke. When Smoke opened the loading gate, the rusted cylinder fell to the ground, causing Pearlie and Smoke to laugh and Cal's face to flame red. "This is the piece you pulled on Sally?" Smoke asked.

The boy nodded, looking at the ground.

Pearlie shook his head. "Cal, you're one lucky pup. Hell, if'n you'd tried to fire that thing, it'd of blown your hand clean off."

Smoke inclined his head toward the bunkhouse. "Pearlie, take Cal over to the tack house and get him fixed up with what he needs, including a gun belt and a Colt that won't fall apart the first time he pulls it. You might also help pick him out a shavetail to ride. I'll expect him to start earning his keep tomorrow."

"Yes, sir, Smoke." Pearlie put his arm around Cal's shoulders and led him off toward the bunkhouse. "Now the first thing you gotta learn, Cal, is how to get on Cookie's good side. A puncher rides on his belly, and it 'pears to me that you need some fattin' up 'fore you can begin to punch cows."

Pearlie had come to work for Smoke in as roundabout a way as Cal had. He was hiring his gun out to Tilden Franklin in Fontana when Franklin went crazy and tried to take over Sugarloaf, Smoke and Sally's spread. After Franklin's men raped and killed a young girl in the fracas, Pearlie sided with Smoke and the aging gunfighters he had called in to help put an end to Franklin's reign of terror.*

Pearlie was now honorary foreman of Smoke's ranch though he was only a shade over twenty years old himself. Boys grew to be men early in the mountains of Colorado.

Smoke's thoughts were interrupted when Pearlie stuffed the last of his bacon and eggs into his mouth and washed it down with a giant drink of coffee. "Ah, that's 'bout the best food I ever ate, Miss Sally."

He paused and glanced at the dough sitting on the counter. "Uh, any idea when those bear sign gonna be ready?"

Sally laughed and pointed at the front door. "You men go on out on the porch and have your cigarettes and I'll let you know."

The three men settled on wooden chairs on the porch and all rolled cigarettes to have with their final cups of coffee.

"When you figgerin' on headin' down Texas way, Smoke?" Pearlie asked.

Smoke glanced at the sky, which was the clear, bright blue of a spring morning. The temperature was still in the low fifties, but it promised to be a beautiful day. "I suspect most of the snow'll be out of the passes by now, so the train shouldn't have any problem making it to Texas. How about we get packed and try to get off tomorrow on the afternoon train?"

"Sounds good to me," Cal said, his face brightening at the prospect of travel to far-off places.

Pearlie nodded. "That'll do."

Trail of the Mountain Man

"You got the boys ready for the spring calving and branding?" Smoke asked.

"Yep. An' the foreman over at Johnny North's has said he'll keep a close watch on the place while we're gone and be sure and help if Miss Sally needs anything."

Smoke flipped his butt over the railing into the dirt. "Good, then it's settled. We'll take the buckboard into town in the morning so Sally can get some last-minute shopping done, and then we'll take off."

Pearlie's nose twitched. "You boys smell anything?" he asked.

Smoke sniffed the air and grinned. "Why I do believe that first batch of bear sign smells like it's about ready."

Cal jumped to his feet and started toward the kitchen, but Pearlie grabbed the back of his belt and jerked him back down. "Don't you know better'n to try an' eat 'fore your betters, boy?" he asked as he sprinted toward the cabin door.

"Take it easy, Cal," Smoke said as he got slowly to his feet. "There'll be plenty to go around."

Cal's face fell. "Not if'n Pearlie gets there first. That boy can eat his weight in bear sign!"

Two

The next morning Smoke, along with Sally and Cal and Pearlie, loaded up the buckboard and headed for Big Rock. Smoke and Sally rode up top, with Cal and Pearlie and their luggage in the back of the wagon.

As they entered the town, Sheriff Monte Carson was standing in the door to his office, drinking coffee from a tin cup and puffing on his battered corncob pipe.

Smoke slowed the buckboard and pulled it to the side of the street in front of Monte's office. After he helped Sally down, she said she would be in Ed and Peg Jackson's general store, picking out the provisions she would need while the men were away on their trip to Texas. She gave a small smile. "Why don't you boys go on over to Longmont's and tell your friends good-bye while I'm shopping, Smoke?"

After she left, Monte gave her an approving look. "You got a good woman there, Smoke. One who knows when to step back an' let her man be with his friends."

Smoke nodded. "I know it, Monte. And I'd appreciate it if you and Mary could drop in on her every once in a while when I'm out of town."

"No problem, Smoke," the sheriff answered.

Pearlie shuffled his feet impatiently. "We gonna go on over to Longmont's, Smoke?" he asked.

Monte cocked an eye at Smoke's foreman. "You must

be 'bout starved, Pearlie, since you probably ain't had nothin' to eat since you left the Sugarloaf this mornin'."

Pearlie rubbed his stomach. "Well, now that you mention it, Monte, I could use a bite or two."

"Damn, Pearlie, it ain't been more'n two hours since you ate last," Cal said as the men walked toward Longmont's saloon down the street.

Pearlie put his arm over Cal's shoulder, speaking in a fatherly tone even though he wasn't more than a couple of years older than the boy. "Cal, like I done tole you, ya' gotta eat ever' chance ya get, 'cause you never know when the next opportunity for grub is gonna present itself."

Smoke led the way through the batwings of Louis Longmont's saloon and, as was his habit from years of having men on his trail, immediately stepped to the side of the door and waited for his eyes to adjust to the gloom of the room before he walked further.

Louis Longmont was, as usual, sitting at his private table in a corner of the saloon, drinking coffee laced with chicory and smoking a long, black cigar.

When he saw Smoke and the others, he grinned and waved them over, calling out to a young, black waiter to come to the table.

After the men sat down, Louis glanced at the waiter. "Johnny, I'm sure these men have all had breakfast already, but that lanky one there on the end has never been known to take a seat in this establishment without ordering some nourishment."

Smoke grinned. "You're right, Louis. We'll all have some of Andre's wonderful coffee, but I'm sure Pearlie will want something extra."

"Just a light snack, to get me through till the train leaves, Louis. How about some flapjacks with blueberry syrup and half a pound of bacon on the side?"

"I see that you're moving very well, Pearlie," Louis said. "I guess that wound you suffered during our excitement last month has healed properly."

Pearlie fingered his flank, where a bullet meant for Cal had punched through his side just under the skin when he'd pushed Cal out of the way.*

He made a face, as though in pain. "Well, it still smarts a mite if'n I move wrong, but I guess the discomfort was worth it to save Cal's hide."

"I swear to God," Cal said, an aggrieved expression on his face. "It wern't more'n a scratch, Pearlie. Hell, Doc Spalding didn't even put a bandage on it!"

The men at the table all laughed as Pearlie assumed an aggrieved expression. "I guess that's the thanks I get for savin' the boy's life," he moaned.

The waiter appeared and began unloading coffee for everyone and a plate piled high with pancakes and bacon, and Pearlie's face lightened as he grabbed a fork and dug in with apparent gusto.

Monte fired up his pipe and leaned back in his chair, looking at Smoke. "I see you got your bags packed in the back of the buckboard, Smoke. You boys plannin' on takin' a trip?"

Smoke explained to him how they were going to go down to Texas and talk to Richard King about buying some of his prize Santa Gertrudis bulls to cross with his shorthorn herd.

"Well," Monte said, glancing out the window, "spring's a good time to travel to Texas, 'fore the sun gets hot enough to melt your pistols."

Louis arched an eyebrow. "Richard King? Seems I've heard the name before."

Smoke laughed. "You should have, Louis. King was a

Heart of the Mountain Man

steamboat operator who became a serious breeder of cattle. He took the native longhorn cows and bred them with expensive blooded bulls to form a breed called the Santa Gertrudis. He bought seventy-five thousand acres down in Nueces County in Texas, just up from the Rio Bravo. He calls his place the King Ranch, and word is it now covers almost a million acres scattered over four counties."

"Whew," Monte said, tipping his hat back, "and I thought we had some large spreads here in Colorado."

"He ships most of his beef and hides out of Galveston on steamboats and sailing ships, but he's agreed to sell me some of his bulls so his stock won't get too inbred," Smoke said.

As Pearlie finished his meal, the men settled into a comfortable discussion of cattle, ranching, and local gossip. As they talked, Smoke thought how lucky he was to have friends like Monte and Louis . . .

He and Monte Carson had become very good friends over the past few years. Carson had once been a well-known gunfighter, though he had never ridden the owl-hoot trail.

A local rancher, with plans to take over the county, had hired Carson to be the sheriff of Fontana, a town just down the road from Smoke's Sugarloaf spread. Carson went along with the man's plans for a while, till he couldn't stomach the rapings and killings any longer. He put his foot down and let it be known that Fontana was going to be run in a law-abiding manner from then on.

The rancher, Tilden Franklin, sent a bunch of riders in to teach the upstart sheriff a lesson. The men killed Carson's two deputies and seriously wounded him, taking over the town. In retaliation, Smoke founded the town of

Big Rock, and he and his band of aging gunfighters
cleaned house in Fontana.

When the fracas was over, Smoke offered the job of
sheriff of Big Rock to Monte Carson. He married a grass
widow and settled into the job like he was born to it.
Neither Smoke nor the citizens of Big Rock ever had
cause to regret his taking the job.

Louis Longmont, on the other hand, owned the saloon
in Big Rock called simply Longmont's, and was Smoke's
friend of many years. Longmont's was where he plied his
trade, which he called teaching amateurs the laws of
chance.

Louis was a lean, hawk-faced man, with strong, slender
hands and long fingers, nails carefully manicured, hands
clean. He had jet-black hair and a black pencil-thin mustache. He was, as usual, dressed in a black suit, with white
shirt and dark ascot—something he'd picked up on a trip
to England some years back. He wore low-heeled boots,
and a pistol hung in tied-down leather on his right side.
It was not for show, for Louis was snake-quick with a
short gun and was a feared, deadly gunhand when pushed.

Louis was not an evil man. He had never hired his gun
out for money. And while he could make a deck of cards
do almost anything, he did not cheat at poker. He did not
have to cheat. He was possessed of a phenomenal memory
and could tell you the odds of filling any type of poker
hand, and was one of the first to use the new method of
card counting.

He was just past forty years of age. He had come to
the West as a very small boy, with his parents, arriving
from Louisiana. His parents had died in a shantytown fire,
leaving the boy to cope as best he could.

He had coped quite well, plying his innate intelligence
and willingness to take a chance into a fortune. He owned

a large ranch up in Wyoming Territory, several businesses in San Francisco, and a hefty chunk of a railroad.

Though it was a mystery to many why Longmont stayed with the hard life he had chosen, Smoke thought he understood. Once, Louis had said to him, "Smoke, I would miss my life every bit as much as you would miss the dry-mouthed moment before the draw, the challenge of facing and besting those miscreants who would kill you or others, and the so-called loneliness of the owlhoot trail."

Sometimes Louis joked that he would like to draw against Smoke someday, just to see who was faster. Smoke allowed as how it would be close, but that he would win. "You see, Louis, you're just too civilized," he had told him on many occasions. "Your mind is distracted by visions of operas, fine foods and wines, and the odds of your winning the match. Also, your fatal flaw is that you can almost always see the good in the lowest creatures God ever made, and you refuse to believe that anyone is pure evil and without hope of redemption."

When Louis laughed at this description of himself, Smoke would continue. "Me, on the other hand, when some snake-scum draws down on me and wants to dance, the only thing I have on my mind is teaching him that when you dance, someone has to pay the band. My mind is clear and focused on only one problem, how to put that stump-sucker across his horse toes-down."

While the other men talked, Smoke smiled at his recollections of Louis and Monte, knowing he was going to miss them on his upcoming trip.

Three

Smoke stood on the train platform, his arms around Sally's neck. "Good-bye, Sally. I'll be back before you know it," he said, staring into her eyes and almost wishing he weren't going.

"Smoke," she began, a serious look on her face.

"I know," he interrupted with a grin. "Ride with my guns loose and loaded up six and six."

She nodded, not smiling. "I'm serious, Smoke. There's liable to still be some of those old wanted posters out on you down in Texas. You know how backward those Texicans are."

"Yes, dear, I'll be extra careful, and I'll make sure Cal and Pearlie watch my back at all times."

She glanced over his shoulder to stare fixedly at Cal and Pearlie. "I'm counting on you boys to keep the big man out of trouble, you hear?"

Pearlie nodded, while Cal looked anxious to get on the train so the adventure could begin.

"I mean it, Pearlie. There'll be no more bear sign if anything happens to Smoke!" she warned.

A look of horror came over his face at the thought. "Don't you worry none, Miss Sally. He'll be safe as if he were in church."

"That'll be the day," she replied with a smile as she hugged Smoke's neck and brushed his cheek with her lips.

"There'll be more of that waiting for you when you get back," she whispered in his ear, a mischievous look in her eyes.

As the train pulled through the mountain passes, most still with quite a bit of snow on the ground from the winter snows, Smoke and the boys moved into the smoking car. They sat at a table and Pearlie pulled out a weathered packet of cards.

"You ready to lose the Sugarloaf, Smoke?" he asked, grinning around a cigarette stuck in the corner of his mouth as he shuffled the cards in the manner of an experienced poker player as Louis Longmont had shown him.

Smoke leaned back and pulled a long black cigar from his shirt pocket. "You boys don't have a chance," he growled. "Louis loaned me a couple of his poker-playing cigars. No way I can be beat long as I smoke these."

Cal's forehead furrowed. "That ain't fair, Smoke! You already beat the tar outta us every time we play. You don't need no special ceegars to hep you do it."

Pearlie began to deal the cards. "Shut up, Cal. Cain't you see he's just funnin' with us?"

They began to play stud poker, using some chips kept on hand in the smoking car for the passengers to use. As the day wore on, the miles passed, and the pile of chips in front of Smoke grew steadily larger, while Cal's and Pearlie's shrank slowly.

A few other men in the car began to gather around, drawn by the lure of a poker game and the evident fun Smoke and the boys were having playing.

Finally, a man wearing a bowler derby and boiled white shirt stepped over, a thin, short cigarillo hanging from his mouth.

"Mind if I sit in?" he asked, pulling up a chair without waiting for an answer.

Smoke pursed his lips. He'd seen men like this hundreds of times in his years on the trail. Tinhorns, they traveled from town to town making a living off suckers who didn't know the difference between a shaved card and one marked with the sharp edge of a signet ring.

Pearlie and Cal looked to Smoke to see what he was going to do. He gave them a sly wink and grinned at the stranger. "Sure, have a seat. This is just a friendly game, however. Might not be up to your standards."

The tinhorn waved a hand. "Oh, I'm not really much of a poker player, so I'll fit right in. My name's Maxwell Gibbons."

"I'm Smoke, and this is Cal and Pearlie," Smoke said, omitting his last name.

Max pulled a small wad of greenbacks from his coat pocket and put them on the table in front of him. "What's the game?"

"Stud poker," Smoke answered as he shuffled and dealt the cards.

Without being obvious, Smoke kept his eye on Max as the game progressed, and the stack of chips in front of the newcomer steadily grew.

He could see Cal and Pearlie becoming more and more frustrated as their money seemed to disappear before their very eyes.

Soon, Smoke had had enough of Max's trickery, and he picked up the deck of cards and stared at the gambler. "I want to show you something, tinhorn," he growled, menace in his voice. Smoke placed the cards on the table and proceeded to cut four aces in a row. Then he picked the cards up, shuffled them, and dealt four hands face-up, giving himself four aces and Pearlie four kings and Cal four queens.

Max's eyes widened, then narrowed as his face flushed bright red. "I . . . I don't understand," he murmured, his eyes shifting around the car to see if anyone was watching.

"Oh, I think you do," Smoke said. He pointed at the signet ring on Max's hand. "You've been shaving the face cards ever since you sat down so they'd be easy to pick out of the deck."

Max pushed his chair back, his hand drifting toward his coat. "You calling me a card cheat, mister?" he said, his voice suddenly harsh.

Smoke leaned back in his chair. "I'll be calling you dead if that hand moves another inch," he said, his voice calm and deliberate.

Max looked in Smoke's eyes, and his face paled at what he saw there. "Uh . . . just who are you, mister?" he asked, letting his hand drop to his side.

"My name's Smoke Jensen."

Max gulped. *"The* Smoke Jensen?"

"There ain't but the one, tinhorn," Pearlie piped up from across the table.

"Uh . . . gosh, Mr. Jensen. I'm sorry 'bout all this. I'll just take my stake and go on about my business," Max said, reaching for his money.

Smoke shook his head. "I don't think so, Max. Just leave it and don't let me see your face again until we get to Texas." He leaned forward toward the gambler. "If I do, I'll be forced to kill you."

"But . . . but where'll I go? The train isn't all that big," Max protested.

Smoke shrugged. "That's up to you, Max. You could always get off at the next station."

"But that's in the middle of nowhere."

"Your choice, tinhorn. Get off and wait for the next train, or take a bullet. Makes no difference to me either way," Smoke said as he gathered up the pile of money and chips and handed them to Cal and Pearlie.

"Damn!" Max muttered as he grabbed his hat and stalked out of the car toward the front of the train. He stopped in the doorway and looked back at the table. "I'll get you for this, Jensen, just you wait."

Smoke didn't answer, but let his hand fall to the butt of his pistol, and Max hastily departed from sight.

"Golly, Smoke," Cal said as he counted the money in front of him. "How'd you know he was cheatin'?"

Smoke grinned. "I've played poker in too many saloons and with too many really good card sharks over the years not to recognize the type, Cal."

"Then, why'd you let him sit in with us?" Pearlie asked as he built himself a cigarette.

"I figured you boys needed a lesson in the realities of life on the trail. Louis Longmont once told me, Smoke, someday a man's going to come up to you and tell you he can make a jack jump up out of a deck of cards and spit in your eye, and you're going to be tempted to bet against him. Don't, he said, because sure as I'm sitting here, you are going to wind up with spit in your eye and an empty bankroll."

Cal and Pearlie laughed out loud. "That sounds like Louis," Cal said. "He has a way with words."

"And it's the truth," Smoke said. "Remember, a man's not going to ask you to take a bet he can't win, so the best thing to do is not bet with strangers."

"What do you want us to do with this money Max left?" Pearlie asked.

"Keep it. You can use it for spending money on the trip."

The train slowed as it pulled into a small town that

wasn't much more than a water stop, and Smoke and the boys saw Max step out of the car ahead, carrying his carpetbag in his hand. As the train pulled out, they waved through the window at him, but he didn't wave back.

Four

James Slade, who called himself the Durango Kid, stood in his stirrups and shaded his eyes against the sun as he surveyed the small herd of cattle in the valley below him.

"Looks like 'bout a hundred head," he said.

Curly Bob Gatling, who was bald as a billiard ball, grunted in reply. He was a man of few words, preferring to let the sawed-off twelve-gauge shotgun he wore in a modified holster on his belt speak for him.

Rawhide Jack Cummings, the third member of the gang, which also included Three-Fingers Juan Gomez, pulled out a Henry repeating rifle and jacked a shell into the chamber.

"Can you see how many men they got ridin' the herd?"

"Appears there's only three or maybe four," the Kid answered.

"Then let's do it," Gomez growled, pulling a Colt Navy revolver from his holster.

Down below, Jimmy Little Deer, an Osage Indian living in the Indian Territories, sleeved sweat off his face. He glanced around at the herd he was watching, glad they seemed to be calm. In this heat, he didn't feel up to chasing a bunch of dogies into the brush of the Oklahoma Territory countryside.

"Hey, Carlos," he yelled, looked across the backs of a

group of beeves toward his riding companion, Carlos Bear Claw. "How about we take our noon now?" he hollered.

Carlos nodded and cupped his hands around his lips to call to the third member of their group, Hank Stalking Horse. The three men were little more than teenagers, but could ride as well as men much older since they'd been raised in a saddle since they were pups.

The three Indian boys walked their mounts to a campfire they had going over on the edge of the herd, and stepped out of their saddles.

"Damn, but I'll be glad when this day's over," Jimmy said as he bent to pour himself a cup of coffee from the pot on the edge of the fire.

Hank paused in the making of a cigarette to look at the horizon. "Do you hear hoofbeats?" he asked.

Jimmy cocked his head, then nodded. "Yeah, maybe the foreman's sendin' somebody to relieve us."

Hank started to laugh at the notion when a loud thump was heard as a bullet smacked him dead center in the chest, knocking him backward and sending him flying spread-eagled onto the hot coals of the fire. Then a distant explosion of gunfire sounded.

"What the . . . ?" Jimmy said, grabbing for the ancient Colt Navy in a worn holster on his belt.

"Rustlers!" Carlos shouted, running for his horse to try to get his Winchester from the saddle boot.

As he leaned over the horse, a bullet shattered his skull, sending brains and blood spraying in the air in a fine, red mist.

Jimmy managed to get his pistol out and get off two wild shots at the four men riding down on him, but they missed their mark.

Curly Bob's shotgun didn't. The twin loads of buckshot took Jimmy square in the chest and blew a hole in his back as big as a bucket, killing him instantly.

The Durango Kid reined in, smoke still pouring from the barrel of his Colt. "Good work, boys," he said. "Now see if these galoots have anything worth takin', then put their hosses on a dally rope and we'll get to roundin' these beeves up."

"How much you think we'll get for 'em in Fort Worth, Kid?"

The Kid pursed his lips, thinking. "They ought'a bring about ten bucks a head, so figger 'bout a thousand dollars, give or take."

Three-Fingers Juan Gomez grinned, exposing a gold front tooth. "Not bad pay for a few days' work runnin' them down to Hell's Half Acre," he said.

"Don't forget," Kid said. "Soon's we get 'em outta the territories, we gotta put a runnin' iron over 'em an' change those brands."

Two days later, after crossing the border into Texas, the men stopped and applied a straight branding iron over the brand of the Osage tribe, changing the brand to one unrecognizable. Then they were back on the trail, headed for Fort Worth, Texas, where they hoped to sell the beeves to someone who cared more about the price of cattle than their origin.

Since the train carrying Smoke and Cal and Pearlie didn't have sleeping cars, it stopped on the way down to Texas for an overnight stay in Fort Smith, Arkansas, to give the passengers a chance for a bath and some good food.

Smoke and the boys got off the train and stretched, trying to get kinks out of their backs that were put there by jolting iron wheels traveling over uneven tracks for several hundred miles.

Pearlie rubbed his gut. "Damn, Smoke. You think we

could get some food here? My stomach's so hungry it thinks my throat's been cut."

"Your stomach's always hungry, Pearlie," Cal observed as he put his hands in the small of his back and bent over backward, trying to loosen up. "I think you were born hungry."

"Hell, Cal. We ran outta Miss Sally's bear sign over twenty-four hours ago an' I ain't et hardly nothin' since then."

Smoke grinned. "I guess those two steaks you put away this morning for breakfast don't count."

"That were more'n six hours ago, Smoke. A body cain't hardly go that long without somethin' to eat."

"All right. Let's go see if we can find a restaurant somewhere in this cow town," Smoke said.

As the boys and Smoke walked down the street toward the center of town, Pearlie glanced to the side and saw a large, wooden structure off in a field by itself, with a chest-high wooden fence around it.

"What do you think that is, Smoke?" he asked.

Smoke followed his gaze. "Unless I'm mistaken, that's the town gallows."

"Gallows?" Cal asked. "Hell, it's got six ropes hanging from it."

Smoke nodded. "Yeah. It's an idea of Hanging Judge Isaac Parker, the federal judge here in Fort Smith. Word is, he was hanging so many men, they had to increase the capacity of the gallows so as not to fall too far behind."

Pearlie's eyebrows shot up. "You mean they hang 'em six at a time down here?"

Smoke turned away. "Yes, that's what I hear, so you boys better be on your best behavior. It wouldn't do to get in trouble in this territory."

Pearlie's expression lightened up when he saw a combination saloon and dining hall down the street. "Now that's what I call hospitality," he said. "You can wet your whistle at the same time you fill your gullet."

Cal stepped to the side, pulling Smoke with him. "Look out, Smoke, it don't do to get between Pearlie and food. He's liable to run you plumb over."

They took seats at a table in the dining room close to the big double doors leading to the adjoining saloon. A large woman wearing a white apron with a hand towel thrown over her shoulder stepped to their table.

"Howdy, gents. My name's Mabel. What can I get for you today?"

Pearlie spread his hands out. "I want a steak this big, with fried taters, sliced onions, and a loaf of baked bread." He hesitated a moment, then added, "An' a jug of beer to go along with it."

Mabel threw back her head and laughed. "Now that's what I like. A man with an appetite. How about you boys?"

Smoke said, "We'll have the same, but bring us some coffee while we wait, please."

"Sure thing, mister," Mabel said, and waddled off toward the kitchen. She glanced back at Pearlie, and gave him a wink as she walked.

Smoke was about to tease Pearlie about his newfound friend when the braying of loud laughter came from the saloon. He glanced through the big door and saw three cowboys rousting a young black man who was trying to mop the floor.

The tallest, a man well over six feet in height, reached out with his boot and kicked the young man in the seat of his pants, sending him sprawling onto his bucket of water, spilling it on the wooden planks of the floor.

Smoke sighed and got to his feet. "I'll be right back," he said, his eyes on the men at the bar.

Pearlie reached out and touched his elbow. "Now,

Smoke, you know Miss Sally said for you to stay out of trouble."

Smoke grinned a hard grin, his lips tight. "Oh, this won't be any trouble. This is gonna be fun."

Both Cal and Pearlie shook their heads and got to their feet, in order to cover Smoke's back in the fracas they knew was coming.

As Smoke walked toward the cowboys, he noticed two men sitting at a nearby table, watching the proceedings with interest. One of the men was dressed in high fashion, wearing knee-high black boots, corduroy trousers, and a bright-red flannel shirt. He sported two ivory-handled six-guns on his hips. The other was dressed less flamboyantly, but was impressive nonetheless. Standing six feet tall, he was lean and wiry and had eyes that Smoke recognized as belonging to a man used to facing death and unbowed by the experience.

Smoke walked to the young man, now on his hands and knees trying to clean up his mess. Smoke reached down and pulled him to his feet.

"What's your name?" he asked.

"Billy Williams, sir," the boy replied.

"Don't you worry none about cleaning that up, Billy." Smoke cut his eyes to the men standing at the bar, watching him with amused expressions. "I'm sure these men will be glad to do it for you, since they caused it."

The smiles left the faces of the men and they looked at each other angrily.

Finally, the tall one stepped forward, hitching his pants up. "Just who the hell do you think you are, mister, mixin' up in our fun like this?" he asked.

Smoke shook his head. "I'm just a man who doesn't like to see three grown men pick on a young boy like this. What else do you boys do for fun? Pull the wings off of flies, kick dogs, slap women?"

The man looked astonished that anyone would speak to him in such a manner. He cast his eyes toward the men sitting at the table nearby, looking to see if they were going to interfere. The one in the knee-high boots just shrugged and took a leisurely drink of his beer.

The cowboy turned back to Smoke. "You apologize for that, or I'll kill ya!" he growled.

Smoke smiled back at him, unconcerned. "Apologize for calling you a low-life pond-scum who picks on children? Why? It's evidently the truth."

"You son of a bitch . . ." the man growled, and went for his gun.

Before his pistol was half out of leather, Smoke had drawn and slapped the barrel of his Colt down across the man's forehead, buffaloing him and knocking him to his knees, senseless.

"Goddamn!" one of the man's companions said, his voice awed. "I didn't even see his hand move."

"He's quicker'n greased lightning," the other man observed, holding his hands well out from his pistol.

Smoke holstered his gun and pointed at the man on his hands and knees in front of him. "You gents with this man?" he asked.

"Yes . . . yes, sir, but we didn't have nothin' to do with what he did."

"But you didn't do anything to stop him, did you?" Smoke asked.

"Uh . . . no, sir," the other man said, his eyes dropping to the floor.

"Then I'd suggest you two fellows clean this mess up, before you get the same thing your friend did."

The two looked at each other, then walked over to the young black boy and took the mop out of his hand. As they started to clean the floor, Smoke winked at the boy and walked back to his table in the dining room.

Just after the waitress brought them their food, the two men who'd been observing the action in the saloon sauntered into the dining area and stood next to Smoke's table.

He looked up from cutting his steak, leaned back in his chair, and gave them a look. "Can I help you gentlemen?" he asked.

He noticed for the first time the shorter of the two men was wearing a gold star on his chest. It appeared to be hammered out of two twenty-dollar gold pieces and said "U.S. Marshal" on it. The man was also carrying a shotgun cradled in his arms.

"Hello, mister," the man with the gold star said. "I'm Marshal Bill Tilghman, and this is my associate, Marshal Heck Thomas."

Smoke nodded; he'd heard of both men, who were famous throughout the West as marshals who always got their men.

"Uh-huh," Smoke said, and continued looking at the men, waiting for them to make their play, whatever it was.

Tilghman glanced at Thomas, who said, "Mind if we ask you what your name is?"

"I'm Smoke Jensen, and this is Cal and Pearlie, friends of mine," Smoke answered.

The two marshals glanced at each other again, clearly surprised a man of Smoke's reputation was in town.

"Do you have business in Fort Smith, Mr. Jensen?" Tilghman asked.

Smoke noticed his hands were tight on the shotgun, as if he expected Smoke to draw down on them.

Smoke shook his head. "No. As a matter of fact, we're on our way down to Texas to buy some bulls for my ranch in Colorado."

Thomas's eyes narrowed. "We've had some reports of stolen Indian Territory cattle being moved down Texas way for sale. You wouldn't know anything about that, would you, Mr. Jensen?"

Smoke smiled. "No. I've made a deal to buy some of Richard King's Santa Gertrudis bulls off the King Ranch. You don't suspect him of selling these stolen beeves, do you?"

Thomas smiled, apparently relieved at Smoke's news. "No, of course not. Mr. King is a highly respected rancher in Texas."

"We may see you later, Jensen," Tilghman said. "Heck and me are gonna be travelin' down to Texas ourselves. We aim to find those rustlers and bring 'em back up here for Judge Parker to deal with."

"Good for you," Smoke said. "Now, do you gentlemen mind? My steak's getting cold."

"Go on back to your meal, Mr. Jensen," Thomas said.

"Nice talkin' to you," Tilghman added as the two men walked off.

After the lawmen left, Pearlie leaned across the table. "I wonder what put a bee in their bonnet. They didn't have no cause to be roustin' you like that, Smoke."

Smoke swallowed the piece of steak he was chewing, washed it down with a gulp of coffee, then answered. "Sure they did, Pearlie. Like it or not, I've still got quite a reputation as a gunfighter, and tracking and fighting gunfighters is what those men do for a living." He shook his head as he cut another piece of meat. "No, I don't blame them for checking me out. In their place, I'd be doing the same thing."

Cal scratched under his arms and around his back. "You think we'll have time for a bath and maybe a couple of hours' sleep here in town 'fore the train leaves again?"

Smoke cut his eyes at Pearlie, who was watching the waitress hand out pieces of pie to a nearby table. "That all depends of if we can get Pearlie out of here before midnight."

Pearlie got a pained expression on his face. "Aw, Smoke. It won't take long to try just one piece of pie."

Five

When they got back on the train, Smoke noticed Marshal Heck Thomas and Bill Tilghman also boarded, though they sat in a different car from the men from Big Rock.

"You think they're followin' us?" Pearlie asked as he shuffled a deck of cards prior to resuming their poker game.

"No," Smoke answered. "They're probably just doing what they said they were going to do, heading down south to try and locate the men who've been rustling cattle from the Indian Territories."

As the train pulled out of the station, Cal glanced out the window at the gallows sitting in an open field, surrounded by its wooden fence.

"I'm sure glad we didn't have no cause to meet that Hangin' Judge Parker," he said.

"I've always thought an innocent man has nothing to fear from the law," Smoke said, "but with Isaac Parker I'm not so sure. Word is his first inclination is to hang a man, whether he's proven guilty or not."

"But that ain't right," Pearlie said.

Smoke nodded. "It may not be right, but it seems to be what the folks out here want from their judge. I guess they feel if the man's not guilty of what he's been charged with, he's probably guilty of something else just as bad."

Cal shook his head. "Helluva way to run a court, if you ask me."

Evidently, Cal and Pearlie were getting to be better cardplayers under Smoke's tutelage, because it took him the entire two-day trip to Fort Worth to win all their money from them.

As they entered the famous cow town, Cal's and Pearlie's eyes were glued to the window, staring at the extensive stockyards with their many cattle pens and slaughter yards on the outskirts of town.

"I never seen so many beeves in my whole life," Cal whispered in awe.

Pearlie nodded. "Yep, quite a few steaks on the hoof out there, all right." He wrinkled his nose. "Guess the folks here in Texas get kind'a used to the smell," he opined.

"You boys think that's something, wait until you see downtown. On the one hand, it's the most opulent city in Texas, and on the other, it's got more whorehouses and gambling dens than any place this side of Dodge City," Smoke said.

"What's that they call the red-light district, Smoke?" Pearlie asked.

"Hell's Half Acre," Smoke answered, "though I've heard it covers a lot more area than that now."

When the train stopped, Smoke and the boys got off and took their gear to the Cattleman's Hotel on North Main Street, supposedly the best hotel in town.

Cal's eyes opened wide at the numerous saloons and gambling houses and places of prostitution that lined the street on either side of the famous hotel. "You wouldn't think such a nice hotel would be smack dab in the middle of all of this," Cal said.

Smoke laughed. "People out here on the frontier have a more pragmatic way of looking at things, Cal. I guess they figure this is where most of the cattlemen stay when they come to town, and gambling and women and whiskey is what they want most after some months on the trail pushing a bunch of stubborn beeves to the market."

They walked through huge double doors into a lobby that was two stories high, with marble floors and polished oak countertops, with heavy overstuffed chairs situated around the room for customers to lounge in as they read the *Fort Worth Star,* a local paper, and had their morning coffee.

"Jimminy," Cal said, staring around at the room. "I ain't never seen such in all my born days."

Though Pearlie tried to look bored with it all, it was plain that he too was impressed with the establishment.

Smoke walked up to the desk and stood there, waiting for a man in a black coat and starched white shirt to wait on him. The man, a snooty expression on his face, glanced at them and then turned around, fooling with some papers on a rear desk and ignoring them completely.

After a minute, Smoke cleared his throat. When the man turned, giving him a disdainful glance, Smoke smiled. "How about this, mister? I jump over this counter, grab you by the neck, and choke you until you learn some manners."

"Why . . . I never . . ." the man started to say, until Smoke made as if to climb up on the counter.

The man cleared his throat and warily approached the boys. "Yes, sir. May I help you?"

"Reservation for three in the name of Smoke Jensen," Smoke said mildly.

The attendant's eyes widened and he swallowed, his Adam's apple moving convulsively. "Did you say Smoke Jensen?" he asked.

"Your hearing is evidently as poor as your manners," Smoke answered, his eyes hardening.

"Uh . . . yes, sir, Mr. Jensen. I have a suite on the top floor. Three bedrooms around a large sitting area."

He pushed a notebook toward Smoke, who took a quill pen from the ink pot and signed his name.

"Where are the baths?" he asked. "My partners and I've been on a train for most of a week and we'd like to get cleaned up."

"The baths are right down the hall from your room. There is an attendant there to take care of any of your needs."

Smoke bent to pick up his valise and then stopped, staring in the man's eyes. "And just what is your name?" he asked.

"Why . . . uh . . . it's Jason, sir."

As Smoke started to leave, Jason asked, "Why would you want to know my name, Mr. Jensen?"

Smoke growled out of the side of his mouth without turning, "I always like to know the name of a man I may have to kill."

Walking up the stairs, Cal and Pearlie burst out laughing. "Why did you say that, Smoke?" Pearlie asked around a grin.

Smoke shook his head. "I never could stand pomposity in a man, or ill manners. Maybe it'll make him think twice before he looks down his nose at a customer just because they're dressed in buckskins."

Down the street, at another fine hotel in Fort Worth, the Durango Kid was registering at the front desk.

"And how many men will be staying?" the clerk asked.

Durango looked over his shoulder, eyeing Curly Bob Gatling, Rawhide Jack Cummings, and Three-Fingers Juan Gomez.

"There'll be three of us, since I suppose you don't allow Meskins to stay here," the Kid answered.

Gomez's eyes narrowed and his lips turned white. "What you mean by that, Kid?" he asked.

"No offense, Juan," the Kid said, "but you'll have to stay down the street over that cantina. This hotel is for whites only."

Gomez stared at the Durango Kid for a moment, then muttered *"Bastardo"* under his breath as he bent and picked up his gear. "I not forget this, Kid," he called over his shoulder as he walked out the door.

The Kid spread his arms. "Hey, Three-Fingers, it's not *my* rule."

Curly Bob shook his head. "You shouldn't ought'a done that, Kid," he said.

"Hell, you want to stay in a place that'll take a Meskin?" he asked. "If you do, head on down to the cantina. I'm sure they'll let you share a room with Gomez."

"That ain't it, Kid," Curly Bob said. "You know Three-Fingers don't like to be called a Meskin. His momma was half-white."

The Durango Kid smiled. "So he says. Anyhow, if he don't like bein' called a Meskin, maybe he ought'a ride with somebody else stead'a me."

"All this jawin' is makin' me thirsty," Rawhide Jack Cummings said. "How's 'bout we head on over to a dog hole an' git some whiskey an' check out the women in this here town?"

"Sounds good to me," Kid said. "Let's dump our gear in our rooms an' see what the local nightlife is like."

On the way to a saloon, they stopped by the cantina at the end of Main Street and asked Gomez if he wanted to join them.

"You sure you want a Meskin to go with you?" he asked, a sarcastic tone to his voice.

"Aw, come on, Juan," Kid said, trying to make amends. "You know I didn't mean no disrespect. It's just I didn't want any trouble at the hotel."

"All right," Gomez said grudgingly, "let us go get drunk and forget about it."

"Now you're talkin', podna," Curly Bob said, throwing his arm around Gomez's shoulders and leading him down the street toward the array of saloons and whorehouses on the block.

Six

Smoke and Cal and Pearlie finished dinner at the Cattleman's Hotel, Pearlie topping his meal of steak and potatoes and canned peaches with a thick slice of apple pie covered with a slab of cheese.

"You think you can still walk after all that food?" Smoke asked.

Pearlie smiled as he wiped a piece of cheese off his chin. "Sure. This little snack was probably enough to get me through the night too."

"Smoke," Cal said.

"Yeah?"

"How about you takin' us out to see the sights. I ain't never been in no big-city saloon or gamblin' halls before."

Smoke pursed his lips. "I don't know, Cal. Sally'd kill me if she thought I was leading you young'uns astray."

"Heck-fire, Smoke," Pearlie interrupted. "What Miss Sally don't know won't hurt her none."

Smoke laughed. "You mean, what she doesn't know won't hurt *me* none."

"Please, Smoke. I don't know when I'll ever get another chance like this," Cal pleaded.

Smoke held up his hands. "All right, but only on one condition."

"Anything!" Cal said, his eyes lighting up at his chance to see the town.

"You boys have got to promise me you won't do any gambling, no matter how much you want to."

"Why, that's easy, Smoke. You done won all our money on the train," Pearlie said, a mischievous look in his eyes.

Smoke took a wad of bills out of his pocket and doled it out to Cal and Pearlie. "You know I wasn't going to keep this, didn't you, Pearlie?"

Pearlie shrugged. "Well, let's just say I hoped you weren't."

Smoke threw some money down on the table and grabbed his hat. "Well, boys, I guess it's time to further your education, though not in a way Sally would approve of."

He stood up. "Let's go see what Hell's Half Acre has to offer."

The Durango Kid, Curly Bob Gatling, Rawhide Jack Cummings, and Three-Fingers Juan Gomez entered the Silver Dollar Saloon, pushing through the batwings and strutting into the place as if they owned it. They were more than a little drunk, this being the third bar they'd visited.

The Kid walked up to a table occupied by a couple of cowboys, who also were well into their cups and had two rather buxom ladies of the night sitting with them.

Kid stepped in front of the younger of the two and laid his hand on the butt of his pistol. "Excuse me, gentlemen, but I think you're sittin' at our table."

The young man glanced up at Kid with bleary eyes. "What the hell you talkin' 'bout, mister? We been here all night."

Gomez stepped around the table to stand behind the cowboy, slipping his Colt Navy out of his holster and holding it where no one could see, the barrel against the boy's backbone. "I don't think you heard my pardner. You at our table, gringo!" he growled in a low voice.

The other man at the table started to get up, until Rawhide Jack put his hand on his shoulder, pushing him back down in his chair. "I wouldn't do that if I were you, podna," he whispered in his whiskey-rough voice, his eyes glittering madly.

"Come on, Jake," the first man said, his face pale with fear. "I think we've had enough for one night."

Jake glanced at the four men standing over them. "Yeah, there's plenty of other places we can spend our money."

As the two men got up to leave, one of the girls whined, "Hey, fellahs, what about us?"

Kid bent down and stroked her cheek with his hand, a leer on his face. "Don't you worry none, pretty lady. We'll take good care of you."

Mollified somewhat, she glanced at her friend across the table and shrugged. "Hell, any port in a storm, I always say."

"What're you girls drinkin'?" asked Rawhide Jack.

"Whiskey. What else?" one answered.

Kid pulled out a wad of bills and handed it to her. "Then why don't you mosey on over to the bar an' get us a bottle or two an' some glasses, honey?"

After the women left, the men took seats around the table, sitting so they could see the rest of the room. Life on the owlhoot trail had taught them to be cautious in new towns.

Curly Bob scratched his chin. "How much money you think we're gonna git for them beeves we got stashed in that corral 'cross town, Kid?"

Kid looked at the many cowmen in the room, all spending money as if it grew on trees. "I figure we'll get 'bout eleven thousand dollars, give or take."

"What's that apiece?" Rawhide Jack asked. "I never was too good at doing sums."

"That'll be three thousand for you and Curly Bob and me, an' two thousand for Three-Fingers," Kid answered as he pulled a small cloth sack out of his pocket and began to build himself a cigarette.

Juan Gomez's eyes widened. "Why for I only get two thousand, Kid?"

Kid cut his eyes at the Mexican. " 'Cause you didn't help much with the brandin' on the way down here, Juanito."

Gomez's face flushed red. He held up his left hand with only three fingers on it. "You know I cannot use running iron with this hand," he snapped.

Kid shrugged. "That ain't my problem, Three-Fingers. I only know we three did most of the work on the trail down here, so it stands to reason we get most of the money."

Gomez started to stand up out of his chair, his hand falling toward his Navy pistol. "Why you son of a . . ."

He stopped when Kid's Colt Army appeared from under the table, pointed at his gullet. "Now don't go gettin' that Meskin temper of yours all fired up, Juan. I'm still the ramrod of this outfit, an' if I say you get two thousand, you get two thousand. *Comprende, compadre?*"

Gomez stared at the pistol in Kid's hand for a moment, as if he were going to draw anyway, but the flat, hard look in Kid's eyes told him he wouldn't hesitate to shoot him dead if he tried.

Finally, he sat back down, his hands on the table, his eyes glittering hate. "We will see, Señor Kid, we will see," he whispered through a voice tight with anger.

Rawhide Jack slapped Gomez on the shoulder. "Come on, Juan. Lighten up an' enjoy the night. We don't get to a town like this very often."

"Yeah, podna, take it easy," Curly Bob said. "Hell, we may get more'n eleven thousand for them beeves anyway."

The conversation stopped as the two whores returned to the table, both carrying bottles of whiskey with no labels on them.

"You boys ready to party?" one asked.

Kid eased the hammer down on his Colt and slipped it in his holster. "Hell, yes!" he shouted, grabbing one of the girls and pulling her onto his lap.

None of the Kid's men noticed two men sitting across the room at a table by themselves, drinking beer and watching their every move.

Smoke and Cal and Pearlie ambled down Main Street, trying to make a choice of the many saloons they passed. As they came to the Silver Dollar, Cal, who was getting impatient to see the inside of a big city saloon, said, "How 'bout this one, Smoke?"

Smoke shrugged. "One's about as good as another," he answered, leading the way through the batwings.

Smoke stepped to the side as he entered, his back to the wall as he surveyed the room and let his eyes get accustomed to the smoky light after the darkness of the street. He'd been too many years looking over his shoulder for someone trying to make a name for himself by killing the famous Smoke Jensen not to be overly cautious when entering barrooms.

As his eyes roamed over the patrons, he noticed Heck Thomas and Bill Tilghman sitting at a corner table to his left. The two men didn't see him enter, their attention being on someone else at the other end of the room.

Pearlie noticed the two marshals also. "Hey, Smoke.

There's them two lawmen who braced us in Fort Smith. Wonder what they're doin' here."

"Me, too, Pearlie. It sure doesn't look like they're having much fun, does it?"

Cal brushed past Smoke and Pearlie. "There's a table over yonder, Smoke," he said, as two men at a table off to the right got up from their chairs and walked toward the stairs with a couple of women on their arms.

"Let's get it," Smoke said, glad the table was across the room from the lawmen. He didn't want to have to put up with any more questions from them tonight.

They took their seats at a table next to four men who were entertaining two women, and who evidently were feeling no pain, for there were two empty whiskey bottles on the table and they were starting on a third.

As they sat down, one of the men at the table next to them glanced over at Smoke and grinned drunkenly. Smoke smiled back and tipped his hat.

Pearlie got up and walked to the bar, returning after a few minutes with a small bottle of whiskey and a pitcher of beer.

"Who's the beer for, Pearlie?" Cal asked, reaching for the whiskey.

Pearlie slapped his hand. "It's for young pups who aren't old enough to be drinkin' whiskey, Cal."

"Hell. A man old enough to get shot ought'a be old enough to drink whiskey if'n he wants to," Cal protested.

"Speakin' of that," Pearlie said as he poured himself and Smoke a small drink, "you ain't been shot in over a month. That ought'a be a record for you."

Cal took a drink of his beer, sleeving the foam off his lips with the back of his arm. "I wouldn't want'a talk too much 'bout that, Pearlie. As I remember it, you were the last one in this group to take a bullet."

Pearlie rubbed his side, a rueful expression on his face.

"Don't remind me. It still hurts when the weather changes."

Smoke leaned back in his chair, thinking about how Pearlie had gotten shot, and how close he'd come to losing his friend . . .

Jim Slaughter was in the process of folding up his ground blanket and sleeping bag when he heard what sounded like hoofbeats coming from the mountain slope on the east side of the camp.

He straightened up, his hand going to the butt of his pistol, and looked toward the sound. He could see nothing through the heavy morning mist, which hung close to the ground like dense fog. Though the sun was peeking over the horizon, it shed little warmth and even less light through the haze.

He glanced over his shoulder toward the campfire, and saw that most of his men were still milling around, grabbing biscuits and beans and coffee, most of them still half-asleep at this early hour.

Damn, he thought, *we're easy targets out here with no sentries left to stand guard.* "Whitey," he called, pulling his pistol and grabbing his rifle from his saddle boot on the ground.

"Yeah, Boss?" Whitey answered from over near the fire.

Before he could reply, four shapes materialized out of the fog like crazed ghosts on a fierce rampage, orange blossoms of flame exploding from the guns they held in their hands.

Their faces were covered with bandannas and their hats were pulled low over their faces as they rode straight into the knot of men around the campfire, shooting as fast as they could pull the triggers.

David Payne, a gunny from Missouri who'd ridden with Quantrill's Raiders, drew his pistol and got off one shot before a bullet took him in the throat and flung him backward into the fire, scattering embers and ashes into the air.

Jim Harris, a tough from Texas who'd fought in the Lincoln County War, had his gun half out of his holster when two slugs tore through his chest, blowing blood and pieces of lung on the men next to him. He only had time for a surprised grunt before he hit the ground, dead.

Slaughter's men scattered as fast as their legs could carry them, some diving to the ground, others trying to hide behind trees or saddles on the ground as the marauders galloped through camp.

An ex-Indian scout called Joe Scarface managed to get his rifle cocked, and was aiming it at one of the riders when an explosion from the direction of the mountainside was followed immediately by a large-caliber bullet plowing into his back between his shoulder blades, which lifted him off the ground like a giant hand and threw him face-down in the dirt, a hole you could put your fist through in his chest.

"Goddamn!" Slaughter yelled, glancing over his shoulder. They were under attack from all sides, it seemed. He dove to the ground behind his saddle as one of the riders, a big man with broad shoulders on a big, roan-colored horse with snow-white hips, rode right at him.

Slaughter buried his face in the soft loam of the ground, and felt rather than saw the bullets from the big man's pistols tear into his saddle and the ground around him as the giant Palouse jumped over him. Miraculously, he was not hit.

"Shit!" he said, spitting dirt and leaves out of his mouth. He recognized that horse. It was the one Johnny West had been riding in Jackson Hole. So he was one of

the bastards who'd been killing his men all along, he realized. The son of a bitch had played him for a fool.

Whitey Jones ran for his saddle, hunched over, expecting a bullet in his back the whole way. As he bent to grab
his Greener shotgun, one of the raiders rode by, his pistol
pointing at the albino.

Whitey whirled, pointing his express gun just as the
rider fired. The bullet grazed Whitey's cheek and tore a
chunk out of his left ear, spinning him around and snapping his head back, blood spurting into his eyes and blind-
ing him momentarily.

Zeke Mayhew, one of the men who'd joined Slaughter's
gang in Jackson Hole, snapped off two quick shots, and
saw one of the riders flinch as one of his slugs hit home.
He grinned and eared back the hammers for another shot
as the man he'd hit leaned to the side and fired point-blank
into his face. Mayhew's head exploded in a fine, red mist
as the .44-caliber bullet blew his brains into his hat.

Two more explosions from the distant mountainside sent
two more men to the ground, one dead and one with his
left arm left dangling from a shattered bone. Milt Burnett
screamed in pain as he grabbed his flopping arm and went
to his knees, just as a gray and white Palouse rode directly
over him, its hooves pounding his chest to pulp. He died
choking on bloody froth from a ruptured lung.

Whitey sleeved blood out of his eyes and rolled onto
his stomach, pointing his ten-gauge at the back of a raider
and letting go with both barrels. Just as he fired, Ben
Brown, one of the men who'd been with Slaughter for
several years, stepped between them, his arm outstretched
as he aimed his pistol.

Whitey's double load of buckshot hit Brown square in
the back, blowing him almost in half as he spun around,
dead before he hit the ground.

Swede, too far from his saddle to get his gun, pulled

his long knife out and stood there, waiting as a rider rode down on him. He bared his teeth and screamed a defiant yell, holding the knife out in front of him.

The rider's eyes grew wide as he saw the man had no gun, and he held his fire, lashing out with his leg and catching Swede in the mouth with a pointed boot as he raced by, knocking out several of his teeth and putting out the man's lights as his head snapped back and he somersaulted backward, unconscious.

Jimmy Silber, thoughts of his thousand-dollar bonus still in his mind, fired pistols with both hands, crouched near the fire. When his guns were empty, he bent over to punch out his empties, but a sound made him turn his head.

He looked up just as a young man on a gray horse rode toward him. The last thing Jimmy saw was a tongue of orange from the man's pistol as the slug tore the left side of his face off and left him standing there, dead on his feet.*

Smoke shook his head at the memories, grinning to himself when he thought of how the boys had teased each other about the incident, even though both had been as close to death as it is possible to be . . .

As Smoke led his friends toward Big Rock, Louis twisted in his saddle and spoke to Pearlie, riding behind him. "How are you doing with that wound? Is it showing any signs or symptoms of suppuration?"

Pearlie stretched his neck and moved his left arm around in a circle to see if there was any pain or soreness. He'd taken a bullet that skimmed along the skin over his

---

Heart of the Mountain Man

his left shoulder blade, burning a furrow half an inch deep but not penetrating any deeper. Though the wound wasn't serious, Smoke and the others were worried about infection.

"No, Louis, it seems to be healin' up right nice. A tad stiff, but no more'n you'd expect."

As he spoke, Pearlie noticed Cal had a wide grin on his face.

"What'a you find so funny, Cal?" he asked suspiciously.

"Oh, a thought just sort'a occurred to me," the boy answered.

"Since when did you start thinkin', Cal?" Pearlie asked. "You ain't got a brain in that empty head of your'n."

"Well, it just seemed kind'a funny to me," he answered. "The four of us rode through them outlaws, guns blazin' and goin' off all around us, an' you the onliest one got shot."

"So?"

"So . . . maybe I ain't the only lead magnet around now. It might just be that you're gonna take my place as the one always seems to take a bullet ever' time we git in a fight."

Smoke and Louis looked at each other, smiling. It was good to see the boys back to normal, bitching and arguing with each other as only the best of friends could.

"I don't see it that way, Cal," Pearlie said.

"Why not?"

"Way I see it, this here bullet I took was probably headed for you, sure as hell, an' I just sort'a got in the way."

"You sayin' you took lead that was meant for me?"

Pearlie nodded. "Yeah, so that means you owe me for savin' you the misery of gittin' shot again."

Cal stared at Pearlie through narrowed eyes. "If'n that's

so, an' I ain't sayin' it is, mind you, I bet I know what you think I ought'a give you for savin' me."

"What's that, Cal?"

"I bet lettin' you have my share of the first batch of bear sign Miss Sally makes when we git home would square things."

Pearlie pursed his lips as he considered this. "Well, now, that just might make things right between us."

Cal shook his head, grinning. "Forget it, Pearlie. I been thinkin' on those bear sign for the past hundred miles. The worst thing 'bout bein' away from home all these weeks has been missin' Miss Sally's cookin', so you ain't gittin' none of my bear sign, no, sirree!"*

Cal looked up from making himself a cigarette and saw the distant look in Smoke's eyes and the slight grin on his face. "What you thinkin' 'bout so hard, Smoke?" he asked, licking the paper and trying to roll the cigarette as expertly as Pearlie did.

Smoke came out of his reverie and shook his head. "Just thinking on how glad I am to be here with you boys," he answered.

"Well, if you're so glad to be with us," Pearlie said, "how about takin' a drink or two of whiskey and joinin' in the fun?"

Smoke picked up his glass and held it up. "Don't mind if I do. Here's to us, boys, let's let her rip!"

---

*Heart of the Mountain Man

Seven

As the evening wore on, Cal and Pearlie became more and more excited by the activities of the saloon, especially the women who were constantly approaching the table and asking if the boys would like to buy them a drink.

Finally, Smoke realized his presence was inhibiting Cal and Pearlie from having a good time. "Boys," he said, "I think I'll just mosey on back to the hotel and give you some space to maybe do some entertaining on your own."

Cal and Pearlie glanced at one another. Then Pearlie grinned. "All right, Boss Man. We'll see ya bright an' early in the morning to see 'bout gettin' them beeves."

As Pearlie said this, the man at the next table cocked an ear. He leaned over the back of his chair and said, "Did I hear you men were interested in buying some livestock?"

Smoke glanced at him, immediately realizing this was no regular cowboy, and he very much doubted he was a rancher either. He wore clothes that were too fancy and had his pistol tied down low on his leg, more in the manner of a gunny than a cowman.

Smoke nodded, however, not wanting to be rude, especially to a man who looked half drunk. "Yes. We're in the market for some bulls. Why do you ask?"

"Well," the stranger said, rubbing his chin. "I got some prime beef on the hoof down at one of the corrals on the edge of town. Don't rightly know how many bulls there are in the bunch, but I'd be happy for you to take a look an' see if they interest you."

Smoke considered this for a moment, then said, "I assume you've got a bill of sale for the animals."

The man's face darkened and he got up from his chair. "Why'd you ask a damn-fool question like that, mister? You implyin' I'm a rustler?"

As he spoke, the man let his hand fall to his pistol butt.

Smoke gently unhooked the hammer-thong off his Colt and stood and faced the man. "I don't know what you are, mister. All I know is you asked me if I wanted to buy some cattle and I asked you if you had a bill of sale. If that bothers you, it's just too damned bad, 'cause it means you're either a poor businessman, or a thief, and in either event I don't think I'd care to do business with you."

"Do you know who you're talkin' like that to, mister?" the man asked.

"No, but I'm sure you're going to tell me," Smoke answered. "Loudmouths always seem to think they're more important than they are."

"I'm the Durango Kid," Kid said, his jaw thrust out belligerently, "an' I aim to kill you for talkin' to me like that."

"You make a move toward that smoke wagon, and you'll be dead before you clear leather," Smoke said calmly, his eyes flat and deadly.

The threat in them must have given Kid some warning, because he asked, "Just who are you, mister?"

"I'm Smoke Jensen."

"Holy shit," Rawhide Jack Cummings said from behind Kid. "You don't wanna mess with Smoke Jensen, Kid. I hear tell he's faster'n greased lightning."

"To hell with him," Kid growled, glancing over his

shoulder at his friends, as if to make sure they were backing his play. "I'll kill him where he stands."

Smoke gave a lazy grin that didn't reach his eyes. "You want to tell me your real name, or do you want Durango Kid on your marker on Boot Hill?" he asked.

An uncertain look crossed Kid's face. He'd never met anyone he couldn't intimidate before, and he suddenly became concerned that just maybe he'd bitten off more than he could chew.

Cal and Pearlie, still sitting at the table, had their hands on their pistol butts, not to protect Smoke from Kid, because they knew he could handle the gunslick, but to guard against Smoke being shot in the back by one of Kid's friends.

Three-Fingers Gomez stepped up to whisper in Kid's ear, "Maybe you better take this outside, Kid. Fewer witnesses."

Kid thought for a moment, then turned and sat back down at his table, saying, "I'm not through with you yet, Jensen."

Smoke shook his head. He looked down at Cal and Pearlie. "You boys be careful, and I'll see you back at the hotel later."

"Yes, sir," Cal said, his face relaxing now that the threat of imminent violence had passed.

When they saw Smoke leaving the table, two girls in revealing dresses ambled over to the table and sat down across from Cal and Pearlie. "You boys lookin' for some company?" one of them asked, a coquettish look on her face.

"Well, I do believe we are," Pearlie answered, signaling the bartender for another couple of glasses.

Walking toward the batwings, Smoke accidently bumped a poker player's back as he brushed past his chair.

Without looking back, Smoke mumbled an apology and continued on his way.

Max Gibbons, the gambler Smoke had braced and had thrown off the train, looked up, his face scowling as he recognized the mountain man.

He threw in his hand and gathered up his chips, raking them into his hat. "Excuse me, gentlemen," he said, "I'll be back shortly."

He slipped his bowler hat on his head and followed Smoke from the building, not sure why, but hoping for some chance to avenge himself to occur.

As Smoke walked through the batwings, Kid watched him with eyes that glittered hate. "I'm gonna go outside an' take care of that hombre," he whispered to his friends. "Watch those men he was with and make sure they don't do nothin' to interfere."

He stood up and walked toward the bar. When he got there, he glanced back to make sure Cal and Pearlie weren't watching, then slipped out the back door, unnoticed in the crowded room.

Smoke walked a few feet down the boardwalk, pausing to stop and build himself a cigarette, smiling to himself at the way Cal's eyes had lit up when the "hostesses" of the saloon asked him to buy them a drink. "Well," he muttered to himself, "the kid's got to learn the facts of life sometime. Might as well be now."

He didn't notice Max Gibbons standing in the shadows just outside the doorway to the saloon, staring at him with undisguised hatred.

He ducked his head and applied a lucifer to his cigarette. As he blew out the match, a voice came from the darkened recesses of the alleyway next to him.

"Hey, Jensen! You ready to settle our differences now?"

Smoke whirled, crouching, his hand dropping toward

the butt of his Colt as he tried to see into the blackness in front of him.

The Durango Kid stepped forward into the scant light from lanterns on the front wall of the Silver Dollar Saloon. He had his pistol in his hand, held at waist level, the hammer already cocked back. "I'm gonna kill you, Jensen, an' then ever'body will know who the fastest gun in the West is," Kid growled, his voice low and menacing.

Smoke's hand twitched. He knew he'd have to draw as fast as he ever had to stand a chance against a man with his gun already drawn and leveled.

Just as he started to make his play, twin gunshots sounded from deep darkness behind the Durango Kid, and the gunman's eyes opened wide and he uttered a sharp scream as the front of his chest exploded in an eruption of blood and bone caused by a bullet passing through his back and exiting out the front of his shirt.

The Kid's body was thrown forward to land sprawled face-downward in the dirt of the alleyway, dead before he hit the ground.

Smoke filled his hand with iron and stared into the alley, noticing a dark figure hightailing it out the rear of the passageway and around the corner of the saloon. Seconds later he heard the back door of the Silver Dollar open and close.

Suddenly, the street was filled with onlookers as men and prostitutes poured out the batwings of the saloon, to stand in a group looking down at the body of the Kid.

Marshals Bill Tilghman and Heck Thomas pushed their way through the crowd, guns drawn, and stepped to Smoke's side.

"I'll take that pistol, Jensen," Tilghman said, his Colt pointing at Smoke's belly.

Smoke let the pistol hang by his finger and handed it to the lawman. "Someone shot him from behind," Smoke said. "I saw him run up the alley and enter the saloon by the back door."

Thomas squatted and examined the two bullet holes in the Kid's back, then used the toe of his boot to flip the Durango Kid over onto his stomach, where a single exit hole of one of the bullets could be seen.

"Somebody drilled him in the back twice, that's for sure," the lawman said, glancing over his shoulder at Smoke.

Max Gibbons stepped to the front of the crowd, grabbing Tilghman by the shoulder. "Jensen did it, Marshal. I saw him," he said, his eyes fixed on Smoke with undisguised satisfaction.

"The tinhorn's lying, Marshal," Smoke said angrily, "and if you give me five minutes with him alone, I'll make him admit it."

Tilghman shook his head. "The only place you're goin' is to the local lockup until I can get you to Fort Smith, Jensen, where Judge Parker will listen to all relevant testimony . . . an' then sentence you to hang by the neck until you're deader'n that fellow on the ground."

Smoke took a step toward Gibbons, who rapidly backed away, until Tilghman grabbed his arms and pulled them behind him.

"Marshal," Smoke protested, "check my pistol. It hasn't even been fired."

"He reloaded it, Marshal," Gibbons said hurriedly. "I saw him do it."

Pearlie elbowed his way through the crowd to stand before Tilghman and Thomas. "Marshal, Smoke Jensen didn't shoot nobody in the back. He don't have to, since he can outdraw anybody in the country."

"We got a witness, mister," Tilghman said, inclining his head toward Gibbons, who dropped his gaze when Pearlie and Cal turned to stare at him.

He put his hand on Smoke's shoulder and pulled him down the street toward the local jail. "You'll have a chance to say your piece at the trial," Thomas said to Pearlie as he followed Tilghman and Smoke down the street.

Smoke turned his head to Pearlie and cut his eyes toward Gibbons, indicating Pearlie should have a talk with him. Pearlie nodded, his eyes flat and angry. "I'll get to the bottom of this, Smoke," he called, then turned and followed Gibbons as he tried to disappear into the crowd.

Eight

The next morning, Pearlie showed up at the jail and asked to speak with Smoke.

Sheriff Billy Jackson pursed his lips, thinking on it for a moment. "I'll have to see that shootin' iron, boy," he drawled, holding out his hands.

Pearlie unstrapped his belt and holster and handed them over.

"I'll give ya' five minutes," the sheriff said, hanging Pearlie's gun on a hat rack. "If'n ya' want more'n that, you'll have to ask the marshal."

Pearlie nodded and followed the sheriff through an iron-clad door into a back room where Smoke lay on a cot, his hands behind his head, apparently asleep.

After the sheriff left, Pearlie walked to stand with his hands on the iron bars of the cell. "Smoke," he called softly, "wake up."

Smoke blinked his eyes open and sat up, yawning.

"How can you sleep at a time like this?" Pearlie asked.

Smoke shrugged. "There's not much else to do in here, Pearlie. What did you find out?"

"We followed Gibbons to his hotel room. Cal's sitting in the lobby now, makin' sure he don't leave town till we get a chance to talk to him."

"Why didn't you ask him about it last night?"

"That Marshal Thomas an' Tilghman were with him

most of the night, takin' down his statement an' writin' it all up legal like."

Smoke made himself a cigarette and stared out the barred window of the cell thoughtfully for a while as he smoked. Finally, he whirled around. "You know, Pearlie, there was something not right about those gunshots last night, and I've been trying to put my finger on it."

"What do you mean, Smoke?"

He shook his head. "They didn't sound quite right, and I think I know why."

"Didn't sound right?" Pearlie asked.

"Yeah. I don't think the Kid was shot with a .44. The shots weren't loud enough, and if it'd been a .44 from that short a distance, both bullets would've gone clear through him."

"So . . . what do you think he was shot with?"

"I think it must've been a .36, probably a Colt Navy or possibly a Scofield."

"But, Smoke," Pearlie said, "you carry a Colt .44 New Model Army."

Smoke grinned. "Exactly my point, Pearlie."

"What do you want me to do about it?"

"Go to the doctor and see if you can get him to dig that bullet out of the Kid. If it's a .36 like I suspect, have him write a letter to that effect and bring it to Fort Smith."

"Why cain't I just have the doc tell the marshals?"

"Because we're leaving for Fort Smith in about an hour. Tilghman and Thomas have three or four other men they're taking back for trial and they seem to be anxious to get on the trail."

"I thought they was after some cattle rustlers."

Smoke shrugged. "Evidently, the man they were after was the Durango Kid, so they've kind'a lost interest in that case."

"But, why don't they go after the men with him?"

"The man who did all the talking, the only one they had evidence against, was the Kid, according to Tilghman. The marshal said they've given a list of the stolen cattle to the local sheriff, and if they surface, he can make the arrest."

"But," Pearlie protested, "what's their hurry to get back to Fort Smith?"

"It's my guess Judge Parker's running low on men to hang, and he wants to keep his reputation up."

"So, what else do you want me an' Cal to do besides talk to the doc?"

"See if you can get Gibbons to admit in front of witnesses that he lied about seeing me shoot the Kid."

"How can we do that?" Pearlie asked.

Smoke grinned. "It's been my experience that two things will loosen a man's tongue faster than anything else."

"What two things?"

"Whiskey, and a woman willing to listen to a man brag."

"The whiskey's no problem, but where are we gonna get a woman willin' to do that for us?"

Smoke's eyes narrowed. "You and Cal looked like you were getting pretty friendly with a couple of women from the Silver Dollar last night. Any chance of sweet-talking one of them into doing it for us?"

Pearlie thought for a moment, then smiled. "I guess so, though our night with them was interrupted by the gunfight."

Smoke reached through the bars and patted his shoulder. "Then you and Cal will just have to get reacquainted with them tonight. And, Pearlie," he added, "spare no expense."

"Where are we gonna git that kind'a money?" he asked.

Smoke handed him a piece of paper with a handwritten

note on it. "Have the telegraph office send this to Sally at the Sugarloaf. She can have all the money you need wired to the bank here in Fort Worth."

Pearlie nodded and took the note. He reached in to shake Smoke's hand. "We won't let you down, Smoke. Me an' Cal'll git the job done."

Smoke smiled. "I know you will, Pearlie. Just make sure you do it fast. From what I hear, Hangin' Judge Isaac Parker doesn't waste any time once he decides to stretch a man's neck."

"You can count on us, Smoke. We'll git what you need 'fore you even come to trial."

"I hope so, Pearlie. I don't like to think of not seeing Sally and the Sugarloaf again."

Nine

Tilghman walked into the back room of the jail and unlocked Smoke's cell. He held in his hands a pair of manacles. "Hold your hands out, Jensen," he said.

Smoke stuck his hands out. "Do I have to wear those, Marshal? I'll give you my word not to try and escape," Smoke said.

Tilghman placed the cuffs on Smoke's wrists and snapped them shut. "It's not that I don't trust you, Jensen," he said, an apologetic look on his face. "It's just that it's the rules. All prisoners have to wear these while bein' transported."

Smoke shrugged. "Yeah, Marshal, we wouldn't want to go breaking any rules, would we?"

"Listen, Jensen," Tilghman replied, his face hard. "We've had over a hundred marshals killed in the line of duty in Judge Parker's jurisdiction, over a third of 'em while transportin' prisoners. So, even if I don't always agree with the rules, I *do* follow 'em."

He led Smoke out of the jail and helped him climb up into an enclosed wagon with bars on the sides instead of wood. Three other hard-looking men were already inside, manacled as Smoke was.

As Tilghman started toward the front of the wagon, Smoke asked, "Isn't Marshal Thomas coming along?"

Tilghman glanced at him, as though considering

whether the question deserved an answer. Finally, he said, "No. We decided he should stay and try to get a line on those cattle stolen from the Indian Territories after all."

Smoke snorted. "You can start with the men riding with the Durango Kid. He tried to sell me some beeves without papers the night he was killed."

Tilghman stopped and turned to look at Smoke. "Why didn't you tell me this earlier?"

"You didn't ask, Marshal. You were too interested in trying to get me to admit to back-shooting the Kid."

"He tell you where they were keepin' those beeves?"

"He said something about a rented corral on the edge of town."

Tilghman nodded, scratching his beard. "That makes sense. They'd blend right in with all the other cattle waitin' for the slaughterin' yards to get to 'em."

"It shouldn't be too hard to find out which one he meant," Smoke said, "if you ask around in the right places."

Tilghman nodded. "Thanks for the tip, Jensen. I'll be sure an' tell Judge Parker how you helped out."

Smoke laughed. "Yeah, maybe I'll get a softer rope around my neck."

"Don't say that, Jensen. Judge Parker is a fair man."

"Uh-huh, and how many men out of the last hundred he's tried has he found not guilty?" Smoke asked.

Tilghman's face burned a fiery red. He mumbled something and turned to go.

"I didn't get that, Marshal," Smoke called.

"Three," Tilghman repeated. "He found three not guilty."

"Sounds like my chances aren't too good then," Smoke said.

"All I can promise you is you'll get a chance to tell

your side of it, Jensen. It'll be up to you to convince Parker you're tellin' the truth."

"Fat chance," Smoke answered.

Tilghman shrugged. "Better than the chance you gave the Durango Kid."

"I told you it wasn't me killed the Kid."

"You know, Jensen, I've been doin' this job for a lot of years, an' outta all the men I've caught and transported, ain't none of 'em ever been guilty according to them. So you can keep on talkin', but ain't nobody gonna be listenin' to you."

He turned to walk toward the sheriff's office. "Now I gotta go tell Heck what you told me 'bout them beeves."

After he left, Pearlie and Cal walked up to the wagon. "Smoke, we got your message to Sally, an' she's gonna be wirin' us the money soon's the bank opens up in Big Rock," Pearlie said.

"She say anything else?" he asked.

"Yeah," Cal said, "she said to tell you her and Monte and Louis would be in Fort Smith by the time you got there an' not to worry. They weren't about to let no judge hang you for something you couldn't do."

Smoke smiled. It was just like Sally to take on the hanging judge, or anyone else who threatened her husband. It reminded him of the time the outlaw Lee Slater and his three hundred bounty hunters had him trapped up in the High Lonesome and she came to the rescue, her guns blazing . . .

"Sally's gone!" Bountiful yelled, bringing her buggy to a dusty, sliding halt.

"What?" Sheriff Monte Carson jumped out of his chair. "What do the hands say?"

"I finally got one of them to talk. He said he took her

down to the road day before yesterday, and she hailed the stage there. He said she had packed some riding britches in her trunk, along with a rifle and a pistol. She was riding the stage down to the railroad and taking a train from there. Train runs all the way through to the county seat. Lord, Lord, Monte, she's just about there by now. What are we going to do?"

Monte led her into his office and sat her down. Bountiful fanned herself vigorously. He got her a drink of water and sat down at his desk. "Nothin' we can do, Miss Bountiful. Sally's gone to stand by her man. And them damn outlaws and manhunters down yonder think they got trouble with Smoke. I feel sorry for them if they tangle with Miss Sally. You know she can shoot just like a man and has done so plenty of times. She's a crack shot with rifle and pistol. Smoke seen to that."

Nearly everyone on Main Street had seen the elegantly dressed lady step off the train and stroll to the hotel, a porter carrying her trunk. As soon as the desk clerk saw her sign her name, he dispatched a boy to run fetch the sheriff.

Sheriff Silva was standing in the lobby, talking to several men, and he nearly swallowed his chewing tobacco when Sally walked down the stairs.

She was wearing cowboy boots and jeans—which she filled out to the point of causing the men's eyeballs to bug out—a denim shirt, which fitted her quite nicely too, and was carrying a leather jacket. She had a bandanna tied around her throat, and a low-crowned, flat-brimmed hat on her head. She also wore a .44 belted around her waist and carried a short-barreled .44 carbine, a bandolier of ammo slung around one shoulder.

"Jesus Christ, Missus Jensen!" Sheriff Silva hollered. "I mean, holy cow. What do you think you're gonna do?"

"Take a ride," Sally told him, and walked out of the door.

Silva ran to catch up with her. "Now you just wait a minute here, Missus Jensen. This ain't no fittin' country for a female to be a-traipsin' around in. Will you please slow down?"

Sally ignored that and kept right on walking at a rather brisk pace.

She turned into the general store, and was uncommonly blunt with the man who owned the store. "I want provisions for five days, including food, coffee, pots and pans and eating utensils, blankets, ground sheets, and tent. And five boxes of .44's too. Have them ready on a pack frame in fifteen minutes. Have them loaded out back, please."

"Now you just hold up on that order, Henry," Sheriff Silva said.

"You'd better not cross me, Henry," Sally warned him, a wicked glint in her eyes. "My name is Mrs. Smoke Jensen, and I can shoot damn near as well as my husband."

"Yes'um," Henry said. "I believe you, ma'am."

"And you"—Sally spun around to face the sheriff— "would be advised to keep your nose out of my business."

"Yes'um," Silva said glumly, and followed her to the livery.

Sally picked out a mean-eyed blue steel that bared its teeth when the man tried to put a rope around it. Sally walked out into the corral, talked to the big horse for a moment, and then led it back to the barn. She fed him a carrot and an apple she'd picked up at the store, and the horse was hers.

"That there's a stallion, ma'am!" Silva bellered. "He ain't been cut. You can't ride no stallion!"

"Get out of my way," she told him.

"It ain't decent, ma'am!"

"Shut up and take that pack animal around to the back of the store."

"Yes'um," Silva said. "Whatever you say, ma'am."

While Sally was saddling up, he turned to the hostler. "Send a boy with a fast horse to Rio. Tell them deputies of mine down there that Sally Jensen is pullin' out within the hour and looks like she's plannin' on joinin' up with her husband. Tell them to do something. Anything!"

"Sheriff," the hostler said, horror in his voice. "Don't look. She's a-fixin' to ride that hoss astride!"

"Lord, have mercy! What's this world comin' to?"

It was nearing dusk when Al Martine and his bunch spotted Smoke high up near the timberline in the Big Lonesome.

"We got him, boys!" Al yelled, and put the spurs to his tired horse.

A rifle bullet took Al's hat off and sent it spinning away. The mountain winds caught it, and it was gone forever.

"Goddamn!" Al yelled, just as another round kicked up dirt at his horse's hooves, and the animal started bucking. It was all Al could do to stay in the saddle.

A slug smacked Zack in the shoulder and nearly knocked him from the saddle. The second shot tore off the saddle horn and smashed into Zack's upper thigh, bringing a scream of pain from the outlaw.

"He's got help!" Pedro yelled. "Let's get gone from here."

The outlaws raced for cover, with Zack flopping around in the saddle.

Smoke looked down the mountain. "Now who in the devil is that?" he muttered.

Sally punched .44 rounds into her carbine and settled

back into her well-hidden little camp in a narrow depression with the back and one side a solid rock wall.

"Who you reckon that was a-shootin' at us?" Tom Post yelled over the sounds of galloping horses.

"I don't know," Crown answered yelling. "But he's hell with a rifle, whoever he is."

Using field glasses, Sally watched them beat a hasty retreat, and then laid out cloth and cup, plate and tableware, and napkin for her early supper. Just because one was in the wilderness, surrounded by godless heathens, was no reason to forgo small amenities.

She opened a can of beans, set aside a can of peaches for dessert, and spread butter on a thick slice of bread. Before eating, she said a prayer for the continuing safety of her man.

"He's up there," Ace Reilly said, his eyes looking at the timberline in the good light of morning. The air was almost cold this high up.

Big Bob Masters shifted his chew from one side of his mouth to the other and spat. "Solid rock to his back," he observed. "And two hundred yards of open country ever'where else. It'd be suicide gettin' up there."

Ace lifted his canteen to take a drink, and the canteen exploded in his hand, showering him with water, bits of metal, and numbing his hand. The second shot nicked Big Bob's horse on the rump, and the animal went pitching and snorting and screaming down the slope, Big Bob yelling and hanging on and flopping in the saddle. The third shot took off part of Causey's ear, and he left the saddle, crawling behind some rocks.

"Jesus Christ!" Ace hollered, leaving the saddle and taking cover. "Where the hell's that comin' from?"

Big Bob's horse had come to a very sudden and unexpected halt, and Big Bob went flying ass over elbows out of the saddle to land against a tree. He staggered to his feet, looking wildly around him, and took a .44 slug in the belly. He sank to his knees, both hands holding his punctured belly, bellowing in pain.

"He's right on top of us," Ace called to Nap. "Over there at the base of that rock face."

Smoke was hundreds of yards up the mountain, just at the timberline, looking and wondering who his new ally might be. He got his field glasses and began sweeping the area. A slow smile curved his lips.

"I married a Valkyrie, for sure," he muttered as the long lenses made out Sally's face.

He saw riders coming hard, a lot of riders. Smoke grabbed his .44-40 and began running down the mountain, keeping to the timber. The firing had increased as the riders dismounted and sought cover. Smoke stayed a good hundred yards above them, and so far he had not been spotted.

"Causey!" Woody yelled. "Over yonder!" he pointed. "Get on his right flank—that's exposed."

Causey jumped up, and Smoke drilled him through and through. Causey died sprawled on the rocks that were still damp from the misty morning in the High Lonesome.

"He's up above us!" Ray yelled.

"Who the hell is that over yonder?" Noah hollered just as Sally fired. The slug sent bits of rock into Noah's face, and he screamed as he was momentarily blinded. He stood up, and Smoke nailed him through the neck. Smoke had been aiming for his chest, but shooting downhill is tricky, even for a marksman.

Big Bob Masters was hollering and screaming, afraid to move, afraid his guts would fall out.

Smoke began dusting the area where the outlaws and bounty hunters had left their horses. The whining slugs spooked them and off they ran, reins trailing, taking food, water, and extra ammo with them.

"Goddamnit!" Woody yelled, running after them. He suddenly stopped, right out in the open, realizing what a stupid move that had been.

Smoke and Sally fired at the same time. One slug struck Woody in the side; the .44-40 hit him in the chest. Woody had no further use for a horse.

Smoke plugged Yancey in the shoulder, knocking the man down and putting him out of the fight. Yancey began crawling downhill toward the horses, staying to cover. He had but two thoughts in mind: getting in the saddle, and getting the hell gone from this place.

"It's no good!" Ace yelled. "They'll pick us all off if we stay here. We got to get out of range. Start makin' your way down the slope."

The outlaws and bounty hunters began crawling back, staying to cover. Smoke and Sally held their fire, neither of them having a clear target and not wanting to waste ammo. They took their time to take a drink of water, eat a biscuit, and wait.

Haynes, Dale, and Yancey were the first to reach the horses, well out of range of the guns of Smoke and Sally.

Haynes looked up, horror in his eyes. A man dressed all in black was standing by a tree, his hands filled with iron.

"Hello, punk!" Louis Longmont said, and opened fire.*

Smoke's eyes cleared and he came back to the present, resolving to leave his memories of Sally until he could see her again in person. It was too painful to think of her while locked away from her touch.

---

*Code of the Mountain Man

He looked at Pearlie. "I just found out Marshal Thomas is going to stay in town. Once you get Gibbons to talk, make sure the marshal is there to hear it."

Pearlie nodded. "Will do. Anything else?"

"How about the doctor?"

"It took fifty dollars, but he's gonna dig the slug out soon as the viewin's over, 'fore the undertaker puts him in the ground."

"Have him talk to Thomas after he gets the bullet out. Thomas will be able to tell the difference if it's a .36 like I suspect."

Pearlie stepped close to the bars of the wagon and whispered, cutting his eyes at the men in the lockup with Smoke, "You gonna be all right, Boss?"

"Sure, Pearlie. These men have more on their minds than doing anything against me. Now, you go get to work, you're burning daylight."

Pearlie touched his hat. "Yes, sir!"

Ten

Smoke settled down in the wagon, his back against the front wall, figuring that way the ride would be marginally smoother over the rough terrain they were going to be traveling over.

The three men with him sat sullenly against other sides of the wagon, their heads down, looking dejected. Finally, one of them, who appeared to be about five feet tall, raised his face to look at Smoke.

"Howdy," he said. "My name's Shorty Robinson."

Smoke nodded. "I'm Smoke Jensen, Shorty. Glad to make your acquaintance."

At the mention of Smoke's name, the other two men glanced up, suddenly interested. "You *the* Smoke Jensen?" a man at the rear asked. He was broad-shouldered, with a thick beard so black it almost appeared blue in the sunlight filtering in through the bars.

Smoke gave a slight grin and nodded.

"My name's Dynamite Dick Bodine," the bearded man said. He cocked his thumb over his shoulder pointing at the other occupant of the wagon. "And this is Jonathan Mayhew."

Smoke nodded again at the other man, who asked, "What are you in here for, Mr. Jensen?"

"You can call me Smoke, since we all seem to be in rather the same predicament."

"All right, Smoke," Mayhew said.

"Tilghman thinks I back-shot an outlaw named the Durango Kid," Smoke said.

Bodine's eyes narrowed. "I never figured a man with your reputation with a six-killer would have to back-shoot anybody."

Smoke shrugged. "I didn't, as a matter of fact, but it doesn't look like Tilghman believes me."

He looked at the men one at a time. "What are you gentlemen charged with?"

Bodine smiled. "I robbed the Union Pacific Railroad. Used a mite too much dynamite tryin' to open the boxcar holding the safe. Blew it an' the man guarding it into 'bout a thousand pieces." He shrugged. "It were an accident, but that don't seem to cut no ice with the marshal there. I figure the Hangin' Judge gonna stretch my neck just as far as if I'd done it a-purpose."

Smoke kept his expression blank.

Bodine continued. "Mayhew there, he's a card shark who shot a man over a poker hand."

Mayhew got a pained expression on his face. "The scoundrel had the effrontery to accuse me of cheating, just because he didn't have the slightest idea of the odds of drawing to an inside straight."

Shorty Robinson smirked. "They got me for killin' two men in a fight. They made fun of my . . . stature, so naturally, I had to show 'em my knife made me just as tall as they was." He gave a short laugh. "An' a lot taller after they was spread out in the street tryin' to hold they guts in."

Smoke shook his head. For traveling companions, these men left a lot to be desired, he thought.

Tilghman came out of the sheriff's office and climbed up on the wagon after hitching his horse to the rear with a dally rope.

"Gentlemen, hold onto your hats, we're headin' out," he said, as he cracked his blacksnake whip over the team leading the wagon.

As they pulled out of town, Smoke saw Cal and Pearlie standing in the doorway of the bank, waiting for it to open. They smiled and waved at him as he passed, evidently trying to keep his spirits up. *Well,* he thought to himself, *I couldn't have better men—and women,* he added thinking of Sally—*trying to get me out of trouble.* It was an uncomfortable thought that his safety depended on other people, since he'd always been a man who depended only on his own strength and intelligence to get him through trouble.

After the wagon passed, Cal turned to Pearlie. "We got to do something, podna. I hate seein' Smoke trussed up like an animal headin' to slaughter."

"Don't you worry none, Cal," Pearlie answered, his eyes hard. "Ain't nothin' gonna happen to Smoke if I have anything to say 'bout it."

A man in a black suit and boiled shirt and high collar unlocked the door and ushered them into the bank.

Twenty minutes later Pearlie and Cal exited with two thousand dollars in fresh greenbacks in their pockets, and a promise that there was more available if they needed it.

They walked down the street to the local doctor's office and knocked on the door.

A slight man with a badly pockmarked face opened the door. "We got your money," Pearlie said, holding up a handful of cash. "Now, let's get to work an' see just what kind'a bullet we find in that galoot on your table."

The doctor took the bills and counted them as he headed back into his surgery suite. Satisfied, he stuck them in his coat pocket and stepped up to a table upon which lay the dead man, who was dressed in a fine suit of clothes for the viewing.

"Here," the doc said, "help me get his coat and shirt off."

After they had the body uncovered, the doctor rolled it onto its stomach. Taking a large scalpel, he enlarged the entrance wound of the bullet that remained in the body. Then he used a long probe to follow the track the slug had made as it coursed into the Kid's chest.

After a few minutes, the doc nodded to himself. "Yep, just as I thought. It's in his right lung."

He went to a side table and picked up an instrument that looked like two small rakes connected to a wheel with a handle on it. "Here, boys, hold these tines in between his ribs while I open the spreader."

He placed the small rakes in between two of Kid's ribs and looked at Cal for help.

Cal's face blanched white and he said, "Uh . . . I don't think . . ." Then he grabbed his mouth and ran from the room.

Pearlie shook his head and stepped up to the table. "Young'un just don't have the stomach for this kind'a work."

The doc smiled. "Not many people do when you get right down to it, son."

He turned the handle and the spreader opened Kid's ribs wide enough for him to get his hand in the chest. He looked at the ceiling while he felt around inside the body, searching with his fingers for the slug he couldn't see.

After a minute, he smiled. "Gotcha!"

He withdrew his hand, and between his fingers was a lead bullet. He handed it to Pearlie after wiping the blood off with a rag.

Pearlie pulled a .44 bullet from his belt and held it up next to the one from Kid's body. He smiled. Sure enough, the .44 was quite a bit larger. Smoke had been right. The Kid had been shot with a .36-caliber gun.

"I'm gonna need you to write a letter to Marshal Thomas tellin' him we took a .36-caliber bullet outta the Kid's body, Doc."

"I'd be glad to, Pearlie. I'd sure hate to see an innocent man hang for something he didn't do."

Eleven

On the trip northward, the men in the wagon began to talk, there being nothing much else to occupy their minds since the scenery was uniformly bleak and unchanging for the most part.

Dynamite Dick Bodine said to Smoke, "I heard you killed over two hundred men. Is that about right, Smoke?"

Smoke tried to keep a pained expression off his face. He'd heard the same question in one form or another many times over the years. "I don't keep a tally of the men I've put in the ground, Dynamite. To me, that'd be too much like notching one's gun butt. To make a man's life, no matter how depraved or worthless, nothing more than a number to be bragged about over a glass of whiskey diminishes not only the man doing it, but the man he killed as well."

"That don't answer the question, Jensen," Dynamite said, his voice becoming harsh.

Smoke's voice became hard as steel as well. "I don't intend to answer, Dynamite. I will say this, though. I never killed a man who didn't draw on me first, or who didn't deserve to be buried forked end up." He hesitated. "And if that's not clear enough for you, I can come over there and try to make it plainer!"

Dynamite's face softened and he dropped his eyes. "I didn't mean nothin' by it, Smoke. Just a question, is all."

"Good," Smoke said, his voice returning to normal. "Then the matter is dropped."

Tilghman, who'd been listening to the conversation, smiled to himself. Maybe this Jensen fellow wasn't the cold-blooded killer he'd been led to believe he was. Tilghman liked a man who didn't brag about his accomplishments. It meant he was sure enough of himself that he didn't have to try to make others think he was bigger'n he was.

The conversation caused Tilghman to reflect for a moment on the men he'd killed in the line of duty over his years as both a local peace officer, and more recently as a federal marshal working under Judge Isaac Parker. Though he felt no guilt about the killings, reasoning as Judge Parker did that he hadn't killed the men, the *law* had, he still felt that he'd failed somehow every time he'd had to shoot someone rather than talking them into surrendering. Finally, he put his mind to other things. The day was far too pretty a one to spend it thinking morbid thoughts.

In Fort Worth, Pearlie and Cal found Marshal Heck Thomas having his breakfast at Aunt Ida's boardinghouse. It wasn't as fancy as the high-priced hotels in town, but it was a lot cheaper, and the food was in fact better, being more like homecooking.

The boys approached Thomas's table. "Marshal," Pearlie began, "I hate to interrupt your meal, but we have some news about the killing of the Durango Kid you might be interested in."

Thomas stared at them as he chewed a bite of wheat cakes for a moment, then washed it down with a drink of coffee and pointed at the chairs across the table from him. "If you're gonna talk business during my breakfast, you might as well grab a seat and have some food while you do it."

Pearlie grinned, and Cal just shook his head. "You don't know what you're doin', Marshal," Cal said. "Pearlie's such a food hog, you're liable to be here all day if we have to wait for him to finish eatin' 'fore he tells you what we came for."

Thomas smiled. "Well, how about you give your order to Aunt Ida over there, an' whilst she's cookin' it, you can tell about your news."

He signaled the heavyset woman wearing a flour-stained apron over to the table.

Pearlie ordered four hen's eggs, a half-pound of bacon, skillet-fried potatoes, and a pot of coffee. Cal just smiled and ordered a short stack of wheat cakes and two eggs.

Thomas smiled after the cook left the table. "I see what you mean about your friend."

Pearlie got right to the point. "Marshal, what caliber gun do you use?"

Thomas's eyes narrowed. "A Colt Army .44. Why?"

"Could I see one of your cartridges?"

Thomas stared at Pearlie as if he had lost his mind for a moment, then pulled a bullet out of his belt and handed it to Pearlie.

Pearlie pulled the bag containing the slug taken from the Kid's body and the note the doctor had written. He handed both to Thomas.

Thomas slowly sipped his coffee as he read the note, then held up the slug next to his .44-caliber cartridge and compared them. "I agree with the doc," he said, raising his eyes to Pearlie. "This does appear to be a .36, and not a .44."

"You know that Smoke Jensen carries only Colt .44's," Pearlie said, "and that's the guns you and Tilghman took away from him."

Thomas pursed his lips and thought for a moment. "You're right, it don't seem to make much sense, but we still got that witness who said he saw Jensen shoot the Kid."

Pearlie leaned back as Cal started to talk, telling the marshal about their run-in with Max Gibbons on the train. "So you see, Marshal Thomas, he's just a tinhorn gambler tryin' to get even with Smoke for kickin' him off the train an' showin' he was a cheat."

"You might be right, son, but how are you gonna prove it?"

"If you'll help us, we plan to get him to admit he lied 'bout Smoke," Pearlie said, sticking a napkin in his shirt as he prepared to dig into the meal Aunt Ida was placing before him.

"And just how do you plan to do that?" Thomas asked.

Pearlie speared some eggs on his fork and glanced at Cal. "You tell him, Cal, an' I'll just get started on this food."

It was almost ten o'clock that evening when a buxom redhead sidled up to the table where Max Gibbons was playing poker. She stood next to him, her hand casually resting on his shoulders and playing with the back of his head as she watched the game.

After a few hands, she leaned down and whispered in his ear, "I just love a man with strong, quick hands. How about we go up to my room and you can practice some of those moves on me?"

Gibbons looked at her, then at the men he was playing with. He'd managed to take most of their money already, so leaving with the woman would be a good excuse to get out of the game with his winnings.

"Boys," he said, stuffing his money in his coat, "I've

just had an offer I am loath to refuse. I shall return later, if I'm not too worn out."

"What's your name, little lady?" he asked as they walked up the stairs hand in hand.

"Ruby. Ruby Redlin," she answered, squeezing his hand and winking at him.

In her room, she slipped out of her dress while he began to disrobe. She lay back on the bed, dressed only in her corset, which emphasized her more-than-ample breasts.

"Say," she said, a thoughtful look on her face. "Aren't you the man who saw that gunman shoot down the Durango Kid the other night?"

Gibbons glanced at her as he pulled off his boots. "Yeah. Why?"

"Oh, I was just thinking it must take an awful lot of courage to stand up and point the finger at a man like that. Why, what if he'd gotten out of jail and come after you?"

Gibbons laughed and crossed the room to lie next to her on the bed. "Jensen ain't never gonna get out of jail, 'less it's to get his neck stretched."

Ruby leaned over and began to rub his chest and stomach, her hand drifting lower and lower. "Well, he really don't have no reason to be mad at you anyway. After all, all you did was tell what he done. I guess it don't take as much courage as I thought it did."

Gibbons bristled at her suggestion that his act didn't take bravery. "Hell, woman. It took a lot more guts than you think it did. Jensen's a well-known killer."

"Yeah, but how could he get angry with you for just telling what you saw?" she asked, her hand disappearing into his shorts.

Gibbons stiffened, laid his head back, and closed his eyes. "Like I said, you don't know all the details," he mumbled, reaching out to grab at the fastenings on her corset.

She leaned over and whispered in his ear, "Then, tell me, darling. I find it *so* exciting."

"That Jensen had the nerve to call me a card cheat," Gibbons said, his hands busy. "So, to get even with him, I lied about what happened out there. He didn't shoot the Kid. Someone else did, but because of me, Jensen's going to hang for it." He leaned back, a proud expression on his face. "That'll teach the son of a bitch to mess around with Max Gibbons."

"Did you see who did shoot the Kid?" Ruby asked, her eyes wide with admiration.

"Naw, it was too dark. But the Kid was facing Jensen when he got plugged in the back."

"Then that was awfully brave of you to lie about a famous gunfighter like that. Just think what he'd do if he ever got out of jail."

Gibbons's face paled for a second. Then he forced a laugh. "Hell, like I said, Jensen's going to be hung. I don't have nothing to worry about."

He buried his face between Ruby's breasts, not noticing the smile that curled her lips as she lay her head back on the pillow, already thinking on what she was going to buy with the money the tall, lean cowboy had given her to get Gibbons to talk.

In the room next to Ruby's, Marshal Heck Thomas sat back from the wall with the small hole drilled in it he'd had his ear against.

He looked at Cal and Pearlie and grinned. "You boys were right after all. The son of a bitch gave a false statement to federal marshals 'bout your friend."

Pearlie slapped his thigh and stood up. "You gonna arrest him now, Marshal?"

Thomas thought on it for a moment, then smiled wickedly. "No. Gibbons is gonna spend some time in Yuma Prison for his lies, so I think I'll just let him finish what he's doin'. It figures to be a very long time 'fore he gets to do it again, at least with a woman, so I'll just let him have his last fling."

"Are you gonna let Marshal Tilghman know he's transportin' an innocent man?" Cal asked, his face worried.

Thomas nodded. "Yeah. Trouble is, Bill's halfway to hell an' gone in some of the worse country there is between here and Fort Smith. I don't have no way to get in touch with him till he reaches Fort Smith. I'll just have to wire the judge with the details of what we've found out so he can let Jensen go when they get there."

"You think there'll be any problem with the judge?" Pearlie asked. "I've heard he sure likes to hang people."

Thomas's face sobered. "Judge Parker is a good man, a God-fearin' man who always tries to do what's right. I'm sure once he's heard the evidence, he'll decide Jensen is innocent."

"And if he don't?" Pearlie asked.

Thomas rubbed his chin. "Well, we could make sure by figuring out just who did shoot the Kid. Then there wouldn't be no doubt of Jensen's innocence."

"Would you mind if we . . . kind'a helped you nose around about that?" Cal asked.

Thomas smiled. "Son, one thing I've learned in all my years out here in the territories, don't never turn down help when it's offered."

Twelve

Marshal Bill Tilghman slowed the team of horses driving the prison wagon near a grove of mesquite trees, pulling it to a stop where both the animals and the prisoners could enjoy some shade. Out on the edge of the Oklahoma Territory Indian Nations, the heat was almost unbearable, even though it was still a couple of months before summer would officially begin.

"Hey, Tilghman," Dynamite Dick Bodine said, his voice raspy and dry. "How 'bout some water back here, or are you tryin' to save the Hangin' Judge the expense of a rope by starvin' us to death?"

Tilghman climbed down from the hurricane deck of the wagon, grabbed a large canvas bag under the seat, and walked back to the rear of the wagon.

He thrust the bag through the bars. "There's some canteens, an' some jerky and biscuits an' a couple of apples apiece for you gents."

The three prisoners riding along with Smoke tore into the bag, grunting in their haste to get water and food. Smoke stayed in his position against the forward wall of the cage.

Tilghman raised his eyebrows. "Ain't you hungry an' thirsty, Jensen?"

Smoke nodded. "Yes, but I can wait until the others

get their fill. I'm more used to going without food and water from my days in the mountains."

Tilghman walked over to stand in the shade of the wagon next to where Smoke reclined. He made two cigarettes from a small cloth sack and passed one through the bars to Smoke. After they both had their cigarettes going, Tilghman said, "I've heard you used to be a mountain man. Is that true?"

Smoke nodded, his mind going back to his early days in the West, riding the slopes with his friend Preacher.

"Yeah. I came out here with my dad when I was just fifteen years old," Smoke said.

Tilghman nodded. "Those must've been some times, what with the Indians an' all."

Smoke laughed. "There were times we'd go a whole year and not see another white man."

"I've been told the Indians pretty much left the mountain men alone."

"Some did," Smoke said, his eyes becoming vague with memories that seemed as if they'd happened only yesterday. "Others came at us every chance they got . . ." *Like the ones attacked my father and me the day we met Preacher,* he thought to himself, his mind going back to the day he and his father first laid eyes on the man known as the first mountain man . . .

Preacher galloped up to the pair, his rifle in his hand. "Don't get nervous," he told them. "It ain't me you got to fear. We fixin' to get ambushed . . . shortly. This here country is famous for that."

"Ambushed by who?" Emmett asked, not trusting the old man.

"Kiowa, I think. But they could be Pawnee. My eyes ain't as sharp as they used to be. I seen one of 'em stick a head up out of a wash over yonder, while I was jawin' with you. He's young, or he wouldn't have done that. But that don't mean the others with him is young."

"How many?"

"Don't know. In this country, one's too many. Do know this: We better light a shuck out of here. If memory serves me correct, right over yonder, over that ridge, they's a little crick behind a stand of cottonwoods, old buffalo wallow in front of it." He looked up, stood up in his stirrups, and cocked his shaggy head. "Here they come, boys . . . rake them cayuses!"

Before Kirby could ask what a cayuse was, or what good a rake was in an Indian attack, the old man had slapped his bay on the rump and they were galloping off. With the mountain man taking the lead, the three of them rode for the crest of the ridge. The packhorses seemed to sense the urgency, for they followed with no pullback on the ropes. Cresting the ridge, the riders slid down the incline and galloped into the timber, down into the wallow. The whoops and cries of the Indians were close behind them.

The Preacher might well have been past his so-called good years, but the mountain man had leaped off his spotted pony, rifle in hand, and was in position and firing before Emmett or Kirby had dismounted. Preacher, like Emmett, carried a Sharps .52, firing a paper cartridge, deadly up to seven hundred yards or more.

Kirby looked up in time to see a brave fly off his pony, a crimson slash on his naked chest. The Indian hit the ground hard and did not move.

"Get me that Spencer out of the pack, boy," Kirby's father yelled.

"The what?" Kirby had no idea what a Spencer might be.

"The rifle. It's in the pack. A tin box wrapped up with it. Bring both of 'em. Cut the ropes, boy."

Slashing the ropes with his long-bladed knife, Kirby grabbed the long, canvas-wrapped rifle and the tin box. He ran to his father's side. He stood and watched as his father got a buck in the sights of his Sharps, led him on his fast-running pony, then fired. The buck slammed off his pony, bounced off the ground, then leaped to his feet, one arm hanging bloody and broken. The Indian dodged for cover. He didn't make it. Preacher shot him in the side and lifted him off his feet, dropping him dead.

Emmett laid the Sharps aside and hurriedly unwrapped the canvas, exposing an ugly weapon with a potbellied, slab-sided receiver. Emmett glanced up at Preacher, who was grinning at him.

"What the hell are you grinnin' about, man?"

"Just wanted to see what you had all wrapped up, partner. Figured I had you beat with what's in my pack."

"We'll see," Emmett muttered. He pulled out a thin tube from the tin box and inserted it in the butt plate, chambering a round. In the tin box were a dozen or more tubes, each containing seven rounds, .52-caliber. Emmett leveled the rifle, sighted it, and fired all seven rounds in a thunderous barrage of black smoke. The Indians whooped and yelled. Emmett's firing had not dropped a single brave, but the Indians scattered for cover, disappearing, horses and all, behind a ridge.

"Scared 'em," Preacher opined. "They ain't used to repeaters. All they know is single-shots. Let me get something outta my pack. I'll show you a thing or two."

Preacher went to one of his pack animals, untied one of the side packs, and let it fall to the ground. He pulled out the most beautiful rifle Kirby had ever seen.

"Damn!" Emmett softly swore. "The blue-bellies had

some of those toward the end of the war. But I never could get my hands on one."

Preacher smiled and pulled another Henry repeating rifle from his pack. Unpredictable as mountain men were, he tossed the second Henry to Emmett, along with a sack of cartridges.

"Now we be friends," Preacher said. He laughed, exposing tobacco-stained stubs of teeth.

"I'll pay you for this," Emmett said, running his hands over the sleek barrel.

"Ain't necessary," Preacher replied. "I won both of 'em in a contest outside Westport Landing. Kansas City to you. 'Sides, somebody's got to look out for the two of you. Ya'll liable to wander round out here and get hurt. 'Pears to me don't neither of you know tit from tat 'bout stayin' alive in Injun country."

"You may be right," Emmett admitted. He loaded the Henry. "So, thank you kindly."

Preacher looked at Kirby. "Boy, you heeled—so you gonna get in this fight, or not?"

"Sir?"

"Heeled. Means you carryin' a gun, so that make you a man. Ain't you got no rifle 'cept that muzzle-loader?"

"No, sir."

"Take your daddy's Sharps then. You seen him load it, so you know how. Take that tin box of tubes too. You watch out for our backs. Them Pawnees—and they is Pawnees—likely to come 'crost that crick. You in wild country, boy . . . you may as well get bloodied."

"Do it, Kirby," his father said. "And watch yourself. Don't hesitate a second to shoot. Those savages won't show you any mercy, so you do the same for them."

Kirby, a little pale around the mouth, took up the heavy Sharps and the box of tubes, reloaded the rifle, and made himself as comfortable as possible on the rear slope of the slight incline, overlooking the creek.

"Not there, boy." Preacher corrected Kirby's position. "Your back is open to the front line of fire. Get behind that tree 'twixt us and you. That way, you won't catch no lead or arrow in the back."

The boy did as he was told, feeling a bit foolish that he had not thought about his back. Hadn't he read enough dime novels to know that? he chastised himself. Nervous sweat dripped from his forehead as he waited.

He had to go to the bathroom something awful.

A half hour passed, the only action the always-moving Kansas winds chasing tumbleweeds, the southward-moving waters of the creek, and an occasional slap of a fish.

"What are they waiting for?" Emmett asked without taking his eyes from the ridge.

"For us to get careless," Preacher said. "Don't you fret none . . . they still out there. I been livin' in and round Injuns the better part of fifty year. I know 'em better than—or at least as good as—any livin' white man. They'll try to wait us out. They got nothing but time, boys."

"No way we can talk to them?" Emmett asked, and immediately regretted saying it as Preacher laughed.

"Why, shore, Emmett," the mountain man said. "You just stand up, put your hands in the air, and tell 'em you want to palaver some. They'll probably let you walk right up to 'em. Odds are, they'll even let you speak your piece. They polite like that. A white man can ride right into nearabouts any Injun village. They'll feed you, sign-talk to you, and give you a place to sleep. Course . . . gettin' *out* is the problem.

"They ain't like us, Emmett. They don't come close to thinkin' like us. What is fun to them is torture to us. They call it testin' a man's bravery. If'n a man dies good—that is, don't holler a lot—they make it last as long as possible. Then they'll sing songs about you, praise you for dyin' good. Lots of white folks condemn 'em for that, but it's just they way of life.

"They got all sorts of ways to test a man's bravery and strength. They might—dependin' on the tribe—strip you, stake you out over a big anthill, then pour honey over you. Then they'll squat back and watch, see how well you die."

Kirby felt sick to his stomach.

"Or they might bury you up to your neck in the ground, slit your eyelids so you can't close 'em, and let the sun blind you. Then, after your eyes is burnt blind, they'll dig you up and turn you loose naked out in the wild . . . trail you for days, seein' how well you die."

Kirby positioned himself better behind the tree and quietly went to the bathroom. *If a bean is a bean,* the boy thought, *what's a pea? A relief.*

Preacher just wouldn't shut up about it. "Out in the deserts, now, them Injuns get downright mean with they fun. They'll cut out your eyes, cut off your privates, then slit the tendons in your ankles so's you can't do nothin' but flop around on the sand. They get a big laugh out of that. Or they might hang you upside down over a little fire. The 'Paches like to see hair burn. They a little strange 'bout that.

"Or if they like you, they might put you through what they call the run of the arrow. I lived through that . . . once. But I was some younger. Damned if'n I want to do it again at my age. Want me to tell you 'bout that little game?"

"No!" Emmett said quickly. "I get your point."

"Figured you would. Point is, don't let 'em ever take you alive. Kirby, now, they'd probably keep for work or trade. But that's chancy, he being nearabout a man growed." The mountain man tensed a bit, then said, "Look alive, boy, and stay that way. Here they come." He winked at Kirby.

"How do you know that, Preacher?" Kirby asked. "I don't see anything."

"Wind just shifted. Smelled 'em. They close, been easin' up through the grass. Get ready."

Kirby wondered how the old man could smell anything over the fumes from his own body.

Emmett, a veteran of four years of continuous war, could not believe an enemy could slip up on him in open daylight. At the sound of Preacher jacking back the hammer of his Henry .44, Emmett shifted his eyes from his perimeter for just a second. When he again looked back at his field of fire, a big, painted-up buck was almost on top of him. Then the open meadow was filled with screaming, charging Indians.

Emmett brought the buck down with a .44 slug through the chest, flinging the Indian backward, the yelling abruptly cut off in his throat.

The air had changed from the peacefulness of summer quiet to a screaming, gun-smoke-filled hell. Preacher looked at Kirby, who was looking at him, his mouth hanging open in shock, fear, and confusion. "Don't look at me, boy!" he yelled. "Keep them eyes in front of you."

Kirby jerked his gaze to the small creek and the stand of timber that lay behind it. His eyes were beginning to smart from the acrid powder smoke, and his head was aching from the pounding of the Henry .44 and the screaming and yelling. The Spencer Kirby held at the ready was a heavy weapon, and his arms were beginning to ache from the strain.

His head suddenly came up, eyes alert. He had seen movement on the far side of the creek. Right there! Yes, someone, or something was over there.

I don't want to shoot anyone, the boy thought. *Why can't we be friends with these people?* And that thought was still throbbing in his brain when a young Indian suddenly sprang from the willows by the creek and lunged into the water, a rifle in his hand.

For what seemed like an eternity, Kirby watched the young brave, a boy about his own age, leap and thrash through the water. Kirby jacked back the hammer of the Spencer, sighted in on the brave, and pulled the trigger. The .52-caliber pounded his shoulder, bruising it, for there wasn't much spare meat on Kirby. When the smoke blew away, the young Indian was face-down in the water, his blood staining the stream.

Kirby stared at what he'd done, then fought back waves of sickness that threatened to spill from his stomach.

The boy heard a wild screaming and spun around. His father was locked in hand-to-hand combat with two knife-wielding braves. Too close for the rifle, Kirby clawed his Navy Colt from leather, vowing he would cut that stupid flap from his holster after this was over. He shot one brave through the head just as his father buried his Arkansas Toothpick to the hilt in the chest of the other.

And as abruptly as they came, the Indians were gone, dragging as many of their dead and wounded with them as they could. Two braves lay dead in front of Preacher; two braves dead in the shallow ravine with the three men; the boy Kirby had shot lay in the creek, arms outstretched, the waters a deep crimson. The body slowly floated downstream.

Preacher looked at the dead buck in the creek, then at the brave in the wallow with them . . . the one Kirby had shot. He lifted his eyes to the boy.

"Got your baptism this day, boy. Did right well, you did."

"Saved my life, son," Emmett said, dumping the bodies

of the Indians out of the wallow. "Can't call you boy no more, I reckon. You be a man now."

A thin finger of smoke lifted from the barrel of the Navy .36 Kirby held in his hand. Preacher smiled and spat tobacco juice.

He looked at Kirby's ash-blond hair. "Yep," he said, "Smoke'll suit you just fine. So Smoke hit'll be."

"Sir?" Kirby finally found his voice.

"Smoke. That's what I'll call you now on. Smoke."*

Smoke came back to the present when Shorty Robinson nudged his arm with a canteen. "Don't you want no water, Jensen?"

Smoke took the canteen, wiped the spout off, then took a deep swallow. It tasted as good as anything he'd ever swallowed.

Thirteen

Smoke drank his fill of the water, sleeved moisture off his lips, and passed the canteen over to Shorty Robinson.

"Here ya go, Shorty."

"Thanks, Smoke," the little man said as he upended the canteen and gulped the rest of the liquid down.

Dynamite Dick leaned over and whispered to Smoke, "Jensen, you think there's any way we can get the drop on the marshal?"

Smoke shook his head, a slow grin appearing on his lips. "Having the Hanging Judge waiting to put a noose around your neck isn't dying fast enough for you, Dick? You want to go to hell a little faster?"

"What's that supposed to mean?"

"Just that Tilghman has a reputation of never having lost a prisoner, though I hear tell he's had to bring a few in dead who didn't start out that way," Smoke said. "You want to commit suicide, go ahead. But me, I'd rather take my chances with Judge Parker. At least a couple of men have survived going before him. . . . None have tangled with Tilghman and lived to tell about it."

Dynamite Dick looked disgusted. "I figgered you for more sand than that, Jensen." He looked over at Shorty and Jonathan Mayhew. "Either of you gents got the guts to try it with me?" he asked.

Both men just shook their heads.

Dick slapped his thigh. "Yellow sons of bitches," he muttered.

Tilghman walked around the wagon, a slight smile on his face as if he'd heard what the men had said. "You'd be smart to listen to Jensen, Bodine," he said. "That way you might live to make it to Fort Smith."

Dick scowled and Tilghman laughed. "All right, men, break's over. Get back in the wagon and we'll get on our way."

Two hours later, when the wagon was halfway across an open prairie with no cover other than the saw grass that grew to knee height, Tilghman pulled back on the reins and jumped down off the hurricane deck. He walked around to the back of the caged area and pulled a long, brass spyglass out of the saddlebags on his horse.

Putting the glass to his eye, he aimed it at the horizon and braced his arm against the side of the wagon to steady his gaze.

Smoke looked out between the bars and could see a cloud of dust, which looked to be about six or seven miles distant.

"Company coming, Marshal?" he asked.

Tilghman nodded without taking the glass from his eyes. "Yeah, an' I don't much think they're friendlies."

"Indians or outlaws?" Smoke asked.

Tilghman looked at him. "Probably a little of both. We've had some reports of some renegade Mescalero Apaches ridin' with some cattle rustlers who've taken to hidin' in the Nations. This is their stomping grounds so I'd bet it's them."

"They got any reason to be mad at you?" Smoke asked.

"Other than the fact they don't much like anybody with a star on his chest, not that I know of," Tilghman replied.

Smoke craned his neck to look on all sides of the

wagon. "Doesn't seem to be anyplace nearby to make a stand."

Tilghman glanced over his shoulder at an outcropping of rock almost five miles ahead of them. "That's the closest, but I don't think I stand a Chinaman's chance of makin' it, leastways not while pullin' this wagon."

Dynamite Dick looked up. "You could always leave the wagon an' take off on your hoss, Marshal," he said with a hopeful glint in his eye.

Tilghman reached in his breast pocket and pulled out a large square of tobacco. Taking a long-bladed knife from a scabbard on his belt, he sliced off a quarter of the square and put it in his mouth. He chewed for a moment, looking off toward the dust cloud, then leaned over and spat a brown stream of tobacco juice into the dust of the trail.

"Yep, I reckon I could, if I's a mind to."

"Then you're gonna leave us an' run for it?" Shorty Robinson asked, not looking as happy about the prospect as Bodine had been.

"Nope," was Tilghman's short answer.

He stepped to his horse and pulled a bright yellow-sided carbine out of a rifle boot next to the saddle. It was an 1873-model Winchester, the one called the Yellow Boy.

He jacked a shell into the firing chamber, placed a box of cartridges on the edge of the wagon next to him within easy reach, and settled in to fight the outlaws.

Smoke made his way within the wagon until he was next to the marshal. "If you want some help, Marshal, I'd be glad to oblige."

Tilghman smirked. "Yeah, but then that'd kind'a be like askin' the fox to guard the henhouse, wouldn't it, Jensen?"

"Have it your way, Marshal. Just don't let your stubbornness get you killed."

* * *

The group of outlaws, rustlers, and murderers crested a small ridge and their leader, Zachary Stillwell, held his hand up, bringing them to a halt. Jaime Gonzalez, his second in command, shaded his eyes with a hand, peering through the heat haze to the wagon in the distance.

"What you make of it, Zach?" he asked.

Zachary smiled grimly. "Why, Jaime, it looks like one of those wagons the U.S. marshals use to take prisoners over to visit the Hangin' Judge in Fort Smith."

George Hungry Bear, a Mescalero Apache renegade, said, "That mean no gold or silver."

Zachary shook his head. "No, but there's usually only the one marshal with the prisoners. It wouldn't be too much of a chore to take him out and maybe get us some more men to ride with us."

Jaime looked around at the men riding with them. "Why for we need more men, Zachary? We got ten now."

"You want to hit that payroll train comin' into Fort Worth next week, don't ya?"

Gonzalez nodded. "Yes. I hear it carry over a hundred thousand dollars."

Zachary smiled. "Then we're gonna need a couple'a extra guns."

"That mean less money for us," Hungry Bear observed.

Zachary shook his head. "Not necessarily. Nobody says they have to survive the robbery. What happens to 'em after we got the gold won't matter to nobody but them."

Gonzalez and Hungry Bear looked at each other and grinned. "Then, let us go free some prisoners," Gonzalez said, whipping the rump of his horse with a short whip he carried on his left wrist.

The ten riders spread out in a line as they galloped toward the wagon, pistols and rifles in their hands, whooping and hollering like Indians on the warpath.

Tilghman calmly leaned to the side, spat in the dirt,

shifted his chaw to his left cheek, and took deadly aim. The explosion of the Yellow Boy kicked back against his shoulder, and seconds later one of the attackers threw his arms in the air and catapulted backward off his mount.

Tilghman jacked another shell in the chamber and muttered, "That's one down."

"Nice shooting," Smoke observed as he watched through the bars.

Tilghman managed to get two more bandits before Zachary Stillwell got smart and pulled his men back out of rifle range.

"What now, Zach?" Gonzalez asked. "We lost three men already, and we ain't got nothin' to show for it yet."

Stillwell motioned with his arm. "Two of you men circle around to the left, an' another two circle to the right. Stay out of range until I give the signal, then start advancing in on the wagon afoot. That'a way you'll make less of a target. Sooner or later, we'll get 'em, 'cause he cain't watch all sides at the same time."

An hour later, when all the men were in place surrounding the wagon, Stillwell held his pistol in the air and fired a single shot.

The men began to creep up on the wagon, keeping low, and keeping up a steady stream of fire at the marshal, who moved quickly back and forth, snapping off shots when he got a glimpse of a head or a rifle barrel, but not hitting anything.

After a second bullet pinged off a bar and ricocheted around inside the wagon, Smoke said, "You got to give it up, Marshal, else we're all going to be picked off."

Tilghman sighed. "You're right, Jensen. I don't have no cause to put you men in danger any longer."

"Get on your horse and hightail it out of here," Smoke said.

"Uh-uh, I ain't leavin' you men to no desperadoes.

Maybe they'll be content with me an' let you men go free."

Tilghman stepped out in the open, put his rifle in the dirt, and raised his hands over his head.

Within a few minutes, the remaining seven outlaws were gathered around the wagon. "Keep a gun on the star-packer," Stillwell told Gonzalez, who held his Colt pointed at Tilghman's belt buckle.

Stillwell walked up to the cage and peered through the bars. "What have we here?" he asked with a grin on his face. "Some bad desperadoes?"

He got the key to the cage from Tilghman's pocket and opened the door, standing back and wrinkling his nose as the four men climbed out.

"Whew, but you're a ripe bunch of monkeys," he said.

"You would be too if'n you'd rode a hundred miles in the back of that hot box," Dynamite Dick Bodine said, grinning.

"And who might you be?" Stillwell asked.

"My handle's Dynamite Dick Bodine."

Stillwell's eyebrows raised. "The train robber?"

"Yep, one an' the same."

Stillwell nodded. "Good, we're plannin' a little job an' your experience will come in mighty handy."

"Be glad to oblige you, mister," Dick said, moving over to stand with the outlaws.

"And how about you?" Stillwell asked the others.

"Them two ain't nothin' but a card sharp an' a street fighter," Dick said, pointing to Mayhew and Robinson, "but that big galoot over there's Smoke Jensen."

Stillwell stared intently at Smoke. *"The* Smoke Jensen?"

Smoke looked steadily back at the outlaw. "One and the same," he said drily.

Stillwell walked up to stand nose-to-nose with Smoke.

"I can use a man with your experience. You interested in joinin' up with us?"

Smoke grinned, but his eyes remained flat. "If it'll get me out of this cage, I am."

Stillwell inclined his head toward Mayhew and Robinson. "What 'bout them? You think they'll be any good to us?"

Smoke shrugged, glancing around at the dead bodies scattered among the scrub brushes and saw grass nearby. "It appears to me you just lost three or four men. I'd think anybody dangerous enough to be in the company of the marshal over there would be an asset to whatever you have planned. Anyway, what've you got to lose? If they don't work out, you can always get rid of them later."

Stillwell laughed and slapped Smoke on the shoulder. "I like the way you think, Jensen."

Smoke pointed at a large canvas bag lying up on the hurricane deck of the wagon. "You mind if I get my guns? The marshal's got them stored in that bag there."

"Go ahead," Stillwell said, turning his attention back to Marshal Tilghman. "I've got some business with the marshal here."

Smoke hurriedly grabbed his belt and holsters along with his large Bowie knife and scabbard out of the sack. He strapped the guns on in their usual manner, right one butt back, left one butt forward, and stuck the knife and scabbard onto the rear of the belt.

He pulled both guns and opened the loading gates, checking to make sure they were still loaded—they were, six and six.

Stillwell pulled his gun and approached Tilghman, grinning. "I've never kilt a U.S. marshal before," he said, "but there's a first time for ever'thing."

Smoke spoke up. "Hold on, Stillwell. That may be a type of trouble you don't want."

Stillwell glanced back over his shoulder, a scowl on his face. "What do you mean, Jensen?"

Smoke shrugged. "It's just that whenever a U.S. marshal is killed, his friends never give up hunting down the men who did it. And more often than not, they end up getting their men."

"Yeah, but if we don't get rid of 'im, he'll just do the same thing," Jaime Gonzalez said, still holding his pistol pointed at Tilghman's gut.

"Not necessarily," Smoke said. "What if we break the wheel on that wagon, and leave the marshal afoot out here in no-man's-land? That way it'll look like he broke down and lost the horses and died of thirst when they find his body . . . if the coyotes and wolves leave anything to be found at all."

Stillwell looked doubtful. "I don't know . . ."

"Plus," Smoke added, "it'll be more fitting for the son of a bitch to die slow and painful-like. A bullet's too easy for him."

Tilghman's eyes narrowed as he stared at Smoke, his expression looking as if he thought maybe he'd misjudged the mountain man after all.

George Hungry Bear snorted through his nose as he laughed. "Jensen think like Indian. It be good to see how the lawman dies."

Stillwell smiled, as if that decided the matter. "All right. Hungry Bear, go over there and break the wheel on that wagon an' unhitch those hosses. We'll take all three of 'em with us until we reach the next town. Should be able to sell 'em for a little somethin' for our trouble."

"Better unload the marshal's pistol and leave it with him. Wouldn't do for him to be found without any iron on him. By the time he reloads it from his belt cartridges, we'll be out of range," Smoke said.

"Good idea," Stillwell said, nodding toward Gonzalez to indicate he should do as Smoke said.

While Gonzalez was busy unloading the marshal's pistol, Smoke stepped up to put his face close to the marshal's. "Thought you were going to see me hang, did you?" he asked, winking at Tilghman where no one else could see. He cut his eyes toward the outcropping of boulders and trees in the distance. "You be careful where you step out here, Marshal. You never know what kind'a snake is going to be in front of you."

Tilghman gave a slight nod to show Smoke he understood. "Yeah, Jensen," he said, his voice bitter. "I wouldn't want to step on any of your relatives."

Smoke laughed and swung up on the marshal's bay horse. He tipped his hat as the others mounted up also. "See ya' around, Marshal," he said, smiling.

"I hope so, Jensen, I hope so," Tilghman said, his face grim.

Gonzalez threw the marshal's Colt in the dirt twenty yards away, and Stillwell and his gang put the spurs to their horses, leaving Tilghman standing in a cloud of dust.

He walked over to his gun, brushed the dirt off, and reloaded it with cartridges from his belt.

He watched the men ride off out of sight and shook his head. "I hope you know what you're doing, Jensen. You're playin' a mighty dangerous game."

He pulled his hat down tight, grabbed a half-full canteen of water from the ruined wagon, and started walking toward the only shelter in sight.

He figured he had about four or five miles to walk in boots that weren't designed for walking just to get out of the sun and wind. *Damn,* he thought, *some days it just don't pay to get outta bed.*

Fourteen

Cal and Pearlie were sitting in Aunt Ida's boarding-house having breakfast when Marshal Heck Thomas approached their table, a grim look on his face.

Pearlie looked up from his plate of bacon, eggs, wheat cakes, and sliced peaches. "Howdy, Marshal," he said. "Pull up a chair and we'll treat you to some good home cookin'."

Thomas shook his head as he pulled out a chair, and signaled Aunt Ida to bring him some coffee. "You boys might not be so generous when I tell you the news."

Cal put his fork down, a worried look on his face. "Why? What's the matter, Marshal? Weren't you able to get in touch with Judge Parker?"

"Oh, I got in touch with him, all right."

"Then why the long face?" Pearlie asked, stuffing another forkful of wheat cakes in his mouth.

" 'Cause he said what I overheard Gibbons say don't amount to a hill of beans in a court of law."

"What?" Cal exclaimed. "But you heard him admit that Smoke didn't shoot that outlaw."

"That's right, Cal, but the judge says that don't count under the law. Seems Gibbons's written statement will stand until and unless he says he lied while under oath."

Pearlie waved his fork in the air. "Then, that's no prob-

lem, Marshal. We'll just traipse on over to the hotel where
that tinhorn is stayin' and make him tell the truth."

"I only wish it were that easy, Pearlie," the marshal
said as he poured a tablespoon of sugar into his coffee
and took a tentative sip.

"Believe you me, Marshal," Pearlie persisted, "Cal an'
me can be mighty persuasive when the need arises."

Thomas smiled. "I don't doubt it, Pearlie. Remember,
I know from experience just how persuasive you an' Cal
are." He hesitated, then said, "I might as well come right
out with it. I went over to Gibbons's hotel myself, just to
brace him with what I heard an' see if he'd agree to amend
his statement."

"What'd the bastard say?" Cal asked.

Aunt Ida interrupted the conversation by appearing at
the marshal's elbow, a stern look on her face.

"You gonna order some food or just sit there slopping
down my coffee?" she asked.

The marshal chuckled and said, "Sure, Aunt Ida, you
know I always eat here when I'm in town."

She was somewhat mollified, and her expression softened.

"I'll have three hen's eggs, scrambled with sweet
cream, half a pound of bacon, fried crisp, an' a short stack
of those wheat cakes Pearlie's wolfin' down."

"That's what I like 'bout you, Marshal," Ida said. "You
eat like a man, not like some greenhorn from back East."

As she turned to go, she winked back over her shoulder.
"I'll even throw in some of those tinned peaches for you
since you been such a loyal customer."

An impatient Pearlie said, "Go on, Marshal, What'd the
bastard say?"

Thomas looked at Pearlie. "Nothin'. Seems he must've
heard about our little eavesdropping session the other

night, 'cause he packed his bags an' took off during the night."

"Took off?" Cal asked. "How'd he do that? He came in on the train with us."

"I asked the desk clerk who was on duty when he left. He said Gibbons had a surrey he'd rented from the livery stable." The marshal smiled grimly. "Guess the tinhorn don't like to ride horses."

"Did the clerk say which way he headed when he left town?" Pearlie asked.

The marshal cocked an eye at Pearlie. "Why? You figgerin' on goin' after him?"

"Marshal Thomas, Smoke Jensen is not only the best friend Cal and me got, he's the best man we know. We aim to clear his name if we have to follow that son of a bitch all the way to San Francisco."

Thomas sighed. "Well, the clerk said he headed northwest outta town, toward Jacksboro."

"Jacksboro?"

"Yeah. It's another cow town 'bout twenty miles from here. Not as big or as famous as Fort Worth, but every bit as cantankerous. If you go there after Gibbons, you'd better ride with your guns loose. The place is a haven for every footpad and murderer in the area, and they don't exactly take to strangers, 'specially if you're not someone riding the owlhoot trail."

Pearlie glanced at Cal. "Finish those eggs, Cal. We got places to go an' we're burnin' daylight sittin' here."

Thomas held up a hand. "Pearlie, let me warn you. If you do manage to find Gibbons an' get him to admit he lied, you got to do it in front of a peace officer or it won't count in court. The deputy sheriff of Jacksboro is an old friend of mine. Name's Johnny Walker. You tell him you're workin' with me on this murder an' he'll be more than glad to help. You get him to put in writin' that Gibbons changed his testimony, an' I'll be able to get Judge Parker to listen."

Pearlie stood up and grabbed his hat. He held out his hand to Thomas. "Thanks for your help, Marshal. We'll let you know soon's we find Gibbons an' get him to talk."

Thomas took Pearlie's hand. "*If* you get him to talk," he said.

"Oh," Pearlie replied, "the sumbitch'll talk, all right, or he'll never talk to anyone again."

Thomas grinned. "Now, Pearlie, don't go doin' nothin' rash. I don't want to have to come after you on another murder charge."

"Don't worry none, Marshal," Cal said with a grin. "I'll keep Pearlie under control."

Thomas shook his head and began to eat his breakfast. "Go on an' get outta here, you two, 'fore I come to my senses and arrest you both."

Fifteen

After riding for ten miles, Zachary Stillwell held up his hand, signaling the men following him to halt.

"This looks like 'bout as good a place as any to make camp for the night," he said, walking his horse up to a copse of cottonwood trees next to a small stream. "This is liable to be the only water 'tween here an' the next town."

Smoke got off Marshal Tilghman's dun, which he'd been riding, and hitched the animal to a branch of one of the trees.

Stillwell's gang now consisted of eleven men, counting the three he'd rescued from Tilghman's cage along with Smoke. The mountain man was busy planning on how he could get away with an extra horse for the marshal without having to kill most or all of the outlaws. He wasn't particularly concerned with saving their lives, being as how they weren't men he respected, but in any gunfight, especially when the odds were so heavy against him, there was a chance he'd lose. And, he reasoned, if he lost, it would also mean the death of a man he did respect, Marshal Bill Tilghman.

George Hungry Bear went about building a campfire, while some of the others broke out cooking utensils and slabs of fatback bacon and dried pinto beans. Smoke took a deep pot down to the stream to fill it with water to cook the beans, noticing that Stillwell followed him.

As he squatted next to the slowly moving water, Stillwell built himself a cigarette and watched as Smoke filled the pot.

"You know, Jensen, I heard a lot about you over the years."

"That so, Zach?" Smoke answered, glancing back over his shoulder at the man standing behind him.

"Yeah. I heard you was 'bout the fastest man alive with a short gun, an' I also heard you never hesitated to send anybody who drew down on you to Boot Hill."

"You heard right, Zach. A man calls the dance on you, someone has to pay the band, and so far, it hasn't been me."

"But what's got me worried, Smoke, is that I never heard nothin' 'bout you bein' a robber. You had some paper on you over the years, mostly for murder of men who goaded you into it, but you were never wanted for robbery or rustlin' or nothin' like that."

Smoke put the pot down on the ground and stretched his back, rubbing his buttocks where Tilghman's saddle had made them sore.

"You're chewing on something, Zach, so why don't you just spit it out and say what's on your mind?"

Smoke noticed Stillwell's hand was resting near the butt of his pistol.

"I was just wonderin' why you agreed to join us on our little trip to take down a train," Stillwell said.

Smoke smiled, using the distraction to turn sideways so Stillwell wouldn't see him loosen the rawhide hammer thong on his right-hand Colt.

"Well, Zach, if you'll remember, I didn't have a whole hell of a lot of choice in the matter. It was either ride with you and your men, or stay with the marshal and get my neck stretched by Judge Parker in Fort Smith."

"So you're sayin' you don't want to help with the train?"

"What I'm saying, Zach, is that I'll ride with you to the next town. Then I'll make my mind up whether to stay the course or not."

"That don't exactly clear my mind on you, Jensen."

"I don't really give a damn about your mind, Zach. That's just the way it is." Smoke inclined his head toward Stillwell's Colt. "Now you can either draw that six-killer on your hip you're playing with and go to work, or get out of my way so we can get some dinner cooked."

Stillwell's face blanched at the ominous threat in Smoke's voice, as if he knew he was seconds away from death. "I didn't mean nothin' by what I was sayin', Jensen," he said quickly, moving his hand so it wasn't near his pistol. "I just wanted to make sure you was on our side."

Smoke bent and picked up the pot of water. "Whose side did you think I was on, Zach? The marshal who was taking me to be hung?"

Stillwell gave a shaky laugh. "No, I guess not."

"Good. Then move aside so I can get us some beans cooking. I'm so hungry my stomach thinks my throat's been cut."

After a supper of fried bacon, pinto beans, and some pieces of jerked meat, washed down with boiled coffee and some whiskey a few of the outlaws had in their saddlebags, the men spread their ground blankets near the fire and stretched out to sleep.

Like most men riding the owlhoot trail, they didn't take the saddles off their horses, but just loosened the belly straps in case they had to make a quick getaway if trouble arrived.

Smoke waited until midnight, when the coals of the fire were almost completely out, before he made his move. He gathered his blanket and moved to Tilghman's horse.

Drawing his Bowie knife, he made the rounds of the gang's horses, quietly cutting each belly strap almost all the way through.

When he was done, he took the reins to one of the horses that had been pulling Tilghman's wagon, along with the marshal's horse, and slowly walked away from the camp.

The moon had set so the night was dark, illuminated only by starlight, as he made his way across the prairie grass back toward where they'd left Marshal Tilghman.

He was still walking, almost a hundred yards from camp, when the sharp crack of a stick behind him made Smoke turn around.

Stillwell stood twenty feet away, a pistol in his hand, his teeth gleaming dully in the faint starlight.

"I knowed you wasn't to be trusted, Jensen," he said. "Now bring them cayuses back to the camp an' we'll see what we're gonna do with you."

Without another word, Smoke drew and fired all in one fluid motion, crouching as he did so. His gun went off at the same time as Stillwell's, and he heard the buzz of the slug as it passed through the brim of his hat.

Stillwell's head snapped back, a black hole appearing in the center of his forehead as the back of his head exploded in a fine red mist, with brains and bone and blood flying around the exiting bullet.

Smoke swung into the saddle and spurred Tilghman's horse into a gallop, hanging onto the reins of the wagon horse so it would follow.

Stillwell's gang jumped out of their bedrolls at the

sound of the shot and made for their horses. They didn't know what was going on, but they knew it meant trouble. As they climbed into their saddles and started to ride away, one after the other hit the dirt as the cut belly straps gave way and they tumbled to the ground.

Smoke smiled at the sight, looking back over his shoulder at the confused melee the men made, scrambling around on foot trying to catch horses running wild with fear.

"That ought to keep them off my back trail until I can get to Tilghman," Smoke muttered as he leaned over the saddle horn and rode as fast as his horse could run.

It was full morning before Smoke arrived at the outcropping of rock and boulders where he'd indicated Tilghman should wait for him.

"Yo, Marshal Tilghman," Smoke called as he approached the hillock, still leading the horse behind him.

He stopped the horses seventy-five yards from the boulders, well out of pistol range, just in case the marshal was feeling trigger-happy after the events of the day before.

Tilghman stuck his head up from behind a rock, his pistol in his hand.

"That you, Jensen?" he called.

"Yeah," Smoke called back.

"You alone?"

Smoke smiled. He was sitting on a horse out in the open, with nothing around for miles.

"You see anyone else, Marshal?" he answered.

Tilghman stood up on top of the boulder. "Then come on in."

Smoke shook his head. "Not while you're holding that Colt. Throw it down on the ground."

"Now why should I do that?" Tilghman asked, not moving to release the gun.

"Because if you don't, I'll just turn these horses around and head on back to Fort Worth by myself, leaving you an awfully long walk back to town."

Tilghman considered his options for a moment, discovered he really didn't have any, and finally threw his pistol off the outcropping.

Smoke walked the horses up to the base of the hillock and got down out of the saddle. He picked Tilghman's Colt up and dusted the dirt off it while the marshal climbed down from his perch on the boulders.

When he got down, he walked over to Smoke. "Why'd you ask for my gun?"

"I didn't know just what sort of frame of mind you'd be in, so I figured better to be safe than sorry."

The marshal's eyes narrowed as he saw the hole in Smoke's hat. "You have some trouble with that outlaw?"

Smoke nodded. "Yeah, Stillwell wasn't too keen on the idea of me bringing you your horse back."

"You kill him?"

"I didn't stop to check, but unless he can live without half his skull, yeah."

"What about the others?"

"I left them on foot chasing down their mounts, with no belly straps to keep the saddles on."

Tilghman looked off in the distance, toward where Smoke had left the outlaw gang. He nodded, as if thinking to himself. "Then I guess I'll just have to go after them then."

"Marshal, there are nine hard cases out there. Don't you think you ought to get some help before you try to apprehend them?"

"In this job, Jensen, a man learns not to rely on getting others to help him."

"Well, it's your funeral."

Tilghman shrugged. "That possibility comes with the badge. You gonna give me my pistol back?"

Smoke stared at the marshal. "If you give me your word not to try and arrest me before I have a chance to clear my name."

"I don't make deals with murderers, Jensen. You should know that."

"I'm not a murderer, Marshal. I just need a little time to prove it."

Tilghman rubbed his chin whiskers. "I guess I owe you that, at least. Tell you what, Jensen. I'll go after the others first, but once I have them in custody, I want you to know I'm coming after you."

Smoke nodded. "Fair enough, Marshal."

He climbed down off Tilghman's horse and handed him his pistol. "Your rifle's still in the boot, and all your ammunition is in your saddlebag."

"What about you?" Tilghman asked.

Smoke inclined his head toward the wagon horse standing nearby. "I'll ride that one on into Fort Worth. I've got to have a word with that tinhorn who lied about seeing me shoot the Durango Kid."

"There ain't no saddle on that bronc," Tilghman said.

"It's better than walking," Smoke said. "Besides, I'm used to riding without a saddle. It won't be a problem."

Tilghman reached his hand out. "Good luck, Jensen. I hope you find the proof you're looking for, 'cause after all you've done, I'd sure hate to be the one to put a rope around your neck."

Smoke shook his hand. "Me, too, Marshal."

Tilghman climbed into his saddle and touched the brim

of his hat. "One way or another, Jensen, I'll be seein' you."

Smoke nodded as Tilghman jerked his horse's head around and trotted off toward the outlaw band.

Sixteen

Louis Longmont took Sally Jensen's elbow and helped her up the steps to board the train. As she stepped aboard, she dropped her purse and he bent to pick it up.

"Whoa, Sally. What do you have in here, stones?" he asked, a quizzical expression on his face.

She smiled slightly and opened the purse for him to look inside. Nestled there was a chrome-plated Smith and Wesson .36-caliber short-barreled pistol.

He glanced up at her. "You planning on robbing this train?"

"No," she answered, "but if anyone thinks they're going to hang Smoke Jensen without having to first deal with his wife, they are sadly mistaken."

Louis looked back over his shoulder as Monte Carson kissed his wife Mary good-bye. Both men were accompanying Sally on the train ride to Fort Smith, Arkansas. They were planning on appearing as character witnesses for Smoke when he came to trial before Judge Isaac Parker. Sally, however, was planning on doing more than that in the event it became necessary. She intended to break Smoke out of jail if the judge refused to listen to reason and sentenced him to hang.

After they'd gotten seated and the train began to move, Louis opened a window next to his seat and took out one of his trademark long, black stogies. He raised his eyebrows at Sally to see if she minded, and she shook her head.

He scratched a lucifer on his pants leg and put the fire to the cigar, inhaling deeply and blowing the smoke toward the open window.

"Do you think the judge will listen to us and believe Smoke is innocent?" Sally asked Monte.

The lawman slowly shook his head, a worried expression on his face. "Not from what I've heard. The word is Judge Parker is a man who believes fully in the law, spelled with a capital L. If he's got a witness who says he saw Smoke shoot a man in the back, then the judge is gonna sentence him to hang, no doubt about it."

"But, Monte, you and Louis both know if anyone says that about Smoke they must be lying," Sally protested.

He nodded. "Of course we know that, Sally. The trick is going to be to convince the judge the man, whoever he is, must be lying for some reason known only to him."

Sally patted her purse, giving Louis a knowing look. "Well, if the man is in Fort Smith, and he intends to lie about my husband, then I might just have to have a word with him before the trial."

Louis grinned. "We'll *all* have a talk with him, Sally, and don't you worry. If he's lying, Monte and I will make him admit it, one way or another."

At that moment, Cal and Pearlie were riding slowly into the city limits of Jacksboro, Texas. Jacksboro, though much smaller, was a town not unlike Fort Worth and twenty-odd miles to the northwest. Built around the cow business also, but on a much smaller scale, the town consisted mostly of cattle pens, butchering houses, hotels, brothels, saloons, and eating establishments.

The streets were awash with horses, buckboards, children, dogs, and men and women. Many people were walking up and down the wooden boardwalks that lined the dirt streets.

"Jimminy," Cal said as he looked up and down the streets wide-eyed. "I ain't never seen so many people in one place at one time just rushin' around in a hurry like."

Pearlie nodded, following Cal's gaze. "Yep. They all runnin' round like they got to be someplace in a hell of a hurry. Wonder what the rush is all about?"

"How do you 'spect we'll ever find Gibbons in all these people?" Cal asked. "There must be twenty or more saloons an' gamblin' houses."

"We'll just have to start at one end of the town an' make our way up an' down the streets till we find the bastard," Pearlie answered. "Sooner or later, he'll show up. Tinhorns cain't hardly stay away from the poker games. They like a man with a powerful thirst for liquor. They always find someplace to get what they need."

"You want to start now?" Cal asked, eyeing the sun, which was nearing the horizon in the west.

"Naw. Let's find a hotel and grab some grub an' maybe a hot bath. My butt cheeks feel like they done growed to this saddle, an' I'm afraid I smell worse'n some of those beeves walkin' down the street over yonder," he said, inclining his head to where a couple of punchers were slowly driving ten head of cattle right down the middle of Main Street.

After they'd gotten rooms at the Star Hotel on Main Street, and partaken of a hot bath in the communal bathing room on the third floor, the boys went to the nearest restaurant and sat down to have some dinner.

The diner was called the Hofbrau, and was run by a heavyset German woman who spoke with a thick, almost guttural accent. Pearlie had to ask her several times what the different items on the menu were, and he finally just let her decide what he should have—"as long as there's plenty of it," he added as she walked toward the kitchen.

After stuffing themselves on pot roast, German potato salad, and two slices of Dutch apple pie, washed down with a pot of coffee that was so strong Cal said he didn't think it needed a cup, they made their way toward the deputy sheriff's office, just off Main Street.

When they walked through the office door, the first thing Cal and Pearlie noticed was the large number of iron-barred cells in the rear of the building, almost all of which were filled with prisoners.

"Seems like the deputy sheriff does a right smart business in this town," Pearlie observed.

Most of the men appeared to be cowboys, probably just off cattle drives, who looked as if they'd partaken of too much cheap whiskey and not enough food.

"Can I help you gents?" a tall, lean man asked from the side of the room. He was sitting behind an oak desk, scarred with numerous spur marks, with his feet up on the edge of the desk and a long, black cigar protruding from his lips. He was dressed in black pants, with a black vest over a boiled white shirt, and had a thin string tie in a bow at his neck. He had a long, handlebar moustache that reminded Cal of pictures he'd seen of Marshal Wyatt Earp in Tombstone, making Cal wonder if the resemblance was calculated on the deputy sheriff's part.

"Howdy," Pcarlie said, striding up to stand before the desk.

The deputy sheriff nodded, his eyes watching Cal and Pearlie closely as if he were trying to figure out if they were here to cause him some sort of problem.

"Somethin' I can help you with?" the deputy asked again.

Pearlie nodded. "Are you Deputy Sheriff Johnny Walker?"

The man nodded, his right hand resting on the butt of his Colt, ready for trouble.

"U.S. Marshal Heck Thomas told us to look you up," Pearlie said. "He said you might be able to help us find a man."

For the first time, Walker gave a slight smile. "Ole Heck said that, did he?"

"Yes, sir," Cal said.

"Well, who is this man an' what's he wanted for?" Walker asked.

"His name's Gibbons, an' he's a tinhorn gambler," Pearlie said. "He gave a false statement to Marshal Thomas 'bout a killin' in Fort Worth; then he skipped out of town."

Walker's face assumed a dubious expression. "You mean Heck sent you all the way down here just to look for a man who's only offense was lyin'?" He laughed and sat up in his chair. "Hell, if I was to arrest ever' man in town who lied, there wouldn't be room for 'em all in the jail. Most of the men in Jacksboro are guilty of somethin' a whole lot worse at some time in their lives. That's why they end up here 'stead of Fort Worth or some bigger town."

Pearlie's voice got a little harder. "This man lied about a friend of ours . . . said he back-shot a man outside a saloon. Now our friend's on his way to Fort Smith to be hanged."

Walker pursed his lips. "Well, now. That's a horse of a different color. And Heck knows this man was lyin' when he said that?"

"Yes, sir," Cal declared. "He overheard the man admit he'd lied, but before he could get him to change his statement, Gibbons left town."

"Why don't Heck just tell the judge the story? That ought to take care of the matter."

"The judge in question is Judge Isaac Parker," Pearlie said. "You ever dealt with him?"

"Oh," Walker said, leaning back in his chair, "that do make it difficult. Ole Judge Parker is a stickler for the legal niceties bein' followed, all right."

"Sheriff," Pearlie said, a bit impatient. "Will you help us? Marshal Thomas said he'd consider it a personal favor."

"Sure, boys. Just let me grab my hat an' we'll get started lookin' for this tinhorn."

As he accompanied them out the door, Walker asked, "What kind'a fellow is this Gibbons? High-class or low-class?"

"What do you mean?" Pearlie asked.

"Well, is he likely to go for a high-stakes game, or try to find one with less money at stake?"

Pearlie glanced at Cal. "I'd figure him more for the high-stakes game. He dresses real nice, an' the night he saw the gunfight he'd been at one of the best saloons in Fort Worth."

"Then we'll start at the north end of Main Street. That's where all the 'gentlemen' gamblers tend to congregate." Walker smiled. "The whores are prettier up there too."

Pearlie grinned. "That should be his sort of place then, 'cause he do appreciate pretty ladies."

"That's how we trapped him into admitting he'd lied," Cal added.

"Oh, tell me 'bout it," Walker said.

As they turned the corner onto Main Street and proceeded northward, the boys told Walker how they'd paid a whore to get Gibbons to incriminate himself.

Walker nodded appreciatively. "Yep. Seems there's a woman behind the downfall of most men, that or liquor, or both."

When they got to the end of the street, he pointed to

several brightly lit establishments. "That there's the Lucky Lady, an' over there's the Double Eagle an' the Cattleman's Palace. Those'd be the ones to start with."

"Which one has the most women in it?" Cal asked.

"Son," Walker said, "this is a cow town. They all chock full of women."

Pearlie pointed. "The Lucky Lady is the closest. Let's try there first."

As they walked through the batwings, the drone of conversation and laughter dimmed for a moment as the patrons saw the star on Deputy Sheriff Walker's vest, then continued unabated when they saw he was just in to look around.

A couple of the girls smiled and waved at Walker, showing he was no stranger to the establishments, and he waved back, a grin on his face.

Pearlie and Cal pulled their hats down low over their faces so Gibbons wouldn't recognize them if he happened to look their way, and they began to weave among the many tables of cardplayers, searching for the man they were after.

It took them over half an hour to ascertain he wasn't in the Lucky Lady, while the deputy stayed at the bar helping himself to a glass of beer, watching them as they searched.

When they were done, he downed the last of his beer and said, "Well, we can try the Cattleman's Palace next. It's right down the street."

Pearlie chuckled. "It's funny, but the Cattleman's is the name of the hotel we stayed in over in Fort Worth."

"Not so funny when you think about it," the deputy said. "Can't throw a stick in either town without hittin' a cattleman, so it's only natural to put the name on places you want them to come to."

Seventeen

Smoke rode slowly toward Fort Worth, but his conscience wouldn't let him be. *Damn it,* he thought, *the marshal doesn't know what he's getting himself into. Those nine men are hard cases who won't give up without a fight.* He shook his head, thinking. *Nine against one is tall odds, even for a man as good with a gun as Tilghman is supposed to be.*

"Horse," he finally muttered to the animal he'd borrowed from the marshal, "we gotta turn around. I couldn't live with myself if I let the marshal go it alone and he got himself killed."

He pulled the mount's head around and began following the marshal's horse's prints toward the outlaw band. As he rode, he checked his pistols one at a time, making sure they were loaded up six and six, and then he filled his pockets with extra cartridges, just in case the upcoming battle lasted longer than he expected.

Smoke stayed well back, just barely keeping Tilghman in sight on the horizon. He knew if the man knew Smoke was coming to help, he'd try and talk him out of it by saying it was his job, not Smoke's, to corral the desperadoes.

No matter. Smoke intended to help only if it looked like the marshal needed it. If he was doing all right by himself, Smoke would stay out of sight.

* * *

It was almost dusk when Smoke saw the marshal up ahead get down off his horse and run crouching to get behind a small copse of trees near the stream where Smoke had left Stillwell's band of men.

"Come on, horse," Smoke said, putting the spurs to the bronc he was riding and circling around to the west of where the marshal was stalking the outlaws. He wanted to come at them from out of the setting sun if he had to intervene, using every advantage he could in the face of superior numbers.

Just as Smoke reached the edge of the small trickle of water, downstream from the bandits, he heard Marshal Tilghman shout for the men to put down their weapons and come out with their hands up.

"Fat chance," Smoke said to himself. "They're gonna come out, all right, with hands filled with iron and guns blazing."

He knew men like those he'd ridden with, men used to riding the owlhoot trail, wouldn't give up without a fight, and most probably a fight to the death.

Sure enough, seconds later as Smoke was getting down off his horse and creeping up the stream toward the men, he heard a volley of gunshots ring out from the group, answered by the booming explosion of Tilghman's Winchester Yellow Boy.

The group of outlaws hunkered down behind the boles of cottonwood trees and in the shelter of the bank of the small stream they were camped next to.

Jaime Gonzalez, who'd taken over leadership of the bandits after Stillwell had been killed by Smoke, glanced over at George Hungry Bear, lying on his stomach behind a fallen log next to him. "Damn it," he shouted, "I thought that marshal was out of it."

"That Smoke Jensen must've gone to help him after killin' Zach," Hungry Bear yelled back.

"You think we can make the hosses?" Gonzalez said, referring to their horses, which they'd tied to another group of trees fifty yards away.

"And do what?" Hungry Bear answered. "Ride them without saddles?"

"I thought you Injuns were good at that," Gonzalez said with a smirk.

"ridden bareaime, I was raised on a reservation. I ain't never my life, an' I don't intend to start now. We got the white eyes outnumber d We just have to send some of the men sneakin' around behind him an' all this'll be over in a little while."

Gonzalez looked to the other side, where the three men they'd rescued from Tilghman were huddled together behind a large, double-trunked cottonwood.

"Hey, Dynamite Dick," he shouted, "how about you and your friends making your way off to the side an' come at the marshal from behind."

Bodine yelled back. "We ain't got no guns, remember? The marshal took 'em from us when we was arrested."

Gonzalez pulled an old Walker Army Colt from his second holster and pitched it over to Bodine. "Take this," he said.

Bodine leaned out from behind the tree to pick up the pistol, and a slug from Tilghman's Yellow Boy almost took his head off.

"Jesus," he yelled, ducking back behind the tree with the gun in his hand. "Hell, Jaime, this thing must weigh four pounds," he said, hefting the Walker in his hand.

"You want me to hold it for you?" Gonzalez said sarcastically.

"What about us?" Jonathan Mayhew yelled.

Gonzalez nodded at Hungry Bear, who scooted back to his saddlebags, pulled out a couple of older-model Army revolvers, and threw them over to the men with Bodine. "Make your shots count," he said. "We ain't got a whole lot of extra ammo."

Mayhew took one of the Armys and handed the other to Shorty Robinson. "I hope you're better with this than I am," Mayhew said.

Robinson expertly flicked open the loading gate and checked the rounds. "Yeah, I guess you tinhorns are more used to deringers than real guns," he opined.

He added, "This works the same way, you get close enough it don't matter where you hit him, he'll go down."

Gonzalez leaned back and shouted at Brooks Sullivan, a cattle rustler who was riding with Stillwell's gang. "Brooks, you an' Willy Jackson sidle on downstream until you get outta sight of the marshal, then crawl on up the hill until you behind him. When Bodine an' his men are ready on the other side, give a whistle an' we'll all charge at once from all different directions."

Brooks nodded and tapped Jackson on the shoulder, pulling him backward down toward the stream behind them.

They crouched down so they'd have the cover of the shallow banks and began to wade downstream, looking back over their shoulders to make sure the marshal couldn't see them.

Once they'd rounded a corner out of sight, they straightened up and began to move faster. "That goddamned lawman ain't gonna know what hit him," Brooks said, glancing at Jackson.

He stopped talking when he saw Jackson's eyes widen in fear, staring ahead of them down the stream.

Brooks jerked his head around in time to see a tall,

broad-shouldered man standing there, his hands hanging at his sides.

"Howdy, gents," the man said, "remember me?"

"Smoke Jensen!" Brooks exclaimed.

"This ain't your fight, Jensen," Willy Jackson said, his voice trembling a little. "Why don't you just ride off an' mind your own business?"

"It's a little late for that, boys. I've anted up in this game. . . . You want to call my bet or fold?"

"Call!" Brooks shouted, and grabbed for his pistol as Willy Jackson did the same.

Smoke's Colt appeared in his hand as if by magic, cocked and spitting lead before the other two men cleared leather. His first slug took Brooks in the center of his chest, knocking him backward to land with his arms outflung on his back in the icy water of the stream.

A split second later, his second slug entered Willy Jackson's open mouth, punching out his two front teeth and continuing on to blow out the back of his neck, almost decapitating him in the process.

Willy spun around, finally managing to get his pistol out of his holster, but never living to pull the trigger. He fell face-down almost on top of Brooks Sullivan, their blood mingling to stain the clear water of the stream a crimson color.

Smoke hesitated long enough to punch out his empties and reload before continuing his journey upstream.

"What the hell was that?" Gonzalez yelled when he heard the shots from downstream.

Hungry Bear started to shake his head, then ducked as a slug from Tilghman's Yellow Boy slammed into the log he was behind and showered his face with splinters and wood dust. "Shit!" he yelled to Jaime. "We gotta get outta here or he's gonna pick us off one by one."

Just as he said it, one of the other men, Sam Best, a

gunman from Tombstone who'd left town at the urging of Wyatt Earp, jumped to his feet and began to run toward the horses.

He'd only gotten twenty yards when his left knee was blown out by a slug from Marshal Tilghman. After he fell to the ground screaming, he tried to crawl the rest of the way, until another bullet took off the back of his head.

Gonzalez peered to the side, seeing that Bodine and Mayhew and Robinson were almost in position to fire on Tilghman's back.

He raised his head slightly to see better, and a bullet from Tilghman hit him exactly dead center in his Adam's apple, tearing a fist-sized hole in his throat. He grabbed his neck with both hands, trying to scream, but finding he had no vocal cords to make a sound with. He gurgled and strangled for a moment on his own blood, until a second shot blew out the left chamber of his heart on its way through his chest. He dropped like a stone, dead before he hit the ground.

Hungry Bear lowered his head and began to chant a death-prayer in his native tongue. He'd never believed in the old ways, but figured if he was going to die, it wouldn't hurt to try to appease the old ones' gods, if they existed.

Finally, he rolled to the side, seeing Roy Bailey, an eighteen-year-old who fancied himself the next Billy the Kid, hiding in a mulberry bush next to a cottonwood off to the side. Bailey, evidently not as brave in a gunfight as he'd thought, had not shown himself since the marshal had attacked.

"Bailey," Hungry Bear whispered hoarsely, "climb up in that tree you're hiding behind an' see if you can get a shot at the marshal."

"But," the kid said, terror in his voice, "what if he sees me?"

"Then he'll shoot you dead, you yellow-belly," Hungry Bear angrily replied, "but if you don't do what I say, I'll kill you myself!"

Slowly, being careful to remain out of sight, the young man began to climb the tree, his Henry thrown over his back on a rawhide strap.

Just then, Dynamite Dick Bodine and Shorty Robinson jumped to their feet from twenty yards behind Marshal Tilghman and began firing their pistols.

Shorty Robinson's second shot took Tilghman in the fleshy part of his left arm, knocking his rifle from his grasp and spinning him around and saving his life.

Bodine's first shot barely missed the marshal when he spun to the side from the impact of being shot, and as was common with the Walker Colts, the second shot exploded in the firing chamber, taking Bodine's first two fingers of his right hand off at the first knuckle.

As Bodine grabbed his hand and fell screaming to the ground, Tilghman drew his pistol and fired from his position lying on his back, hitting Shorty Robinson in the belly, doubling him over as he grabbed at the hole in his stomach, trying without success to keep his intestines in.

Jonathan Mayhew started to point his pistol at the marshal, had second thoughts, and threw it to the ground, raising his hands over his head. Evidently, he figured he had a better chance with Judge Parker than with the angry-eyed lawman, who was drawing a bead on his face.

"I give up, Marshal," Mayhew shouted. "Please don't kill me!"

"Lie down on your face an' spread your hands out, Mayhew," Tilghman growled. "An' if you reach for that pistol, you're a dead man!"

Hungry Bear looked up at Roy Bailey, hidden in the branches of the cottonwood, his rifle cradled in his arms. "You got a shot?" the Indian asked.

"Naw," Bailey replied, "he's lying down an' I can't get a bead on him."

"Wait a minute," Hungry Bear said, "I'm gonna go out there with my hands up. When he shows himself to arrest me, you plug him good. You understand?"

"Right. You get him to stand up, an' I'll take him down," Bailey replied, more brave now that he knew he couldn't be seen.

"Marshal," Hungry Bear shouted without raising his head up.

"Yeah?" Tilghman replied.

"You've kilt all of us 'cept me. I'm gonna throw my gun out and give myself up."

"Then come on, but don't try nothin' fancy, or I'll drill you through an' through," the marshal replied from his position on the ground.

Hungry Bear pitched his pistol over the log and stood up, his hands held high over his head. He stepped over the log and began to walk toward where Tilghman lay.

When Hungry Bear was out in the clear, away from his gun, the marshal stood up, motioning with his Colt for Mayhew to follow him toward the Indian.

Mayhew and George Hungry Bear stood in front of Marshal Tilghman, their hands up. "You men are under arrest," Tilghman said, reaching behind his back to pull out some manacles to put on their wrists.

A sudden shot rang out from the direction of the grove of trees near the stream, and Tilghman whirled around, crouching, pointing his pistol toward the sound.

A body, still holding a Henry repeating rifle, fell from a tree to land with a resounding thump on the hard-packed dirt. Roy Bailey squirmed once, calling out for his mamma; then he quivered for a moment and died, still holding his rifle.

A tall, dark figure stepped from the cover of the trees,

his hands above his head. "Don't shoot, Marshal," the man called. "It's Smoke Jensen."

As Smoke approached, the marshal shook his head, grinning. "Jensen, I thought you was on your way to Fort Worth."

Smoke shrugged, lowering his hands and holstering his Colt. "I was, but I thought you might need a little backup."

"That you I heard shootin' over downstream a while back?"

Smoke nodded. "Yeah. A couple of the gang were on their way to sneak up on your back. I let 'em know that wasn't appreciated."

Tilghman laughed. "Yeah, I heard how you told 'em, with a .44, it sounded like."

"You need some help with that arm?" Smoke asked, noticing the marshal's wound.

"If you could keep a gun on these galoots, I'll tie it off with my bandanna. Then we can get 'em on their horses for the ride back to the wagon."

"No problem, Marshal." Smoke glanced around. "You ought to have enough broncs to pull it the rest of the way."

"Yeah, an' you can get back on your way to Fort Worth to finish your business there."

As Smoke started to ride away, the marshal added, "Jensen, I want you to know I'm grateful for what you did here today."

Smoke nodded.

"But, Jensen, I've never let my personal feelin's interfere with my work as a U.S. marshal. Even though you probably saved my life by doin' what you did, if you're still wanted for murder when I get to Fort Smith, I gotta tell you, I'll be comin' after you, just like any other wanted man."

"I appreciate the warning, Marshal, and I would expect nothing less," Smoke said.

"Just wanted you to know not to expect any special treatment 'cause of today."

"Don't worry about it, Marshal. I'm going to get this mess cleared up so there won't be any need of you having to track me down."

"I hope so, Jensen, for your sake, 'cause I always get my man, one way or another."

Eighteen

As he rode toward Fort Worth, Smoke realized he had to do some heavy thinking. It wasn't going to be enough to get that tinhorn who said he'd seen Smoke shoot the Durango Kid in the back to recant his testimony. Smoke was going to have to find the culprit who did the shooting to really clear his name. After all, he'd been the one found standing in the alleyway over the dead man's body.

Smoke began to go through various possibilities in his mind. Murders weren't all that uncommon in the West, especially in cow towns like Fort Worth. Bumping a man's arm at a bar, stepping on his toes, or even stealing a whore he was wooing was often grounds for senseless killing and violence. But to cold-bloodedly shoot a man in the back spoke of a hatred more intense than that usually occasioned by a barroom fight or imagined insult.

He figured it had to be someone with a powerful hate, or a real good reason to see the Kid dead, who did him in. As he thought back over the events of that night, he remembered the Kid had said they'd only just gotten to town with their beeves the night before, so it would be unusual for him to have made such a deadly enemy so quickly.

Smoke nodded as he continued to think it through. That meant the most likely suspects were the men riding with the Kid. One or more of them would probably have reason to want the outlaw dead. "Money or women," Smoke muttered to himself, thinking extreme violence usually had one or the other of those two ancient motives behind it.

"Now all I have to do is track down the men who were riding with the Kid and find out which one of them had the most reason, and the opportunity, to shoot him dead," he said in a low voice to the back of his horse's head. "I just hope they're still in town," he added, thinking it would be difficult if not impossible to trail them if they'd gone on their way without telling anyone where they were headed.

In Jacksboro, Cal and Pearlie had failed to find the gambler Gibbons on their first night of searching.

"I'm sorry, boys," Deputy Sheriff Johnny Walker said after trailing them through most of the saloons along Main Street. "I got to get back to my duties, but I'll tell you what. You find that galoot, see if he's willin' to change his story, an' I'll write it all down for Marshal Thomas, and I'll even send a wire to Judge Parker over at Fort Smith."

"Thanks, Sheriff," Pearlie said. "If we find him, I'll guarantee he'll tell the truth."

"I hope so, boys, 'cause if he don't change his story, I'm afraid the hangin' judge is gonna live up to his name with your podna."

After the deputy sheriff left them at the lobby of their hotel, Cal asked, "What now, Pearlie? You want to walk around the rest of the night an' see if'n we can find Gibbons some more?"

"Naw," Pearlie said. "If he was gonna gamble tonight, he'd already be at the tables. Maybe he was so tired he took the night off to get some rest."

"Or maybe he found hisself a girl to spend the night with," Cal said.

Pearlie nodded. "That's a possibility. I suggest we get some shut-eye an' start out first thing in the mornin'. If we don't find him by lunchtime, we can take a nap an' be fresh an' ready to try again tomorrow night."

"I just hope we're not too late for Smoke," Cal said in a low voice, a sorrowful expression on his face.

"Don't you worry none 'bout Smoke," Pearlie said. "He's been in plenty worse situations than this. He can take care of himself."

"It's not Smoke I'm worried about," Cal said as they climbed the stairs toward their room. "It's that Hangin' Judge. From what I hear, he's a mite too anxious to use that rope of his."

As soon as Smoke got to Fort Worth, he went to the Cattleman's Hotel, where he'd left Cal and Pearlie.

He walked up to the desk clerk. "Can I have my key?"

The man looked up from his register, a startled look on his face. "But . . . but I thought you were on your way to Fort Smith." It was the same snooty dandy that had been on duty when Smoke and the boys first arrived.

Smoke smiled reassuringly. "New evidence came in, Jason, so Marshal Tilghman let me go. Now, I'd like to get to my room, get a bath, and catch a little shut-eye, after I talk to my friends."

Jason shook his head. "Your friends left the other day."

"Left?"

"Yep. They were asking all over town about that gambler fellow—I can't bring his name to mind—and then they heard he went to Jacksboro, so they went after him."

"Oh. Well, has my suite on the top floor been rented out?

"No, sir."

"Then give me the key and see if you can get the bath boy to heat up some water."

"But, it's the middle of the day," the dandy said, his face aghast at the idea of anyone bathing before darkness came.

"Jason," Smoke said, his patience wearing thin. "I haven't bathed in almost a week. Get the water hot and give me a key before I come across that desk and teach you how to do your job!"

"Yes, sir, Mr. Jensen," Jason said, sleeving sweat off his forehead with the back of his arm as he handed the key across the desk to Smoke.

After his bath, Smoke slept the rest of the afternoon, getting up just after sundown. He dressed in clean clothes, electing to wear black trousers, a white shirt under a black vest, and no coat, since the cool spring nights were mild.

He ate a hearty dinner at the Cattleman's Hotel, then went looking for the Kid's friends. He knew the Kid and his men had liked the Silver Dollar, for that was where he'd first met them, so he headed there to begin his search.

He eased through the batwings and stepped to the side, as was his habit, observing the room for possible danger before entering. He didn't know if Cal and Pearlie had talked with Marshal Heck Thomas, or even if the marshal was still in town, but he didn't want to meet up with him until he'd had a chance to do some looking around.

He saw no one familiar, so he made his way to the bar and ordered a mug of beer. It looked to be a long night of searching, so he stayed away from whiskey.

He took his mug and leaned back with his elbows on the bar, looking for the women who'd been entertaining the Kid and his friends the night of the killing.

Building himself a cigarette, he drank and smoked

slowly, waiting for one or another of the women to show themselves.

Finally, while on his second beer, Smoke saw one of the women come down the stairs, her arm around the waist of a drunken cowboy.

He got the bartender's attention and nodded at the girl. "What's that lady's name?" Smoke asked.

The man chuckled. "She ain't exactly a lady, but her name's Dolly."

Smoke grinned. He glanced at the barman. "Seen Marshal Thomas around lately?"

"No, thank goodness. Word is he's ridin' around to all the local ranchers, askin' some questions 'bout stolen beeves." The man began wiping the bar down with a soiled rag. "Good thing too. Ever' time he comes in here I lose business. Ain't nobody likes to drink and carouse with a U.S. marshal lookin' over their shoulders."

Smoke threw a coin on the table and touched his hat. "Thanks for the information."

The man raised his eyebrows. "You want to . . . talk to Dolly?"

Smoke nodded. "Yeah. I'm going to go over to that table in the corner. Why don't you send her and a bottle of whiskey over?" he said, adding another coin to the one on the bar.

"Yes, sir," the man said, sliding the coins into his pocket.

Smoke carried his beer to the table and took a seat, his back to the wall, just in case the Kid's friends happened to come in. He was relieved he didn't have to worry about running into Marshal Thomas for a while. It made things a whole lot simpler.

After a few minutes, he saw the bartender whisper into Dolly's ear. She glanced his way, smiled, and disengaged herself from the grasp of the drunken cowboy. Grabbing the whiskey bottle and a couple of glasses from the barman, she began to walk toward Smoke, grinning and waggling her hips as she moved through the crowd.

She took a seat next to Smoke at the table, sitting so close their hips touched.

"Howdy, cowboy. Max over at the bar said you asked for me special."

"That's right," Smoke said.

She deftly pulled the cork from the bottle and poured them both drinks, hers slightly heavier than his.

Clinking glasses, she said, "Here's to a good night, an' a mornin' without a hangover."

Smoke touched glasses and took a small sip of his whiskey.

Dolly leaned over and whispered in his ear. "You want to drink for a while, or just head on upstairs?"

"Let's talk for a while," Smoke said.

She raised her eyebrows. "Well, mister, a drink'll buy you a little time, but for serious talk, it's gonna cost you more than that."

Smoke pulled a double eagle gold coin from his shirt pocket and placed it in her hand.

Her eyes widened. "Twenty dollars? Hell, cowboy, for that much you get all night."

Smoke laughed. He knew the going rate for all night was closer to five dollars, but he didn't say anything.

He kept the conversation to generalities until Dolly had downed several drinks. He was hoping to get her drunk enough to not be suspicious when he began asking her questions about the Kid and his men.

After a while, she stared at him. "I don't remember entertainin' you before, mister, an' believe me, I'd remember you."

"No, we haven't met before."

"Then why'd you ask for me? Somebody give you my name?"

It was the perfect opening for Smoke. "Yeah. I saw you with some men several days ago. A tall man dressed in black, a Mexican with three fingers on his left hand, and two other gents."

"Oh, them," she said, a chill in her voice.

"You remember them?" Smoke asked.

"Sure," she said, shrugging her shoulders. "The only one in the group who was willin' to spend any money went an' got himself shot before I could get him upstairs."

"Oh?" Smoke asked, pretending to be surprised.

"Yeah. An' the other galoots were so cheap they thought buyin' me an' Suzie a few drinks entitled them to take liberties, if you know what I mean."

Smoke nodded.

"We finally told them how the cow ate the cabbage," she said, slurring her words a little. "If you wanna play, you gotta pay."

Smoke laughed out loud. He was beginning to like this Dolly. She was plainspoken, but had more personality than most women in her line of work.

"Have they been back?" Smoke asked, an innocent expression on his face.

"Naw," she said. "When they found out we wasn't givin' it away, they kind'a lost interest. Said they had to sell some cattle 'fore they could spend that kind'a money on whores," she added, an insulted look on her face.

"You know where they are now?" Smoke asked.

Her eyes suddenly became sharp, showing she wasn't as drunk as she'd been pretending to be.

"Oh, so this isn't 'bout you an' me, it's 'bout them cowboys, ain't it?"

Smoke figured he had nothing to lose by being truthful. "Yes, it is."

Her expression became shrewd. "What's it worth to you if I can find out where they're stayin'?"

"You can keep that double eagle and I won't make you earn it."

She smiled, looking him up and down. "Now, who said I'd mind earnin' it with you?" she asked.

He shook his head. "You can keep the coin and I'll give you another just like it, if you let me know next time you see them, or can find out what hotel they're staying at."

She grinned. "Now you're talkin'. Where're you stayin', cowboy?"

"The name's Jensen, and I'm at the Cattleman's Hotel."

She raised her eyebrows at the mention of his hotel, which was about the swankiest in town.

"Well, I'll start askin' around. I should hear somethin' by tomorrow night."

He put his hand over hers. "Dolly, be careful. These men are dangerous. Don't let them find out you're asking around about them."

She bent down and pulled the hem of her dress up, exposing a garter on her leg holding a double-barreled derringer. "You think they're dangerous, honey, you ain't seen Dolly at work!"

Nineteen

Cal and Pearlie, after sleeping most of the afternoon, arose just before sundown and went to a local eatery for dinner. Pearlie, as usual, ate enough for two men, while Cal, who was worried about Smoke, hardly touched his meal.

"You got to put some vittles in your gut, Cal," Pearlie said as he stuffed a large piece of corn bread in his mouth. "You cain't do Smoke no good if'n you're famished."

"I'll eat when we get that statement from Gibbons," Cal replied sullenly. "I just don't have no appetite, thinkin' of Smoke in that jail in Fort Smith."

"All right then," Pearlie said, "let's get to it."

He paid their bill and they walked out onto Main Street. "Where do you think we ought'a try next?" Cal asked.

"Well, we tried all the highfalutin places last night, an' didn't see hide nor hair of the galoot," Pearlie drawled. "Maybe he's short of cash an' cain't afford the high-stakes games. Tonight, let's hit the places down by the Mexican quarter. Maybe we'll find him there."

They turned left on Main and walked five blocks, then took another left toward the cattle yards where the lower-class part of town was. Its residents were mainly Mexicans, blacks, and working-class whites, and the area had several cantinas and bars that were downright dangerous to enter.

According to Johnny Walker, even he didn't go into the area at night unless backed up by at least two other deputies. As they walked, Cal and Pearlie both loosened the rawhide hammer-guards on their pistols, ready in case of trouble.

In the third place they entered, which had the unlikely name El Gato Negro, The Black Cat, they found their man. The saloon was made of adobe and had a low ceiling and dirt floors. With the few lanterns and hazy, smokey air, it was hard to see more than ten feet in front of your face, but the boys recognized Gibbons's flashy yellow and black plaid coat from across the room.

"There the sumbitch is," Pearlie growled, loosening his Colt in its holster. "You sidle on around to get between him an' the back door, an' I'll ease on up to him from the front."

"Pearlie," Cal said, staring at the table Gibbons was sitting at.

"Yeah?"

"Watch your back. Those men he's playin' with look awful hard to me."

Pearlie nodded. Cal was right. At the table with Gibbons were two Mexicans with long, handlebar mustaches, both wearing large Colt Army pistols on their belts and knives in scabbards stuck in their pants. A huge, six-foot-tall black man wearing an undershirt and pants held up with a rope was the fourth man at the table.

Cal moved through the crowd of drunken men until he was standing in front of the rear door, the one leading back to the privy in the alley behind the saloon. He leaned back against the wall next to the door and let his hand rest on the butt of his pistol, sweating nervously as he watched the milling crowd in the small room.

Pearlie walked over to stand behind and to the side of Gibbons, out of sight of the gambler. He noticed most of the money and poker chips at the table were piled in front of the tinhorn, and that the other men at the table were staring at Gibbons with ill-concealed anger.

Gibbons must have known he was in over his head, for when he turned and saw Pearlie standing beside him, he grinned nervously and greeted Pearlie like an old friend.

"Why, Pearlie, how're you doing?" he asked, turning in his chair to face him.

Pearlie nodded at the pile of money in front of Gibbons. "Pick up your winnin's, Gibbons," he said in a low, hard voice. "We got to talk."

"Gladly, my boy, gladly," the gambler said, taking off his hat and raking the bills, chips, and coins into it.

"Wait a minute, *señor*," the Mexican next to Gibbons said harshly. "The gringo has won all our moneys. He cannot leave."

Gibbons held out his hand in a placating manner. "Don't worry, Jose," he said. "I'm just goin' out to the privy to relieve myself and talk to these gentlemen for a moment. I'll be right back."

"You better, mistuh," the large black man said, "or I'll cut you up real good."

Pearlie noticed the man had a machete stuck through the rope in his pants.

Gibbons nodded, smiling and grinning as sweat ran down from his forehead to drip off his chin.

"Come on, Pearlie, let's go out back and settle this."

Pearlie followed him out the back door, picking up Cal on the way. Once outside, he grabbed Gibbons and swung him around. "Are you gonna change that lyin' statement you gave to Marshal Tilghman, or am I gonna have to beat the shit outta you?" Pearlie asked.

Gibbons held up his hands, palms outward. "Pearlie, I'll sign anything you want if you'll get me out of here. These men are not very gracious losers, and I'm afraid they plan to do me bodily harm if they don't win their money back."

A soft sound from behind him made Pearlie turn around. The Mexicans were standing there, both with large pistols in their hands. One of them held up a pair of aces. "You left these behind you, *señor,*" he said to Gibbons. "They fell out of your coat when you left the table."

"Why," Gibbons said, his voice quavering at the sight of the cards, "those aren't mine!"

"Lying gringo," the Mexican said, letting the hammer down on the pistol. It exploded, sending a .44 slug slamming into Gibbons's chest, flinging him backward to land half in the privy, his head resting against the seat.

Both Mexicans turned their pistols on Cal and Pearlie, who were standing there openmouthed at the suddenness of the violence.

"Please be so kind as to not move, *señors,*" one said while the other walked over to Gibbons's dead body and removed his hat. The man emptied the money out of it and set it gently back down on Gibbons's skull.

"Adios, señors," the other said, and they took off running down the alleyway.

"Goddamn!" Pearlie exclaimed, bending over Gibbons to check for signs of life. Finding none, he grabbed Cal and pulled him down the alley away from the direction the Mexicans took. "Let's get the hell out of here before someone comes out and accuses us of killin' Gibbons," he said, breaking into a run.

"But . . . but what about Smoke?" Cal said, jogging beside Pearlie as they rounded a corner.

"We're gonna have to find some other way to clear him," Pearlie said. " 'Cause Gibbons sure as hell ain't gonna change his statement now."

* * *

Pearlie and Cal walked back over to Main Street and entered Deputy Sheriff Johnny Walker's office. As usual, Walker was sitting back in his chair with his feet up on his desk, sipping coffee out of a stained mug.

"Howdy, boys," he said, smiling. "You find that tinhorn yet?"

Pearlie nodded. "Yeah, we found him. Trouble is, a couple of Mexes put a .44 slug in his chest. He's lyin' in the privy out behind the Black Cat cantina."

Walker pursed his lips, staring at Pearlie. "I don't suppose there're any witnesses to say you boys didn't do it, are there?"

Cal shook his head. "Sheriff, you know we needed him to save our friend's life. We wouldn't't've killed him."

After a moment, Walker nodded. "I suppose that does make sense."

"Are you gonna go over there and check it out?" Pearlie asked.

"You say you're sure he's dead?"

"Deader 'n a stone," Pearlie said.

Walker shrugged. "Then I don't see no sense in botherin' about it tonight. I'll amble on over there at first light in the morning."

"Sheriff," Cal said, "after the gunshot, no one even came out of the cantina to see what was happenin'."

The deputy laughed. "No, I don't s'pect they did."

"Isn't that a little strange?" Pearlie asked.

"You boys know how many men get killed in that area ever' night?"

The boys shook their heads.

"Enough so's it not nothin' anybody over there gets too excited about. Hell, they'll probably go on using the privy too, after movin' him to the side a bit, an' not even say nothin' about it."

"What do you suggest we do now?" Pearlie asked.

"Seems to me, your only chance of helpin' your friend is to find out who really killed the man in Fort Worth. Was it me, I'd go back there and see what I could dig up."

Pearlie looked at Cal. "He's right, Cal."

"Then let's go," Cal said. "Smoke don't have too much time left."

Twenty

Sally, followed by Monte Carson and Louis Longmont, walked right by the clerk guarding the door to Judge Isaac Parker's chambers.

"Hey, miss, you can't do that . . ." the young man began, starting to rise from his chair.

Sally, without pausing, turned steel-hard eyes on the boy and pointed her finger at him. "Sit!" she said, putting her hand on the door and pushing it open.

The young clerk stared openmouthed at Louis and Monte as they followed Sally into the room. Louis glanced back over his shoulder with a sympathetic look at the man. "Women," he said, and shrugged as he walked into the room.

Parker looked up from his desk, tilting his head to see over the half-glasses on his nose. "What is the meaning of this interruption of my work?" he asked imperiously.

Undaunted, Sally strode right up to the front of his desk and stood there, staring down at the judge. He was in his mid-thirties, dark-haired, and wore a dark gray suit coat and vest over a white shirt and black bow tie. His face appeared stern and his visage was serious, and Sally thought to herself, *Here is a man who thinks he is doing God's own work. He'll be pompous and take himself too seriously, I'll bet.*

"My name is Sally Jensen, and I've come to talk to my husband."

The judge shook his head and leaned back in his chair. "I don't handle visitation of prisoners, ma'am. You'll have to speak to the Superintendent of Jails. Didn't my clerk inform you of that fact?"

"I'm afraid the young man didn't have a chance to inform us of anything, Your Honor," Louis said.

Parker cut his eyes to Louis. "And just who might you be?" he asked.

Louis gave a short bow. "I'm Louis Longmont, Your Honor. Pleased to make your acquaintance."

Parker's eyes roamed to Monte Carson, who took off his hat and held it in both hands in front of him. "I'm Monte Carson, Judge. Sheriff of Big Rock, Colorado."

Parker steepled his hands under his chin and glared at the group standing in front of his desk.

"I presume you all have some reason for being here?"

"We've been to the Superintendent of Jails, Judge Parker," Sally said, "and he said there is no one in jail by the name Smoke Jensen."

"Ah, so you're Smoke Jensen's wife," Parker said, his eyes softening a little. "I've heard a great deal about your husband, especially in the last couple of weeks."

Sally held her chin up high. "Then you know Smoke couldn't possibly have shot a man in the back."

The judge leaned forward. "I notice you didn't say your husband couldn't possibly have shot the man, just that he didn't do it in the back."

Sally looked at the judge as though he was a simpleton. "Of course he could have shot the man, given adequate provocation. My husband is a famous shootist, Judge, and this is the West. On occasion, men come up to Smoke to try and get a reputation, or to prove their bravery. Most times, he can talk them out of trying his hand with a gun, but sometimes it just isn't possible and he has to kill them. He regrets it, but he simply does not instigate confrontations, and he is so proficient with firearms that he does not need to shoot anyone in the back."

"I see," the judge said, leaning back in his chair. "So your husband has killed many men, Mrs. Jensen?"

Sally's eyes became flat, and she gave him a look that would curdle milk. "As have you, Judge Parker."

Parker looked offended. "Surely you're not comparing *me* to a gunfighter?"

"No," Sally said simply, "a gunfighter shoots in self-defense and puts his own life on the line, while you hide behind those law books on your shelves and make your judgments with no risk to yourself." She hesitated. "But the end result is the same, one man left alive, one man left dead."

Sally regretted her words almost immediately. She could tell by the hurt look on the judge's face that he was wounded by her accusation, and remembered hearing that he often shed tears when sentencing a man to die by hanging.

He looked off out his window, which overlooked the scaffold in the distance on which so many men had died by his pronouncements.

"Please, Mrs. Jensen, take a seat," he finally said, waving his hand at a group of chairs near his desk.

Sally, Louis, and Monte sat down, waiting to see what Parker had to say.

After a moment, he spoke, his eyes soft now with none of their former arrogance. "First of all, Mrs. Jensen, I'll tell you what I tell all of the men I sentence to hang. It is not me that is killing these men, it is the law, the law they broke when they murdered or raped or robbed someone. I am only its instrument, carrying out the justice demanded by the men who wrote the laws in the first place and by the society which demanded a code of conduct that, if broken, must be punished."

"I know that, Judge Parker, and I apologize if I offended you. But you must also realize that I am fighting for my husband's life. He's a man I know as well as one can know another human being, and I *know* that he could not have done the crime of which he is being accused."

"Then he will be set free, Mrs. Jensen. On that you have my word."

"Excuse me, Judge," Louis interrupted, "but it is not as simple as that. You and I both know that innocent men have been convicted of crimes they did not commit. That is a fact, and that is what we aim to prevent if we can help it."

Before the judge could respond, Monte leaned forward in his chair. "Judge, we heard someone had given testimony that he saw Smoke shoot the man in the back. Is that true?"

Parker looked at a stack of papers on his desk and thumbed through them looking for a copy of the wire he'd received. "Ah, here we are," he said, holding up a telegram. "You are right, sir, there is such a testimony on record." He read further for a moment, then added, "However, Marshal Heck Thomas says he has evidence the man was lying in his statement and is taking steps to get it revised."

The three visitors looked at each other, relief on their faces. "There, Judge, I told you so," Sally said.

He held up his hand. "Hold on a moment, Mrs. Jensen. As I told Marshal Thomas in a reply to his telegram, the original statement will hold if the witness does not recant his testimony. That is the law."

"So, even though a sworn peace officer of this court tells you the witness is lying, you're still going to rely on perjured testimony?" Louis asked, disgust in his voice.

The judge spread his hands. "I have no choice, Mr. Longmont. As I said, it is the law."

"Then the law is in error," Louis said angrily.

Sally, trying to head off a confrontation, said, "May we see my husband, Judge Parker?"

"Oh, I thought you knew," he answered.

"Knew what?" Sally asked.

"There has been some delay in his arrival here. Marshal Bill Tilghman was bringing him, along with three other miscreants, overland by caged wagon, and he has failed to arrive on schedule."

"What has happened to them?" she asked, a worried look on her face.

"I do not know, Mrs. Jensen. We have received no word from either Marshal Tilghman or any other law enforcement officers concerning these prisoners."

"Well, what are you doing about it?"

The judge looked uncomfortable, and wouldn't meet Sally's eyes as he replied, "Mrs. Jensen, you have to realize, our U.S. marshals each cover thousands of square miles of wilderness territory. They go out alone, and come back alone. We simply do not have the manpower to provide them with adequate backup. They are, in a very real sense, on their own out there."

"Do you really expect me to just sit here and wait to hear if my husband is alive or not?" Sally asked, rising from her chair.

For the first time in the meeting, the judge grinned, slightly. "No, Mrs. Jensen. After meeting you, I am quite sure that is the last thing a lady such as yourself would do."

He bent his head and scribbled a quick note. "If you will give this to one of the marshals in the main office, one of them will show you on a map the route Tilghman would most likely take to bring your husband here from Fort Worth."

He leaned back, still smiling. "And then, you may go out to meet him, or to see what might have befallen him on the trip here."

She took the note and turned without another word, hurrying out the door.

Louis took the time to tip his hat at Judge Parker. "Thank you for your courtesy, sir."

Parker's eyes remained on Sally's back as she left the room. "She is quite a woman, isn't she?" he murmured, almost as if to himself.

Louis smiled. "She is that, all right!"

"This Jensen fellow may or may not be a murderer, but after meeting his wife, I'd say either way, he is one of the luckiest men in the world."

Louis nodded. "You are right, Judge. They just don't make them like Sally Jensen very often."

Louis paused when he got to the door. "In fact," he added, looking back over his shoulder, "I'm quite sure she is unique among women."

After Louis and Monte and Sally had gone, Parker got a fresh sheet of paper and began writing a telegram to be sent to Marshal Heck Thomas in Fort Worth.

"Marshal Thomas, I have come to believe you may be correct in proposing Jensen's innocence. Spare no expense in investigating the aforementioned affair. I want to get at the truth in this matter."

He signed it at the bottom and called in his clerk to get it sent at once.

Twenty-one

Dolly, the prostitute Smoke had talked to about the Durango Kid's men, waited until the bartender began to shut the Silver Dollar Saloon down before making her move.

She checked the loads in the derringer in her garter, then made her way down Main Street to the Star Hotel. She knew the men who'd been riding with the Durango Kid were staying there, but hadn't mentioned the fact to Smoke Jensen, thinking she might be able to get more money from the men by not telling of their whereabouts than from the big, handsome cowboy who'd braced her in the saloon.

Dolly, on her own since the age of fourteen when her stepfather raped her and then threw her out of the house, had learned the hard way that a girl had to take care of herself, because sure as hell no one else was going to do it.

When she stepped through the door of the Star, the clerk, dozing at the main desk, woke up and scowled at her. "We don't allow no whores in here," he said in a nasty tone of voice.

Dolly glared at him for a moment, then forced herself to smile. After all, the one thing she'd learned in her years earning a living on her back was that a smile would get most of what she needed from most men.

"Excuse me, sir," she said, laying it on thick, "I have personal business with some of your guests. I am in possession of information they urgently need. I'm sure they would be most . . . upset if you kept me from seeing them."

"What guests?" the man asked suspiciously.

"Misters Juan Gomez, Jack Cummings, and Bob Gatling," she answered sweetly.

Evidently the man knew whom she was talking about and didn't want to anger them. As he remembered, they were indeed hard-looking men.

"Top of the stairs on the left, Rooms 302 through 304," he said, immediately laying his head back down on the desk and resuming his nap.

Dolly climbed the stairs, looking around at the lavish furnishings of the elegant hotel. It wasn't often . . . Hell, it was never that she got to see such opulence. She felt sure she'd been right in her decision not to tell the tall man about where these men were staying. If they could afford this hotel, then they could afford to pay her a lot of money to keep their secret. The thought she'd be walking into danger never entered her mind. In her profession, danger was an everyday occurrence and was accepted as the price of doing business.

She knocked on the door to Room 302, fluffing her hair a bit to make herself appear more attractive.

A gruff voice, slurred a bit by too much alcohol, called out, "Who is it?"

"A friend," Dolly answered in as sweet a voice as she could manage.

After some rumbling noises inside, indicating the man was putting on his pants and boots, the door opened a crack. One eye peered out, checking the corridor behind Dolly to make sure she was alone before opening the door fully.

Three-Fingers Juan Gomez opened the door and stepped out into the hall, a Colt hanging from his right hand. "What do you want? I didn't order no girl."

"I have some information I thought you might like to have," Dolly said. "It concerns your friend who was killed the other night."

"Yeah? What is it?" he asked.

Dolly glanced up and down the hall. "I don't believe you'd want me to go into it out here in the corridor where just anyone could overhear."

Gomez considered this for a moment, then stepped aside, letting her into his room. She crossed the small space and took a seat in a chair by the window, arranging her skirts as she sat so she could get to her derringer quickly if the need arose.

"All right, tell me," he said gruffly, flopping on the bed, putting his feet up, and crossing his hands behind his head as he lay back against the pillows.

"Well," Dolly said, dropping her gaze demurely, "the information is rather important, and I was hoping you'd offer to pay me for my trouble in bringing it to you at such a late hour."

Gomez smiled cruelly. "I ain't payin' you nothing, girl. Now you tell me what you got to tell me or I'll just have to beat it outta you."

Dolly smiled, causing Gomez to assume a worried expression. He wasn't used to women not being afraid of him when he threatened them.

"I'm sorry, sir, but I've already been offered twenty dollars for the information from another fellow. If you don't want to pay, that's fine."

She started to get up from her chair. "I'll just go to this other gentleman and sell him what I know."

Gomez was off the bed and across the room in a flash. He grabbed Dolly by the throat, his eyes wild with anger.

"Don't you go threatenin' me, you little whore!" he screamed. "Now, you gonna tell me or do I have to hurt you?"

Without taking her eyes off Gomez's face, Dolly reached under her skirt and brought out the derringer. She thumbed back the double hammers with a loud metallic click, and stuck the twin barrels under the point of Gomez's chin.

"Just how do you plan to hurt me, sir, with what little brains you have scattered all over the ceiling?" she said in a calm, low voice.

Gomez's eyes rolled downward and he released Dolly's throat, holding his hands high above his head. "Be careful with that . . . miss," he stammered. "It's liable to go off."

She smiled into his eyes. "If it does, you'll never hear it, Pancho," she said derisively.

She pushed him back and walked over to his bed, where he'd laid his Colt. She picked it up and let the hammers down on the derringer. "The Colt makes a much nicer hole than that little popgun, don't you think?" she asked.

Gomez didn't answer. He couldn't take his eyes off the barrel of the Colt, which was pointing at his groin.

"Perhaps I'm talking to the wrong man," Dolly said. "Why don't we wake your friends up and see if they might be more reasonable about paying me for information that is vital to your survival."

She put the gun under her overcoat and followed Gomez as he went to the adjoining rooms and managed to get his friends awake. They all gathered in Curly Bob Gatling's room. The three men sat next to each other on the bed, while Dolly sat across the room in a chair, the big Colt resting on her lap.

"Now, gentlemen, what am I bid for what I know?"

The three looked at each other. Finally, Curly Bob said, "We can give you twenty dollars."

She smiled and shook her head. "I told the Mex here I've already been offered twenty dollars and I wouldn't have had to go to all this trouble. No, gentlemen, you're going to have to sweeten the pot a little to ante up in this game."

The men put their heads together, whispering quietly among themselves for a moment, then looked back at Dolly. "We might be able to get forty dollars together, but that's all we got. We got some beeves for sale, but we ain't got the money for 'em just yet."

Dolly pursed her lips, thinking. Forty dollars was all right, especially if it was all they had. After all, she reasoned to herself, there was nothing to keep her from selling the same information to the man who called himself Smoke after she'd made her deal here.

"All right," she said, "get it."

The men fumbled in their pockets, finally having to go to some saddlebags lying on the dresser to get the money together. Curly Bob took the handful of crumpled bills and reached across the room to hand it to Dolly. She took the bills without taking her hand off the Colt.

"Now, just what is so all-fired important that we'd be willin' to pay forty dollars to hear?" Rawhide Jack Cummings asked, the first time he'd spoken since Dolly entered the room.

"Two things," Dolly said. "Word on the street is that Marshal Heck Thomas is going around to all the local ranchers checking up to see if anyone sold you those beeves you're wanting to sell. So, if you plan to get rid of them and get out of town, you'd better hurry."

"What makes you think our cattle are stolen?" Gomez asked, trying to assume an innocent expression.

"Oh, please," Dolly said, laughing. "I've been entertaining cowboys for years now, and if you three ever earned a dime herding or selling beeves, I'll eat this here Colt."

Curly Bob chuckled. He was beginning to like this woman. She knew how to read men. "What else do you have for us?" he asked, smiling at her.

"There's this tall, good-looking gent, goes by the name Smoke Jensen, asking around town about you boys." She raised her eyebrows. "Seems he wants to meet with you in the worst way."

"Jensen?" Gomez asked. "I thought the marshal arrested him an' hauled his ass off to Fort Smith."

"Must have been a quick trip," Dolly observed.

"What's he want with us?" Rawhide Jack asked, puzzled.

"Says he wants to talk with you boys about finding out who killed your friend, the Durango Kid."

"That don't make no sense," Curly Bob said. "I thought Jensen killed him."

Gomez, who'd begun to sweat at the mention of Smoke Jensen, stood up. "That all you got to say?" he asked, his voice rough.

"Yes, for now," Dolly replied, also standing up and moving toward the door. "However, if I hear anything else, I'll be sure to give you gentlemen a chance to buy it. That is, if you live long enough to sell those beeves you've got stashed at the edge of town."

Gomez took a step toward her, but Dolly eared back the hammer on the Colt. "Now, Pancho, don't do anything stupid, all right? I'd hate to wake everyone in the hotel up by blowing your guts all over the wall."

Gomez stopped and backed up, sweat pouring from his forehead.

Dolly cocked her head. "I can see that the idea that Smoke Jensen wants to talk to you about your friend's death has upset you."

She glanced at Curly Bob and Rawhide Jack. "Perhaps you gentlemen better have a talk with your friend here before Smoke finds you. It appears to me he might know more than you do about who shot the Kid."

Dolly opened the door and stepped out into the hall. "I'll just leave your pistol in the next room on my way out. But, gentlemen, don't try and come after me for a little while, because I may just stand out here in the hall to see if anyone tries to open this door. Good morning, gents, I'll see you later."

After she eased the door shut, Curly Bob stepped around to stand in front of Gomez.

"Just what the hell did she mean about you knowin' somethin' 'bout the Kid's murder?"

When Gomez's eyes shifted back and forth and he refused to meet Curly Bob's gaze, Gatling knew Dolly had been right.

"Out with it, Three-Fingers. What did she mean?"

Gomez whirled around. "I don't know what she's talkin' about. She's just some crazy whore!"

Curly Bob stepped over to the bedpost where his holster was hanging. He pulled out his pistol and pointed it at Three-Fingers Gomez.

"We been ridin' together a long time, Three-Fingers. It'd be a shame for me to have to drill you 'cause you tryin' to feed me some bullshit."

Gomez wilted, sitting on the edge of the bed with his head in his hands. "I just couldn't stand it no more," he moaned. "The Kid always ridin' me 'bout me being Mexican, tellin' me I wasn't gonna get my fair share of the money from the beeves, me havin' to stay over on the west side of town an' all."

Rawhide Jack stood up and began to pace the room. "So, you tellin' us you shot the Kid in the back?"

Gomez looked up, his face red with shame. "I don't know what came over me, boys. When the Kid went out in that alley to brace Jensen, I snuck out the back door to see if he'd get shot. 'Fore I knew it, my six-gun was in my hand an' I shot him in the back. All that anger just kind'a boiled outta me an' I shot him deader 'n shit."

"Goddamn it, Three-Fingers, we was partners," Rawhide Jack said angrily.

"You was partners," Gomez answered. "Remember, the Kid said I wasn't gonna get a fair shake when we divvied up the money."

Curly Bob held up his hands. "All right, it's over and done with now, an' I gotta agree with Gomez. The Kid did ride him awful hard."

"Yeah, but now we not only got this Marshal Thomas on our back trail, we got Jensen to worry about," Rawhide Jack said.

Curly Bob nodded. "That's true, but I think I see a way outta our troubles." He glanced at Gomez. "Three-Fingers, didn't you say you met a *vaquero* up from Mexico over at the cantina wanted to buy our beeves the other night?"

Gomez looked up, hope in his eyes. "Yeah, only he wasn't offerin' as much as the Kid wanted."

"Well, thanks to you, the Kid ain't around no more to object, is he?"

"No," Gomez admitted, "an' bein' as how we're only splittin' the money three ways 'stead of four, it'll be almost the same amount to us anyway."

"That's about the first smart thing you've said since I met you," Curly Bob said. "Now, my idea is to sell those beeves to the Mex as fast as we can to get some ready cash so we can hightail it outta Fort Worth."

"That might get the marshal off our backs, but what about this Jensen feller?" Rawhide Jack asked.

"We might just have to use some of Three-Fingers' share to buy us some insurance," Curly Bob said, a grim smile on his face as he stared down at Gomez.

"While we're over at the cantina makin' our deal with the Mex, we'll see if we can't find some hard cases who might want to earn some spendin' money by takin' Jensen out."

"What do you mean, out of my share?" Gomez asked.

Curly Bob pointed the gun at Gomez. "It was you who caused him to be on our backs; it's only fair you pay to get him off them."

Gomez nodded, knowing he didn't have a hell of a lot of choice in the matter.

Twenty-two

Three-Fingers Gomez led Curly Bob Gatling and Rawhide Jack Cummings to the cantina where he'd first talked to the *vaquero* from Mexico who wanted to buy their beeves. The cantinas stayed open all night, not closing early like the more upper-class establishments in the wealthier part of town.

As they entered the cantina, the men had to strain to see through the thick clouds of cigar and cigarette smoke that hung in the air like a morning fog. The smell of stale beer and whiskey and vomit was strong enough to make their eyes water, and the noise of drunken Mexicans and blacks laughing and talking in loud voices made their ears ring.

"You see your man?" Curly Bob asked, having to put his lips close to Gomez's ear to be heard over the din.

Gomez looked around the room, finally seeing the buyer in a far corner sitting at a table with two Mexican whores and two other cowboys.

He pointed, then led the way across the room toward the man.

"Señor Trujillo," he said. *"Buenas noches."*

The *vaquero* looked up through bleary, bloodshot eyes. "Ah, my friend Gomez. How are you this fine evening?" he said, only slurring his words slightly.

Three-Fingers pulled up a chair from a nearby table

and sat next to Trujillo. "I'm fine. I have reconsidered your offer and wonder if you still want to buy our cattle?"

"*Sí*," Trujillo said, his eyes becoming more alert. "But I can only pay what we discussed before."

"That's fine," Gomez said, "as long as we can make the deal tonight."

"Why the rush, *señor?* Sit, drink, and enjoy the company of the fine *señoritas* here at the cantina. We can talk business later."

Gomez shook his head. "No, Señor Trujillo. It must be tonight. My compadres and I must be on the trail early in the morning."

Trujillo's eyes narrowed with suspicion. "You have trouble, no?"

"We have much trouble, *señor,* and if we don't sell you those cattle tonight, you won't be able to buy half the number from anyone else with what you have to spend."

Trujillo nodded. "All right. Make out a bill of sale and I will give you the moneys."

Gomez looked over his shoulder at Curly Bill, who nodded. Gomez pulled out a piece of paper, and wrote he was selling the cattle to Trujillo and listed the price. When he pushed the paper across the table to the Mexican, Trujillo grinned, grabbed a leather wallet from inside his coat, and handed it to Gomez. He stuck out his hand and they shook on the deal.

Gomez got up from the table and walked to the bar, followed by Curly Bob and Rawhide Jack. He counted the money in the wallet, ordered tequila all around, and when the drinks arrived, leaned back against the bar and surveyed the other inhabitants of the place.

"Now," Gomez said, "we've got to find some men willing to take money to get rid of Smoke Jensen."

Curly Bob took a deep drink of the tequila, made a

face, and said in a hoarse voice, "That shouldn't be too hard from the looks of the men here."

Rawhide Jack, after seeing the effect the tequila had on Curly Bob, took a tiny sip, then put the glass back down on the bar without finishing it. He pointed to a table in a far corner of the room, occupied by six men who were all wearing pistols in holsters tied down low on their thighs. Two of the men had bandoliers of rifle shells crisscrossed on their chests.

"Those gents look the type," he said.

"Why don't you go have a word with them?" Curly Bob said to Gomez. "I think it'd go better if you went alone. You'll probably have to speak Mex to 'em anyway."

Gomez nodded and started toward the men, but Curly Bob grabbed his arm.

"Don't offer 'em more'n you have to. We need some of that money to travel on."

He stared at Curly Bob for a moment, then reached over to the bar and grabbed the bottle of tequila, taking it with him to the table.

Curly Bob watched as Gomez sat at the men's table and began pouring them all drinks from the bottle of tequila.

"Man knows how to bargain," Rawhide Jack said.

"You know, Rawhide, I been wonderin' if we might not ought'a think 'bout moseyin' on down the road alone. Could be that stickin' with Gomez is gonna get us hanged right along with him if that Jensen feller comes after us."

Rawhide Jack's eyes strayed back to Gomez. "You might be right, Curly. We'll just have to play it by ear. One thing, though, from what I heard 'bout Jensen, if he do come after us, it would be good to have an extra gun along. I'd hate to face him without a whole lot of firepower."

"There is that to consider," Curly Bob said.

After a few minutes, Gomez and two of the men at the table got up and walked out the door.

Curly Bob and Rawhide Jack followed.

Gomez talked in a low voice to the men, then pulled out the leather wallet Trujillo had given him and counted out a number of bills. He handed them to the men, who grinned, stuffed the bills in their coats, and went back into the cantina.

"Well?" Curly Bob asked.

"It is done," Gomez answered. "I described Jensen to them, said they couldn't miss him bein' as how he's 'bout the biggest man in town."

"They gonna do it?" Rawhide Jack asked.

"Yeah. They said for us to stay outta sight until tomorrow evening an' they'd hunt him down and put a window in his skull." Gomez grinned. "I told 'em he'd probably be over at the Silver Dollar talking to Dolly, tryin' to find out where we were stayin'."

Curly Bob nodded.

Gomez looked at him, his eyes flat. "I told him as long as they were doin' it, I'd pay an extra fifty dollars if Dolly happened to get caught in the cross fire."

"Why'd you do that?" Rawhide Jack asked.

" 'Cause she's figured out I gunned down the Kid. I don't want her talkin' to no lawmen after we're gone."

"We gonna wait around to pay 'em after it's over?" Curly Bob asked.

"Hell, no," Gomez answered with a grin. "I'm hightailin' it outta town tonight. I ain't waitin' around to see how it all turns out."

"Where you figuring on headin' to?" Rawhide Jack asked.

Gomez scratched his chin for a moment, then smiled. "I think I'll head down south, toward Galveston. Might just catch me one of those steamboats and take a little cruise on around to the East Coast."

"That's not a bad idea," Curly Bob said, looking at Rawhide Jack. "Even if Jensen does survive the fracas with the Mexes, he'll never be able to track us on a boat."

Rawhide Jack thought for a moment, then shook his head. "I'm afraid I'm gonna have to pass, boys. The one time I was on a boat, I got so sick I like to puked my guts out."

Gomez looked at him suspiciously. "Well, what *are* you gonna do?"

"I'm gonna head on over to Jacksboro. I heard that's where a lot of fellers go when they on the run from the law, or somebody else who might be huntin' 'em. I figure the town's big enough to get lost in for a while, 'specially if'n it's full of other men on the hideout too. After all, Jensen ain't gonna be lookin' for me. I didn't kill nobody."

Gomez started to say something, his face red with anger, but Curly Bob grabbed his arm. "Come on, Three-Fingers. Rawhide's right. Makes better sense if'n we split up anyhow. If Jensen does come lookin' and askin' around, he'll be lookin' for three men ridin' together, not two."

"All right," Gomez admitted. "But you better keep your mouth shut about what you know, Rawhide, or it won't only be Jensen come lookin' for you."

Curly Bob glanced at the horizon, where specks of light could be seen.

"Come on, boys. It's gettin' on toward dawn an' I want to be in the saddle 'fore sunup."

The three men walked rapidly back to the hotel, split the rest of the money, and packed their bags, then headed to the livery stable where they'd left their horses.

They paid off the boy at the stable and rode out to the edge of town.

They sat there for a moment, looking at the two roads leading away, one south, one north.

"Adios," Gomez said, sticking out his hand to Rawhide Jack.

Jack took it and smiled. "Good luck, boys."

Curly Bob grinned. "Luck don't hardly have nothin' to do with it, Rawhide. You ride with your guns loose, you hear?"

Rawhide waved and started his horse up the north trail while Gomez and Curly Bob turned south toward Galveston.

Twenty-three

Sally and Monte and Louis were less than ten miles out of Fort Smith when they saw a man riding a wagon coming toward them in the distance.

Sally spurred her horse into a full gallop and raced toward the man.

As she pulled the horse to a stop, she noticed the man was holding a Winchester Yellow Boy cradled in his arms, the hammer cocked.

She grinned. "Are you Marshal Tilghman?"

He glanced over her shoulder at Monte and Louis, who were just arriving, and moved the rifle a bit so it covered all three.

"Yeah."

She inclined her head at the rifle. "Are you expecting trouble, Marshal?"

"Expectin' it or not, it usually seems to find me. Who are you an' what can I do for you?"

"My name is Sally Jensen, and I was told you were bringing my husband to Fort Smith to stand trial for murder."

Tilghman nodded and seemed to relax just a bit. "I was."

"What do you mean, was?" Sally asked, moving her horse a little to the side so she could see in the back of the cage. "Isn't Smoke with you?"

"No, ma'am," Tilghman answered shortly.

"Well, where is he?"

"On his way back to Fort Worth, I 'spect."

"Marshal," Sally said, her exasperation clearly showing in her voice. "Would you please tell me what's going on?"

"Mrs. Jensen, why don't you get down off that horse and climb up here on the hurricane deck with me? That way I can tell you while I keep this wagon headin' toward Fort Smith. I'm already a couple'a days late an' I'd kind'a like to keep movin'."

Sally jumped down off her horse, handing the reins to Monte Carson, and climbed up on the wagon with Tilghman.

He snapped the reins and got the wagon moving, setting his rifle in the boot next to his feet while he drove.

"Now, Marshal, what about my husband?"

"I'm fixin' to tell you the damnedest story you ever heard, ma'am," the marshal said, grinning as he glanced sideways at her.

Sally shook her head. "Marshal, if you knew Smoke like I do, you'd know nothing you can say about him will surprise me."

Half an hour later, when Tilghman had finished telling Sally about the confrontation with Zachery Stillwell and his gang, and Smoke's subsequent rescue of the marshal, Sally just nodded.

"That's just like Smoke. He never could stand to see an underdog get beaten without joining in to help."

The marshal glanced at her as if he didn't much like being called an underdog, but then shrugged as if he knew what she'd meant by it.

"So, you *do* believe my husband's innocent of the charges against him, don't you, Marshal?"

Tilghman thought on it for a moment, then slowly nodded his head. "Yes, ma'am, I do. I just can't see a man who did what your husband did for me bein' a back-shooter."

He paused to build himself a cigarette, holding the reins between his knees while he put the tobacco in paper and licked it. Striking a match on the side of the wagon, he lit the cigarette, turning his head to the side to blow the smoke away from Sally.

"Course, you understand that it don't much matter what I think 'bout Smoke. Under the law he's still a wanted man an' I got to bring him in, soon's I get these galoots to the jail in Fort Smith."

Sally nodded. "I understand you have to do your duty, Marshal Tilghman, but it is good to know you don't truly believe Smoke is capable of shooting a man in the back."

"No, ma'am. I think that gambler fellow Gibbons was lyin' when he said he saw Smoke do it. I just don't know why . . . yet."

"So, you intend to question the gambler more about his accusations?" she asked.

"Yes, ma'am. I do. In fact, that's top of my list of things to do, once I get Smoke back in custody."

"You plan to head back to Fort Worth as soon as you drop these prisoners off at the jail?"

"Well, that's a mighty long ride, ma'am. I'll probably take the day to rest up, take a bath, an' get some shut-eye 'fore I try to ride all the way back there."

Sally thought for a moment. "Marshal, doesn't a train run between Fort Smith and Fort Worth?"

Tilghman looked at her. "Yes, ma'am. The Southern Pacific makes a daily run down there."

"How about if we all go by train? We'll get there much sooner, and you can sleep while the train's taking us there."

Tilghman frowned. "That'd be a right nice idea, ma'am, 'cept the U.S. Marshals Service don't pay for no train rides. They expect us to use horses to get back an' forth."

"Oh, for heaven's sake, Marshal. I'll pay your fare. It's important for me to find Smoke before someone else tries to arrest him and causes him to do something that might get him in more trouble than he's already in."

Tilghman smiled at her and slapped the reins to get the horses to move faster.

"You're right intent on takin' care of your man, ain't you, ma'am?"

"You're damned right, Marshal. So get those horses moving, because we're burning daylight."

"Gid'yup!" the marshal yelled at the horses, grinning as they took off at a slow lope, pulling the wagon as fast as they could.

Cal and Pearlie were riding southeast down the trail toward Fort Worth, talking about what they were going to do when they got there.

"Our only chance now is to talk to the men with the Durango Kid on the night he was killed. Maybe they'll know somebody who might have had it in for the Kid enough to shoot him in the back like that," Pearlie said.

The road from Jacksboro to Fort Worth was narrow and not much traveled, so Pearlie and Cal took notice when they saw a lone rider approaching them from a distance on the trail.

"Looks like we got company coming," Cal said.

"Yeah," Pearlie answered. He pulled a pocket watch from his pants pocket and looked at the time. "Hell, it's almost noon. Why don't we stop for a bite to eat. Maybe he'd like to join us."

Cal looked at Pearlie. "Don't tell me you're offerin' to share your grub with a stranger."

Pearlie shrugged. "Why not? 'Fore we left, I had that German lady fill my saddlebags with enough food for three or four men for the trip."

Cal laughed. "Well, since you usually eat enough for two, that don't leave a whole lot for him an' me."

"You'll just have to make do," Pearlie said. "Besides, I want to see what the news outta Fort Worth is, see if this man's heard anything 'bout Smoke or the killin'."

Cal and Pearlie pulled their horses off the trail, and Cal began to gather some rocks to make a fire while Pearlie got his saddlebags off his horse and began to unload the sack lunches the lady at the Hofbrau had prepared for them.

He had a package of cold fried chicken, a container of German potato salad, and three cans of sliced peaches spread out on his ground blanket when the man on the horse pulled abreast of them.

Cal had the water in the coffeepot boiling, and was just adding in spoonfuls of coffee when he looked up to see the man slow his horse.

"Jimminy," Cal whispered to Pearlie, "that's one of the galoots was at the table with the Durango Kid the night he was killed."

Pearlie nodded, turning his back to the man so he wouldn't hear. "Be careful and keep your hand next to your gun in case he recognizes us," Pearlie said. "I'm gonna invite him to sup with us."

"They were all pretty drunk that night," Cal said. "I doubt he'll remember us, since it was the Kid did all the talkin' to Smoke."

"Just keep your guns loose," Pearlie said, "just in case."

He straightened up and turned to face the man on the

trail. "Howdy, mister. We're just about to take a noonin'. Care to join us?"

Rawhide Jack, tired and dusty from being up all night and on the trail all morning, welcomed the chance to get out of the saddle and take a break.

"Don't mind if I do, mister," he called, turning his horse's head off the trail to ground-rein it next to Cal and Pearlie's mounts under a nearby tree.

Jack dusted off his butt and stretched as he walked over to the fire. "You gents headed toward Fort Worth?" he asked.

"Yeah," Pearlie said. "We've just come from Jacksboro, on our way to see the big city."

Jack squatted next to the fire and took the cup of coffee Cal handed him with a nod of thanks. "Boy, this sure smells good after sucking in trail dust all day."

"You comin' from Fort Worth?" Cal asked, an innocent expression on his face.

"Yep."

Pearlie lay on his left side on the edge of his ground blanket and began to eat the chicken. "Got some fried chicken here, if'n you want some," he offered.

Jack's eyes lit up. "Sure do," he said, sitting cross-legged across from Pearlie. "I'm so hungry I'd almost trade my hoss for some."

"Dig right in," Pearlie said, winking at Cal, who stayed over by the fire so he'd be behind Jack.

As Jack ate, he stared at Pearlie for a moment. "You look kind'a familiar. I ever seen you before?"

Pearlie shook his head. "Nope, not that I recollect."

"How 'bout some of that tater salad?" Jack asked.

Pearlie handed the bowl over to the man and continued to munch on a chicken leg.

"How're things in Fort Worth?" Pearlie asked. "Plenty of action there?"

" 'Bout all you could want, an' then some," Jack said with a grin. "Prettiest girls I ever seen in all my born days."

"What hotel you stay at?" Pearlie asked.

"The Star, but it's kind'a expensive for my tastes," Jack answered. "There's plenty more won't take all your drinkin' money to let you have a bed."

Pearlie laughed, shifting his body a bit so he could get at his pistol quickly if need be.

"Is it pretty rough over there? We heard the other day a man got back-shot outside one of the saloons."

Jack's eyes dropped and his face became more serious. "There's some trouble, if you go to the wrong places. Were I you, I'd stay in the nicer saloons. Not so much gunplay there."

"How 'bout that cowboy got shot?" Cal called from behind him. "You see it?"

Jack swiveled his head to glare at Cal. "Why you so interested in one shootin'? Hell, there was three men killed in gunfights the week I was there."

Suddenly, Jack stiffened and he stared harder at Cal. "You look mighty familiar to me too. I know you boys from someplace."

Pearlie eased his pistol out of his holster and had it pointed at Jack when he turned back around. "Yeah, we do know you, mister. We were sittin' with Smoke Jensen the night your pardner, the Durango Kid, got hisself shot dead."

Jack's hand moved toward the gun in his holster, until Pearlie thumbed the hammer back on his Colt. "I wouldn't do that if'n I were you, mister, 'less you wanna meet up with the Kid sooner than you planned to."

"Goddamnit," Jack said, slumping where he sat. "I knew I'd seen you boys before. I just couldn't remember where."

Cal eased up behind Jack and lifted the man's pistol from his holster, then moved around to sit across from him.

"Now, you gonna tell us what you know about that night, or are we gonna have to *make* you tell us?" Pearlie asked, his voice low and hard, his eyes flat and dangerous.

"Hell, you were there too," Jack said. "You know as much about it as I do."

Pearlie shook his head. "No, sir, I don't think so. Our friend Smoke Jensen has been accused of shootin' the Kid in the back, an' we know for a fact he wouldn't do somethin' like that. Now, you know the Kid better'n we do, so you probably know who had reason to shoot him."

Jack stared at the ground before him. "I don't know nothin'," he said sullenly.

Pearlie winked at Cal. "Cal," he said, "go add some wood to the fire, get the coals nice an' hot."

Cal winked back. "Yeah?"

"Then get that brandin' iron outta my saddlebags. I can see we're gonna have to do some powerful persuadin' to get this man to talk."

Jack's eyes flicked up. "What? What do you mean, branding iron?"

Pearlie shrugged. "We're out here twenty miles from nowhere. Won't nobody hear you scream, an' I *do* intend to get the truth outta you, one way or another."

"Wait just a minute," Jack pleaded. "You can't just go around brandin' a man to make him talk."

Pearlie glanced down at his pistol, pointed at Jack's chest. "Oh? Well, Mr. Colt here says I can do just about anything I want to do out here."

"But, if I tell you who shot the Kid, he'll kill me."

Pearlie's heart beat faster at the man's admission he knew who had shot the Durango Kid. "And if you don't tell me, you'll spend the next couple of hours in more pain than you can imagine."

Jack's face fell and he slumped again. "All right. It was Three-Fingers Gomez who shot the Kid."

"Who is Three-Fingers Gomez?" Pearlie asked.

"He was the Mex sittin' with us that night at the Silver Dollar."

"Why'd he shoot the Kid?" Cal asked from behind Jack.

"The Kid had been ridin' him pretty hard all week, makin' him stay down in Mexican Town, not lettin' him have a fair share of the money we were gonna get from selling our cattle."

"Your cattle?" Pearlie asked with scorn. "You mean the cattle you stole?"

"Yeah, that's what I mean," Jack answered, completely defeated now.

Pearlie pointed at the chicken on the ground blanket. "Go on an' eat your fill, mister, 'cause when you finish you're gonna go back to Fort Worth with us an' clear our friend's name."

"But then the marshal will put me in jail."

Pearlie shrugged again. "Better'n being branded, ain't it?"

Twenty-four

Smoke walked around Fort Worth, checking with the desk clerks at most of the hotels near the center of the city. He figured the Durango Kid and his cohorts would probably have stayed somewhere near the Silver Dollar Saloon, where he'd first seen them. The problem was, none of the clerks would tell him if men fitting their description were staying at their hotels. They all said it was against hotel policy, but Smoke thought they just didn't want any trouble in their places.

Finally, discouraged that he'd ever find the men unless he ran into them on the street or in a saloon or bar, he returned to the Silver Dollar, hoping Dolly had been able to find something out about their whereabouts.

He bought a mug of beer from the bartender and told him if he saw Dolly, to send her over to his table. He found one that was empty in a corner of the room, where he could sit with his back against the wall, as usual. He did this both out of long-standing habit, and because he wanted to keep an eye out for the three men as well as for Marshal Heck Thomas. He didn't know if Thomas would believe that Tilghman had let him go or would try to re-arrest him.

He was on his second beer when he saw Dolly at the bar, talking to the bartender. She glanced over at him, stared a moment as if trying to decide whether to speak to him or not, then finally shrugged and walked over to his table.

"Hello, Dolly," Smoke said. "Grab a seat."

"Uh, Mr. Jensen, I'm a working girl. I got to keep circulating or the boss man will get mad."

"That's all right. I guess you don't have any news for me anyway."

She looked down at him, noticing he was looking discouraged. She stepped around the table and pulled up a chair next to him. "Listen, Smoke, if you'd like to . . . hire my services, we could go up to my room and talk for a while."

He smiled at her. "Don't think I'm not attracted, Dolly. You are a right handsome woman. But I'm a married man who loves his wife very much. I have never strayed and I'm not about to start now." He hoisted his beer glass to her. "So, thanks, but no."

Dolly was touched. She'd been with hundreds of men, a lot of them married, and she respected a man who wouldn't think of cheating on his wife. It was something she didn't often see.

She chewed on her lip for a moment, thinking about what she should do. "You really want to talk to those men, huh?"

He looked into her eyes. "Dolly, I'm a wanted man, wanted for a murder I didn't commit. If they can't help me clear it up, then in all likelihood, I'm going to hang for something I didn't do."

He took another drink of his beer. "It's either that or go to running for the rest of my life. Either way, my life is over if I don't discover who did kill the Durango Kid."

Dolly made up her mind. She glanced over her shoulder to see if anyone could hear her, then leaned over close to Smoke. "I know where they're staying," she whispered.

Smoke was about to ask her where when, out of the

corner of his eye, he saw something that didn't make sense. He turned his head to see four Mexicans enter the saloon. The men were hard-looking gunnies, all wearing pistols tied down low on their legs, two of them carrying rifles.

The Silver Dollar was a high-class saloon right in the center of the wealthiest part of Fort Worth. Men like this just didn't come here to drink or to gamble. The hair on the back of Smoke's neck stirred when he saw them stand in the doorway, looking around as if searching for someone. He knew instinctively it was him they were looking for.

"Dolly," he said urgently, "get the hell away from here!"

"What?" she asked with a surprised expression on her face.

When one of the men in the group saw him and said something to the others, pointing his finger in Smoke's direction, Smoke shoved Dolly aside and flipped the table up on its edge, ducking behind it.

The first man drew a pistol and started walking toward Smoke, firing at the table as he approached.

Smoke drew his right-hand Colt and rolled to the side just as several slugs punched their way through the thin wood of the table. He came to rest on his stomach and aimed and fired in one fluid motion. His first bullet took the Mexican in the forehead, blowing the top of his scalp off and showering surrounding tables and gamblers with blood and brains.

Women started screaming and men began to shout and dive for cover as the remaining three Mexicans opened fire.

Smoke hit the second man in the stomach with his second shot, doubling him over just in time for Smoke's third bullet to enter the top of his head and shatter his skull, dropping him like a stone to land face-down in spilled beer and spit and peanut shells.

The other two men began to fire their rifles, shooting and jacking the levers and shooting again. Bullets pocked the wooden floor on all sides of Smoke as he rolled again, first one way, then the other, trying to escape the fusillade of slugs.

As the room filled with heavy layers of gun smoke, making it difficult to see, Smoke leaped to his feet and jumped up on a nearby table, hoping to see over the low-lying cloud of smoke.

He could barely make out the two men, their large Mexican sombreros just visible sticking up out of the smoke.

Whipping out his left-hand gun, Smoke began firing with both hands as rapidly as he could cock and pull the triggers.

The sombreros jerked twice each, then disappeared as the men dropped out of sight into the smoke.

Smoke stepped down off the table and walked toward the men, his guns held waist-high in front of him.

He stepped over the first two bodies, seeing they were dead as dirt, and kept walking, blinking his eyes against the acrid sting of the cordite and smoke in the air.

The third man was lying on his back, open eyes looking upward as if they were trying to see the hole in the center of the forehead that Smoke's .44 had drilled there. He too was dead.

The fourth man was on his stomach, crawling on hands and knees toward the batwings of the saloon, moaning and cursing in Spanish, his left arm dragging behind him, a trail of blood on the floor between his legs as he crawled.

He'd dropped his rifle, so Smoke used the toe of his boot to kick the man over onto his back. The right side of his head had a deep furrow in it, all the way down to where bits of brain could be seen in the hole.

Smoke knelt next to the man, cocked his Colt, and put it against the gunman's nose. "Who paid you to do this?" he asked.

The bartender ran up holding a shotgun in his arms, and squatted next to Smoke in time to hear the man say, "Gomez . . . *hombre* with *tres* fingers . . . paid us to kill Smoke Jensen."

Smoke looked at the barman. "You hear that?" he asked.

The bartender nodded. "Gomez, he said."

Smoke looked back down at the man, whose eyes became unfocused as blood began to pour from his ear.

"Amigo," Smoke said, "whatever he paid you, it wasn't enough."

The man tried to smile, choked once, and died.

Twenty-five

Smoke stood up and took a deep breath. His heart was hammering and his mouth was dry from the excitement of the gunplay. *No matter how many times this happens,* he thought, *it doesn't get any easier to kill a man.*

He glanced down at the hunks of flesh and blood that only minutes before had been living, breathing human beings, with hopes and aspirations just as real and poignant as those of anyone else in the saloon. No matter the men had taken money to end another's life. They were still men with souls and minds that to them were the most important things in the world. It was no small thing to take all that a man is or ever hopes to be and change it in the blink of an eye to a lifeless pile of meat, cooling rapidly in the spring evening.

He looked around at the shambles of the saloon, the overturned chairs and tables, men and women coming out from their hiding places, horrified, scared looks on their faces, some openly weeping at the terror they'd experienced just moments before.

He saw several other lifeless bodies scattered around the room, three men and one woman who hadn't moved fast enough to get out of the way of the murderous onslaught of the four hired killers. People who were dead in some small way because of him and who he was. That also was not an easy thing to live with.

He glanced over to the table where he'd been sitting, looking to see if Dolly was all right, and saw her legs sticking out from under an overturned table in the corner. He holstered his pistols and rushed to her side.

She lay there, curled in a fetal position, with blood on her chest just below her right shoulder. He gently touched her face and her eyes opened, cloudy with pain and suffering.

"Dolly," he said in a low voice as people began to gather around. "You doing all right?"

She gave the sarcastic smile he'd grown to appreciate over the past two days and shook her head slightly. "No, I'm not all right. I've been shot, you big blockhead."

He grinned back at her. With his practiced eye, he examined her wound. There was no bright red liquid pumping from the hole in her chest, and there was no foam on her lips or bubbling in her breathing. Evidently, the bullet had missed her lung. She would most probably survive if infection didn't set in and if she could get medical help soon.

Smoke looked up at a gambler standing over them. "Go and get a doctor . . . now!" he ordered, and the man turned and ran from the room.

The bartender came over and squatted next to Dolly, taking her hand in his. "Don't worry none, Dolly," he said. "We've sent for the doc."

She glanced at him and whispered thanks, then looked back at Smoke.

"Mr. Jensen, I gotta tell you something."

"What's that, Dolly?" Smoke asked.

"The other night, after you were here, I went to see those men you were looking for."

Smoke didn't say anything, but merely nodded. He'd suspected as much.

"You see, I knew where they were staying, but I wanted

to see if they'd pay me more not to tell you than you would to know."

He put his hand on her cheek. "Don't worry about it, Dolly. Just rest until the doctor gets here."

She shook his hand off, an earnest expression on her face. "No, I gotta say this, just in case . . . well, just in case."

Smoke nodded. "Go on."

"When I was talking to them, I got the idea that the Mexican—name of Gomez, I think—had something to do with the death of that man they're saying you shot."

"He tell you that?" Smoke asked skeptically.

She grinned, and there were specks of blood on her teeth, not a good sign.

"Yeah, but only 'cause I took his gun away from him and he didn't have much choice."

Smoke remembered something about the night of the killing. "Do you know what kind of gun it was?" he asked.

Dolly's forehead wrinkled in puzzlement at the question. "Sure, it was a Colt . . . a Navy model."

Smoke nodded. That made sense, since the gun that'd been used to kill the Kid was a smaller caliber than the .44 most men carried, and most of the Navys were .36-caliber.

He put his hand back on her cheek. "Thanks, Dolly. By telling me that you may have saved my life."

She leaned her face into his hand, then her expression got serious. "Now, you go on and get outta here before the law gets here, Smoke, or you won't be able to go and find those men."

She was right, Smoke thought. The town sheriff or maybe even Marshal Thomas would be there shortly after hearing all the commotion.

He glanced up at the bartender. "Will you stay with her?"

The man nodded and squeezed her hand. "Sure, mister. But like she says, if you're gonna git, you better git fast."

Smoke stood up just as Sheriff Billy Jackson walked through the batwings and began to look around, a pistol in his hand.

The bartender inclined his head toward the rear of the room. "Out the back door 'fore he sees you. I'll make sure he knows you had nothin' to do with all this."

Smoke touched his shoulder. "Thanks, and make sure the doc takes good care of Dolly. Tell him to spare no expense and I'll make sure he gets paid."

"Will do," the barman said.

As the sheriff began to question the people in the saloon, Smoke ducked his head and made his way slowly out the back door. Once in the alleyway, he moved at a fast pace toward his hotel room, knowing the sheriff would soon be there to get his side of the story of the gunfight at the Silver Dollar Saloon. He couldn't afford to be detained, either by the sheriff or by Marshal Thomas if he happened to be in town.

Just before he got to the hotel, he saw three riders coming up Main Street. Two of the figures looked familiar, even at the distance they were down the street.

Cal and Pearlie, he thought. *Thank God, I can use some help in this business.*

He stepped into another darkened alley and whistled softly as they came abreast of his position.

Pearlie jumped at the sound and whipped his pistol from its holster, twisting in the saddle and pointing it at the barely seen figure in the darkness.

"Who is it?" he said in a harsh voice.

"Smoke," Smoke called softly.

"Smoke!" Cal said, jerking his horse's head around and trotting his animal over near the alley. "We got good news for you."

Smoke inclined his head at the man in the saddle next to Pearlie. "Who's that?" he asked.

"That's Rawhide Jack Cummings," Cal answered, looking back over his shoulder. "He's one of the men who were ridin' with the Durango Kid."

"What're you doing with him?" Smoke asked.

"That's the news we got to tell you," Cal answered.

Smoke looked around, up and down the street. "We need to talk, but I can't go back to the hotel. The sheriff's gonna be there looking for me shortly."

Cal thought for a moment, then said, "Why don't Pearlie an' me get some new rooms? You can keep this galoot covered an' bring him up the back stairs after we get settled."

Smoke nodded. "That sounds good. I'll just take him down the alley behind the hotel, and you can call down to me and tell me what rooms you're in."

Thirty minutes later, Smoke took Rawhide Jack up the back stairs to rooms on the same floor as his old room, but down the hall a ways.

Once they were all gathered together, Cal and Pearlie quickly filled him in on their tracking of Gibbons to Jacksboro and his subsequent death at the hands of the disgruntled poker players.

Smoke nodded. "I never figured him to last long in the business of card-sharking. He just wasn't good enough at it to fool anyone for very long."

He cut his eyes over at Rawhide Jack, who was sitting in a chair by the window, a hangdog expression on his face. "Tell me about this one," Smoke said, pulling his makings out of his pocket and building himself a cigarette.

As he took a deep puff and tilted smoke out of his

nostrils, Pearlie told him about how they'd trapped Raw-hide Jack on the way to Jacksboro.

"And he says he knows who killed the Durango Kid?" Smoke asked.

"Tell him, Jack," Pearlie said.

"You go to hell!" Jack said defiantly. "I've done all the talkin' I'm gonna. You won't dare do nothin' to me here in town."

Smoke grinned, but the smile never touched his eyes. "Mister," he said in a voice as hard as ringed steel, "I've just killed four Mexican *bandidos* that said you boys paid them to gun me down. Now," Smoke added, taking the cigarette out of his mouth and looking at the glowing red end, "I'm not much one for torture, but I *do* aim to get at the truth. After killing four men, putting a few minor burn holes in your hide don't sound too bad to me."

Rawhide Jack stared at the cigarette and sweat popped out on his forehead.

"You wouldn't dare," he said, though the fear on his face belied his false bravado.

"Pearlie," Smoke said as he started to get up out of the chair, "take your bandanna and tie it around Jack's mouth. We wouldn't want to disturb the other guests with his screaming."

When Pearlie got up off the bed, Jack held up his hands. "No, now hold on a minute. I guess it won't hurt none to tell my side of it."

Smoke sat back down and crossed his legs. "Go on," he said, leaning back in his chair.

"The Kid, Curly Bob Gatling, Three-Fingers Gomez, an' me, we rustled some cattle from some Injuns over in the Nations a couple of weeks back. After we changed the brands, we drove 'em here and stuck 'em in a corral at the edge of town, plannin' on sellin' 'em and usin' the money to pay our way out to California."

Smoke nodded, finishing his cigarette and stubbing it out on the bottom of his boot.

"While we was tryin' to find a buyer, the Kid kept raggin' on Gomez, treatin' him like dirt an' tellin' him he wasn't gonna get an even share of the loot 'cause he didn't do the same amount of work in the drivin' an' brandin' of the beeves."

"So, the Kid was the leader of your gang?" Smoke asked.

Rawhide Jack frowned. "We wasn't no gang nor nothin'. Just a few men tryin' to make a livin'."

"Go on," Smoke said, a disgusted look on his face.

"Well, when the Kid called you out and followed you out of the saloon, while we were all watching the front of the place, Three-Fingers Gomez snuck out the back door. He said he didn't know what came over him, but when he saw the Kid standin' there, he just drew his pistol and plugged him in the back. When everybody else ran out the front door to see what had happened, he came back in the rear door and just walked on out the front with all the other onlookers."

"And that's when Gibbons, pissed off 'cause you'd humiliated him on the train, must've got the bright idea to get back at you by claimin' he saw you do the shootin'," Pearlie said to Smoke.

Just then, they heard a pounding coming from down the hall and a loud voice yelling, "Come on out, Jensen, we know you're in there!"

"It's time to tell your story to the sheriff, Jack," Smoke said, getting up from his chair. "And if you don't, then either I or my friends here will kill you dead before you can get out of town."

"But they'll arrest me for stealin' those beeves," Jack said, his eyes wide with fright.

Smoke walked up to him. "I don't care about the cattle.

You can leave that part out, for all I care. But you'd better be real clear when you tell them Gomez admitted to you he shot the Kid in the back, or you're a dead man as sure as I'm standing here." Smoke paused. "You can also tell him that Gomez was the one hired the Mexicans to shoot me down."

He gave a small smile. "After all, Gomez isn't here to dispute your story."

Rawhide Jack nodded, his mind working over the possibilities that he might get out of this with his hide intact. Finally, he looked up and nodded. "All right," he said, knowing he really didn't have any other choice.

It was almost midnight by the time Fort Worth sheriff, Billy Jackson, had the stories all straight. He'd taken Smoke, along with Rawhide Jack, Cal, and Pearlie, over to his office under armed guard.

True to his word, Rawhide Jack told the sheriff the same story he'd told Smoke, leaving out the part about the rustled cattle.

Jackson finally leaned back in his chair and told his deputies to give Smoke and Cal and Pearlie their guns back. "An' lock that sumbitch up in a back cell till I can talk to Marshal Thomas 'bout him in the morning," he added.

After Rawhide Jack was escorted to a cell, Smoke asked the sheriff, "When is Marshal Thomas due back in town?"

"I don't know," the sheriff said. "Right now, he's out traipsin' around to all the ranches in the area lookin' for some beeves stolen from the Indian Nations a few weeks back."

"Was anyone hurt in the theft?" Smoke asked.

The sheriff nodded. "Yeah, seems three young braves was gunned down. Evidently, they never stood a chance."

Smoke's face became hard. "Sheriff, Rawhide Jack left out some details in his story. You might want to ask him about some cattle he and his friends sold to a Mexican *vaquero* night before last. If you hurry, you might even be able to catch up with the herd before it gets to Mexico."

"You mean that sumbitch . . . ?"

Smoke nodded. "And, if you get a chance to talk to Marshal Thomas, would you be sure to tell him I'm innocent? I don't want him out looking for me on the old warrant."

"Will do, Mr. Jensen. And thanks for your help, boys. I know the marshal will be glad to get this cleared up."

"Come on, Cal, Pearlie," Smoke said, standing up and grabbing his hat. "We need to get some shut-eye if we're gonna head down to Galveston after Gomez and Gatling."

"Why don't you boys let the law handle this?" Sheriff Jackson asked.

" 'Cause the law doesn't move fast enough to catch them before they sail off to God knows where," Smoke said. "And since I have to go down that way to the King Ranch anyway, I might as well kill two birds with one stone."

The sheriff laughed. "I sure as hell wouldn't want you on my back trail, Jensen."

Smoke's face was serious when he said, "No, Sheriff, I don't believe you would."

Twenty-six

Smoke came instantly awake to a light tapping at his hotel room door. Reaching over, he pulled his Colt from its holster hanging on the bedpost and walked on tiptoe over to the door.

When he eased it open, his heart began to beat wildly. Sally was standing in the hall, smiling demurely at him.

"Is this the room of the famous gunfighter Smoke Jensen?" she asked, a teasing tone in her voice.

Smoke grinned widely and stepped back to let her enter.

"How did you get up here?" he asked. "I would have bet that Jason fellow at the front desk wouldn't approve of a woman calling on a male guest in his hotel."

"He didn't," Sally said, her lips curling slightly, "until I showed him this." She opened her purse and let Smoke see the shiny surface of her short-barreled Smith and Wesson.

He slammed the door closed, threw his gun on the bed, and wrapped his arms around her, hugging her so tight she almost couldn't breathe.

"When did you get here?" he asked without letting her go.

"Less than an hour ago. Monte and Louis and I came in on the train from Fort Smith with Marshal Tilghman. We went straight to the sheriff's office and he told us you were here in the hotel."

Smoke stepped back. "What time is it? We've got to get on the train to Houston."

Sally smiled and began to remove her clothes. "Don't worry, we've got hours yet before the train leaves. Plenty of time for us to . . . say hello."

Later, a much refreshed Smoke and Sally joined their friends along with Marshals Bill Tilghman and Heck Thomas at breakfast in the hotel dining room.

It took a while for everyone to tell their part of the story, but by the time Pearlie was on his second helping of everything, all were up to date.

Over final cups of coffee and cigars and cigarettes, Tilghman asked Smoke, "What do you plan to do now?"

Smoke took a sip of his coffee, then leaned back in his chair. "I plan on taking the Cottonbelt train down to Houston, and from there heading on over to Galveston to see if I can head off Gomez and Curly Bob Gatling before they get on that steamer."

Tilghman glanced at Thomas, pursing his lips as if trying to think of a way to say what was on his mind. "You know, it ain't your job to do that, Smoke."

When Smoke started to speak, the marshal held up his hand. "And technically, you're still wanted for the murder of Jim Slade, the Durango Kid."

"What?" Smoke exploded. "You know I didn't do that. You've got the testimony of a U.S. marshal that the witness was lying, and the testimony of the killer's partner that he admitted he shot the Kid."

Tilghman gave a slight smile. "I know all that, but the fact of the matter is you've been formally charged with the crime. It don't matter what I know, but what the court rules after considering all the evidence. You're gonna have to go before Judge Parker and be declared not guilty before the charges can be dropped."

"That's bull . . ." Smoke said, then paused and glanced at Sally sitting next to him. "Dung, and you know it!" he went on.

Tilghman shrugged. "Yeah, I know it is. But I'll tell you what. If Heck here agrees," he said, glancing at his friend, "I don't see any reason why you can't stop by Fort Smith on your way back to Colorado. After you get your beeves from the King Ranch, you gotta drive 'em pretty near there anyway to get 'em home."

Smoke stared at the two marshals. "You'd trust me to do that?"

Tilghman and Thomas looked at each other and nodded. "Sure," Tilghman said.

"What are you two going to do about Gomez and Gatling?" Smoke asked.

"Well, our first job is to get those beeves back the *vaquero* bought from the Kid's partners. So, Heck's gonna take a few deputies and get on the trail after 'em."

"And what are *you* going to be doing?" Smoke asked.

"Why, I plan to book passage on the Cottonbelt too," Tilghman answered.

"That's why you're so ready to trust me to come back to Fort Smith," Smoke said. " 'Cause you're going to be right by my side the whole time."

"Well," Heck Thomas said, "truth of the matter is, we'd kind'a hate to have to chase Gomez an' Gatling all the way to the East Coast. Be much easier if they just happened to still be in Galveston when Bill here gets there."

Tilghman looked directly into Smoke's eyes. "And I would trust you to keep your word, Smoke. You've proven that to me on several occasions already."

Monte pulled a pocket watch out of his coat and announced, "If we're gonna catch that train, we'd better get a move on."

Smoke hired a private car on the Cottonbelt so the group could all stay together on the two-day journey down to Houston. From Houston, they'd have to either rent or buy horses for the fifty-mile trip down to Galveston, since the train didn't go that far.

As they sat at tables in the car, drinking brandy, Monte, Louis, Cal, and Pearlie played with a deck of cards. Pearlie was anxious to show Louis what he'd learned from Smoke about the game of poker. Louis just grinned, figuring he'd show Pearlie a few things he hadn't yet learned.

Bill Tilghman, Sally, and Smoke sat at a table alone, talking about the past.

"It must be exciting work, Marshal," Sally said, "spending all your time hunting dangerous men."

Tilghman nodded. "It is, Mrs. Jensen. Human beings are about the most dangerous game there is to hunt. One of the few animals who'll shoot back at the hunter."

As he spoke, Smoke's mind went back to the time he'd hunted down the men who'd killed his father . . .

After meeting up with Preacher, Smoke's father Emmett told Preacher that he was going out looking for the three men who killed Smoke's brother and stole some Confederate gold. Their names were Wiley Potter, Josh Richards, and Stratton. Emmett went on to tell Preacher that he was going gunning for those polecats, and if he didn't come back, he wanted Preacher to take care of Smoke until he was grown up enough to do it for himself. Preacher told Emmett he'd be proud to do that very thing.

The next day, Emmett took off and left the old cougar

to watch after his young son. They didn't hear anything for a couple of years, time Preacher spent teaching the young buck the ways of the West and how to survive where most men wouldn't.

During that time, Smoke became about as natural a fast draw and shot as Preacher had ever seen, the boy spending at least an hour every day drawing and dry-firing the twin Navy Colts he wore.

Two years later, at Brown's Hole in Idaho, an old mountain man found Smoke and Preacher and told Smoke his daddy was dead, and that those men he'd gone after had killed him. Smoke packed up, and he and Preacher went on the prod.

They arrived at Pagosa Springs, Pagosa being an Indian term for healing waters, just west of the Needle Mountains, and stopped to replenish their supplies. Then, they rode into Rico, a rough-and-tumble mining camp that at that time was an outlaw hangout.

Smoke built a cigarette as his mind wandered, lighting it and taking a deep puff, remembering how it had been for the young boy and his old friend in those rough and rowdy days . . .

Smoke and Preacher dismounted in front of the combination trading post and saloon. As was his custom, Smoke slipped the thongs from the hammers of his Colts as soon as his boots hit dirt.

They bought their supplies, and had turned to leave when the hum of conversation suddenly died. Two rough-dressed and unshaven men, both wearing guns, blocked the door.

"Who owns that horse out there?" one demanded, a

snarl in his voice, trouble in his manner. "The one with the SJ brand?"

Smoke laid his purchases on the counter. "I do," he said quietly.

"Which way'd you ride in from?"

Preacher had slipped to his right, his left hand covering the hammer of his Henry, concealing the click as he thumbed it back.

Smoke faced the men, his right hand hanging loose by his side. His left hand was just inches from his left-hand gun. "Who wants to know—and why?"

No one in the dusty building moved or spoke.

"Pike's my name," the bigger and uglier of the pair said. "And I say you came through my diggin's yesterday and stole my dust."

"And I say you're a liar," Smoke told him.

Pike grinned nastily, his right hand hovering near the butt of his pistol. "Why . . . you little pup. I think I'll shoot your ears off."

"Why don't you try? I'm tired of hearing you shoot your mouth off."

Pike looked puzzled for a few seconds; bewilderment crossed his features. No one had ever talked to him in this manner. Pike was big, strong, and a bully. "I think I'll just kill you for that."

Pike and his partner reached for their guns.

Four shots boomed in the low-ceilinged room, four shots so closely spaced they seemed as one thunderous roar. Dust and birds' droppings fell from the ceiling. Pike and his friend were slammed out the open doorway. One fell off the rough porch, dying in the dirt street. Pike, with two holes in his chest, died with his back against a support pole, his eyes still open, unbelieving. Neither had managed to pull a pistol more than halfway out of leather.

All eyes in the black-powder-filled and dusty, smoky

room moved to the young man standing by the bar, a Colt in each hand. "Good God!" a man whispered in awe. "I never even seen him draw."

Preacher moved the muzzle of his Henry to cover the men at the tables. The bartender put his hands slowly on the bar, indicating he wanted no trouble.

"We'll be leaving now," Smoke said, holstering his Colts and picking up his purchases from the counter. He walked out the door slowly.

Smoke stepped over the sprawled, dead legs of Pike and walked past his dead partner.

"What are we 'posed to do with the bodies?" a man asked Preacher.

"Bury 'em."

"What's the kid's name?"

"Smoke."

A few days later, in a nearby town, a friend of Preacher's told Smoke that two men, Haywood and Thompson, who claimed to be Pike's brother, had tracked him and Preacher and were in town waiting for Smoke.

Smoke walked down the rutted street an hour before sunset, the sun at his back—the way he had planned it. Thompson and Haywood were in a big tent, which served as saloon and cafe, at the end of the street. Preacher had pointed them out earlier and asked if Smoke needed his help. Smoke had said no. The refusal had come as no surprise.

As Smoke walked down the street, a man glanced up, spotted him, then hurried quickly inside.

Smoke felt no animosity toward the men in the tent saloon; no anger, no hatred. But they'd come here after him, so let the dance begin, he thought.

Smoke stopped fifty feet from the tent. "Haywood! Thompson! You want to see me?"

The two men pushed back the tent flap and stepped

out, both angling to get a better look at the man they had tracked. "You the kid called Smoke?" one said.

"I am."

"Pike was my brother," the heavier of the pair said. "And Shorty was my pal."

"You should choose your friends more carefully," Smoke told him.

"They was just a-funnin' with you," Thompson said.

"You weren't there. You don't know what happened."

"You callin' me a liar?"

"If that's the way you want to take it."

Thompson's face colored with anger, his hand moving closer to the .44 in his belt. "You take that back or make your play."

"There is no need for this," Smoke said.

The second man began cursing Smoke as he stood tensely, legs spread wide, body bent at the waist. "You're a damned thief. You stolt their gold and then kilt 'em."

"I don't want to have to kill you," Smoke said.

"The kid's yellow!" Haywood yelled. Then he grabbed for his gun.

Haywood touched the butt of his gun just as two loud gunshots blasted in the dusty street. The .36-caliber balls struck Haywood in the chest, one nicking his heart. He dropped to the dirt, dying. Before he closed his eyes, and death relieved him of the shocking pain by pulling him into a long sleep, two more shots thundered. He had a dark vision of Thompson spinning in the street. Then Haywood died.

Thompson was on one knee, his left hand holding his shattered right elbow. His leg was bloody. Smoke had knocked his gun from his hand, then shot him in the leg.

"Pike was your brother," Smoke told the man. "So I can understand why you came after me. But you were wrong. I'll let you live. But stay with mining. If I ever see you again, I'll kill you."

The young man turned, putting his back to the dead and bloody men. He walked slowly up the street, his high-heeled Spanish riding boots pocking the air with dusty puddles.

After Smoke shot and killed Pike, his friend, and Haywood, and wounded Pike's brother, Thompson, he and Preacher went after the men who killed Smoke's brother and stole the Confederates' gold. They rode on over to La Plaza de los Leones, The Plaza of the Lions. It was there they trapped a man named Casey in a line shack with some of his *compadres*. Smoke and Preacher burnt them out by setting the shack on fire, and captured Casey. Smoke took him to the outskirts of the town and hung him.

After the hanging, the sheriff of the town put out a flyer on Smoke, accusing him of murder and offering a ten-thousand-dollar reward.

Preacher advised Smoke they should head up into the mountains and go into hiding, but Smoke said he had one more call to make. They rode on over to Oreodelphia, looking for a man named Ackerman. They didn't go after him right at first. Smoke and Preacher sat around doing a whole lot of nothing for two or three days. Smoke wanted Ackerman to get plenty nervous. He did, and finally came gunning for Smoke with a bunch of men who rode for his brand . . .

At the edge of town, Ackerman, a bull of a man, with small, mean eyes and a cruel slit for a mouth, slowed his horse to a walk. Ackerman and his hands rode down the street, six abreast.

Preacher and Smoke were on their feet. Preacher

stuffed his mouth full of chewing tobacco. Both men had slipped the thongs from the hammers of their Colts. Preacher wore two Colts, .44's. One in a holster, the other stuck behind his belt. Mountain man and young gunfighter stood six feet apart on the boardwalk.

The sheriff closed his office door and walked into the empty cell area. He sat down and began a game of checkers with his deputy.

Ackerman and his men wheeled their horses to face the men on the boardwalk. "I hear tell you boys is lookin' for me. If so, here I am."

"News to me," Smoke said. "What's your name?"

"You know who I am, kid. Ackerman."

"Oh, yeah!" Smoke grinned. "You're the man who helped kill my brother by shooting him in the back. Then you stole the gold he was guarding."

Inside the hotel, pressed against the wall, the desk clerk listened intently, his mouth open in anticipation of gunfire.

"You're a liar. I didn't shoot your brother; that was Potter and his bunch."

"You stood and watched it. Then you stole the gold."

"It was war, kid."

"But you were on the same side," Smoke said. "So that not only makes you a killer, it makes you a traitor and a coward."

"I'll kill you for sayin' that!"

"You'll burn in hell a long time before I'm dead," Smoke told him.

Ackerman grabbed for his pistol. The street exploded in gunfire and black powder fumes. Horses screamed and bucked in fear. One rider was thrown to the dust by his lunging mustang. Smoke took the men on the left, Preacher the men on the right side. The battle lasted no more than ten to twelve seconds. When the noise and the gunsmoke cleared, five men lay in the street, two of them dead. Two more would die from their wounds. One was shot in the side—he would live. Ackerman had been shot three times: once in the belly, once in the chest, and one ball had taken him in the side of the face as the muzzle of the .36 had lifted with each blast. Still Ackerman sat in his saddle, dead. The big man finally leaned to one side and toppled from his horse, one boot hung in the stirrup. The horse shied, then began walking down the dusty street, dragging Ackerman, leaving a bloody trail.

Preacher spat into the street. "Damn near swallowed my chaw."

"I never seen a draw that fast," a man said from his storefront. "It was a blur."

Later, the editor of the paper walked up to stand by the sheriff. He watched the old man and the young gunfighter walk down the street. He truly had seen it all. The old man had killed one man, wounded another. The young man had killed four men, as calmly as picking his teeth.

"What's that young man's name?"

"Smoke Jensen. But he's a devil."*

Smoke came out of his reverie as Sally asked him a question.

"What did you say, dear?" he asked.

"Daydreaming, huh?" she said.

"Yeah. Just sitting here gathering wool, thinking about old times like some old codger on a porch in his rocking chair," Smoke said.

Across the table, Tilghman nodded. "It's a disease common to all of us who live by the gun," he said. "Some-

---

*The Last Mountain Man

times, the memories of those times when your life hangs by the thread of who's the quickest with a six-killer are overpowering."

Twenty-seven

Sally poured tea for herself and stirred in some sugar.

"That's an interesting way of putting it, Marshal Tilghman," she said. "How did you get in the marshaling business anyway?"

Tilghman added a dollop of brandy to his glass and took a sip, thinking on how to put it.

"When I was about eight or so, my father went off to fight in the Civil War, and my older brother, Richard, became a drummer boy. I was left alone as the 'man' of the place. Let me tell you, it was quite a job for a boy of eight to help keep food on the table, plough the fields with an old mule, bring in the crops, and take care of my mother at the same time."

Sally nodded. "I can see it must have made you mature quite early."

"Yep, an' it didn't help any when my dad came back from the war blind and my brother married and moved away."

"What'd you do?" Smoke asked.

"The only thing I could do. I kept workin' the farm and takin' care of Mom and Dad. Then, after they died—this was in the summer of '72—I got work as a professional buffalo hunter. I'd become a pretty fair hand with a rifle, shotgun, knife, an' pistol during my years takin' care of the farm, so the work kind'a came natural to me."

"I've read stories about the old buffalo hunters, Buffalo Bill Cody and Wild Bill Hickok, but I've never met one," Sally said. "What was the life like?"

"Well, that summer of '72, me an' a group of men made a camp near where the Kiowa and Bluff Creeks come together, 'bout fifty miles from Dodge City. We built a dugout large enough for all fourteen of us, and one for the horses an' mules too. After a while, we'd just about shot all the buffalo for miles around, so we moved southward and made another similar camp on the Kiowa Creek. Now, just south of there was the Cimarron River on the edge of the Gloss Mountains, home of the Cheyenne."

Tilghman stopped to pull a cigar out of his pocket and put a lucifer to it, while Smoke refilled his brandy glass.

"Now, the Cheyenne just naturally resented us white men comin' in an' shootin' up all their buffalo. One day, when we got back from an afternoon of shootin' damn near ever'thing in sight, we found the camp destroyed . . . tents shredded, equipment smashed, and everything just generally torn up."

Sally glanced at Smoke, her mouth open. "Did you then leave the area?"

"The other men wanted to, but I was a young buck, full of piss an' vinegar." He paused, his face reddening. "Excuse me, ma'am. Sometimes my mouth forgets I'm in the presence of a lady."

Sally laughed. "Marshal, I've lived among cowboys too long to be offended by earthy language. You go ahead and tell your story in your own words. It's a fascinating tale of the old West."

"Yes, ma'am. Like I said, to me the attack was a personal insult, an' I wasn't about to stand for it. So, after the others took off, I hid in some tall prairie grass near the camp, figurin' the Injuns would come back to see what we'd done."

He took a drag on his cigar, a sip of his brandy, and continued. "Sure enough, I'd only been there a couple'a hours when three of 'em came back. One of 'em had a rifle, but the other two only had these long, nasty-lookin' knives. When they saw me, they charged right at me, whoopin' and hollerin' to beat the band. Guess they figured it'd scare me off like the others."

"And did it?" Sally asked, forgetting all about her tea and letting it get cold untouched on the table before her.

"No, ma'am. I let the hammer down on my shotgun, and a full double load of buckshot hit the lead one in the stomach, killin' him right away. The second one, seein' my gun was empty, ran up at me with that big knife in his hand, figurin' on gettin' my scalp. I clipped him hard under the chin with the butt of the shotgun and knocked him on his . . . uh, down in the grass, unconscious. The third one jumped on my back, intent on cuttin' my throat, an' we wrestled around a bit 'fore I was able to turn that knife into his own throat."

"What happened to the one you knocked down?" Sally asked.

Tilghman chuckled. "Oh, when he got up an' saw what'd happened to his friends, he took off runnin' an' never looked back."

"I'd venture a guess that you had no further problems with the Cheyennes on that hunt," Smoke said.

"Nope," Tilghman replied. "As a matter of fact, a few days later we had the best hunt of the year at that particular spot."

"So the other hunters returned after you'd gotten rid of the Indians?" Sally asked.

"Yeah. They showed up the next day, all carryin' their big Sharps buffalo rifles, ready to do some shootin'."

"What caliber Sharps did you use?" Smoke asked, interested, since he'd had lots of experience with the gun called the Sharps Big Fifty, a .52-caliber weapon, when he was up in the mountains with Preacher in his early days.

"Oh, I didn't use a Sharps," Tilghman replied. "I used a shotgun."

"What?" Smoke asked, astounded. "How on earth could you kill a buffalo with a shotgun?"

Tilghman laughed. "You sound just like my old huntin' partners. They asked the same question."

"Well?"

"I made some special loads for my shells. Instead of buckshot, I substituted a single lead slug in the shell."

"Why did you do that?" Sally asked.

Tilghman glanced at Smoke. "Smoke will know what I mean when I say I didn't much like the way the Sharps kicked. I was afraid it'd knock me off my feet or give me a broken shoulder."

"And did it work?" Smoke asked, thinking back to the times he'd had to put a poultice on his shoulder after firing his Sharps Big Fifty.

"Only too well," Tilghman replied. "The best thing was, I could fire while ridin' my pony, without having to jump down an' fire from the ground like my partners. In less than half an hour that first day, I'd bagged a dozen buffalo. I guess the number I got total that year was over four thousand, while the combined total of all my partners taken together was less than half that."

"Did they finally see the light?" Smoke asked, smiling at the innovation of this marshal.

"Oh, yeah. 'Fore long, all of 'em wanted to use shotguns 'stead of Sharps."

Sally tasted her cold tea, made a face, and got up to make herself another cup. When she returned to the table, she asked, "What did you do after you gave up buffalo hunting, Marshal?"

"When the buffalo got scarce, sometime around '75, I rode on over to Dodge City, just to see what was goin' on. I met Charlie Basset, who was sheriff of Ford County, an' he asked me if I'd consider bein' his deputy."

Tilghman shrugged. "Heck, I didn't have nothin' else goin' on, an' I'd never been a lawman before, so I said I'd give it a shot."

"Wasn't Dodge City very . . . rough back then?" Sally asked.

"Yes, ma'am. On my second day on the job I had a run-in with a local gunman named Texas Bill. When he saw my shiny new badge, he stepped in front of me on the boardwalk and blocked my path. I told him, 'You'll have to turn your guns in or leave town. It's a new ordinance.' "

"Did he draw on you?" Smoke asked, enjoying the tales of towns he'd been in himself.

"Not then. He just said, 'Never heard of it. If you want 'em, come an' take 'em from me.' "

"Did you?" Sally asked.

Tilghman smiled at the memory. "Being new to the job, I didn't quite know what to do. It seemed a small thing to shoot a man over, so I just slugged him."

"You knocked him out?" Smoke asked, laughing.

"Yeah, an' then two of his buddies jumped on me an' I had to knock them out too. Once they was all out cold, I just got some citizens to help me carry 'em to jail."

"Those were certainly rough times in Dodge," Smoke said.

"You're right, Smoke, an' it went from bad to worse. In early '76, Mayor Dog Kelly, who owned the Alhambra Saloon, wired Wyatt Earp over at Wichita to come to Dodge an' take over from the town marshal. Old Dog had heard a bunch of Texas cowboys were on their way to

Dodge an' he didn't think Bat Masterson an' I could handle it alone."

"So that's how Wyatt got to Dodge?" Smoke asked. "I always wondered."

Tilghman nodded. "Uh-huh, an' he brought Neal Brown an' Bat's brother, Ed, with him."

"I assume everything went all right and you were able to control the cowboys," Smoke said.

"Yes, but it weren't easy. Back then the town was full of toughs, men like Doc Holliday, Ben Thompson, and even the worst of 'em all, Wes Hardin. After a while, Bat Masterson was elected sheriff of Ford County an' hired me to stay on as his deputy."

"And how was that?" Smoke asked.

"It was all right, but I soon tired of it an' homesteaded me a few hundred acres, built me a cabin, an' married a widow woman named Flora Robinson. I partnered up with Neal Brown an' just took life easy for a while."

Smoke wanted to ask more about the wild days and times Tilghman had lived in, but noticed Sally trying to stifle a yawn across the table.

He took a final drink of his brandy, and stood up. "Well, Marshal, this has been most interesting, but I see my wife is about to fall asleep at the table. We'd better call it a night."

Tilghman glanced at Sally, a chagrined look on his face. "Sorry, ma'am, hope we haven't bored you to death with all this man talk about the past."

"Oh, no," Sally protested. "It was very interesting and exciting, but as you know, Marshal, we've been on trains for the better part of three days and I am just exhausted." She stood up and held out her hand. "I hope we'll be able to continue the stories tomorrow."

"I'm done wore out talkin' 'bout myself, ma'am, but maybe you can get Smoke to tell us some of his adventures up in the mountains back before white men came here," Tilghman said, shaking her hand.

She looked at her husband. "Getting Smoke to talk about himself is like pulling teeth, but I'll try. Good night, Marshal."

"Good night, ma'am."

Twenty-eight

The private car the group was riding in was divided into three parts; private sleeping quarters for Sally and Smoke, a bunk room for the other men, and the main part of the car.

After Sally and Smoke retired, Tilghman walked over to the poker table, where Louis Longmont was giving Cal and Pearlie and Monte Carson a lesson in cardsmanship.

"You boys have markedly improved your skills at poker," Louis said with a grin. "It took me almost two hours to clean you out."

They'd been playing with poker chips that came with the car, not for real money, but losing still stung the boys. "I've just never seen such a run of luck," Pearlie complained, throwing his last hand down on the table.

Cal shook his head. "I don't believe luck had nothin' to do with it, Pearlie," he said. "If I remember correctly, you had just as many good hands as Louis. You just didn't win as much with 'em as he did."

Monte smiled approvingly. "That's the most important lesson you can learn about poker, Cal. Luck may determine who wins a particular hand, but at the end of the night, luck has nothing to do with who has the most chips."

Louis nodded. "The sheriff's right, boys. You got to know when to hold them and when to fold them, when to bet big and when to ease into a hand to make the most money from your luck when it hits."

Pearlie frowned. "I guess I still got a lot to learn then."

Louis smiled. "Don't feel too bad, Pearlie. You didn't learn to handle a cow pony or a mean steer overnight. It took you a lot of years and a lot of sore behinds before you could stay in the saddle in the middle of a stampeding herd, didn't it?"

"You got that right, Mr. Longmont."

"Well, the same is true of any other skill, even poker. You have to get your butt kicked a few times before the lessons sink in, but then you don't forget them."

"Gentlemen," Tilghman said, "I'm gonna hit the hay. It's been a long day, an' tomorrow don't figure to be any shorter. Good night."

The other men agreed and all decided to hit the bunks.

As Bill Tilghman lay there, images from his past kept flicking through his mind, brought on by his retelling the story of his early days to Smoke and Sally. As he finally dozed off, the images turned into dreams. He occasionally moaned in his sleep as the recollections were reenacted in his thoughts . . .

After Tilghman left Dodge City, he met up with Chris Madsen and Henry "Heck" Thomas, and they all hired on to bring law to the town of Perry, where they became known as the "Three Guardsmen." One of their first duties had been to track down the members of the Doolin Gang, headed by Bill Doolin.

One night, on patrol with Heck Thomas, Tilghman noticed a crude dugout cabin several hundred yards off the trail they were riding.

"Heck," he said, pointing with his head, "there's a place

I ain't never seen before. You hang here while I go check it out."

He pulled the head of his bay around and walked it through the light underbrush to the doorway of the dugout. The night was wild, with heavy winds and light rain moving almost sideways in the gale.

Tilghman knocked, then pushed the door open and stepped inside, taking off his hat and flinging water off it to the floor. When he looked up, he noticed in the dim light of a lantern hung from a nail on the wall that both sides of the interior were lined with bunks, covered with hanging blankets.

At the end of the room, a large river-stone fireplace was blazing, sending out welcome waves of heat into the room. In the center of the open space between the bunks, a man sat with a Winchester rifle across his lap.

"Howdy," Tilghman said, brushing more water from his slicker. "I'm lookin' for Bee Dunn's place. How far is it from here?"

"That's for you to find out," the man replied sourly.

"Well, I's just passin' by with my fightin' dog and thought maybe I could get Bee to match a fight," Tilghman said, keeping his voice light and calm. "He told me a while back he thought his dog could beat mine."

Tilghman, every lawman instinct in him crying out danger, noticed the man's eyes flicking to the sides to look at the bunks on either side of the room.

"I done tole you to find it on your own," the man growled.

"All right, I'll do that, but this fire sure feels good," Tilghman said, rubbing his hands and stamping his feet in front of the blaze, using his movements to cover his looking at the bunks. He noticed the tips of several rifle barrels sticking out from behind the blankets, all aimed at him.

"I guess I'll be goin'," Tilghman said from his place near the fire. "Which way does a fellow go to get out of here?"

"The same damned way he came in."

Without betraying the terror he felt, Tilghman calmly backed toward the door, jamming his hat back down on his head. "Well, adios, stranger. I'll just let myself out an' see if I can find the Dunn place on my own."

The man in the chair didn't answer, but his hands were tight on the rifle in his lap and his eyes were cold and hard as he watched Tilghman back out the door.

As fast as he could, Tilghman rode back to the trail where Heck was waiting.

"What'd you find out?" Heck asked.

"I couldn't see much, it was too dark," Tilghman replied. "But one thing's sure. There's a passel of men hidin' out in there, an' we're gonna need help to bring 'em in."

They rode over to Pawnee and enlisted the help of Chief Deputy John Hale, who formed a posse. When they got back to the cabin, the only occupant left was the man in the chair.

"What's your name, mister?" Tilghman said after they'd disarmed the man of his rifle.

"Will Dunn," the man replied, still in a surly mood.

"Where are the men who were hidin' here when I was here before?" Tilghman asked after checking the bunks and finding them empty.

"The outlaws is already gone. An' you would be too, lawman, if Bill Doolin hadn't kept his men from shootin' you in the back as you left."

"What do you mean?" Heck Thomas asked.

"They was all here, ever' one of Doolin's gang . . . Bill Doolin, Red Buck, Charley Pierce, Tulsa Jack, and Little Bill Raidler. Old Red Buck sure wanted to kill you, Marshal," Dunn said to Tilghman, smiling as if he agreed with the sentiment. "He was all ready to shoot you in the back, but Bill Doolin stopped him by grabbin' his gun hand."

"Why'd he do that?" Tilghman asked, a puzzled expression on his face.

Dunn snorted, "Doolin said Bill Tilghman is too good a man to be shot in the back." He shook his head. "Red Buck was plenty peeved off at being stopped. . . . He must have a powerful hate for you, Marshal."

Tilghman felt a chill up his spine at the close call he'd had, but it wasn't to be his last by a long shot.

Bill Tilghman groaned and turned over in his bunk, the near miss in his dreams leading him to his next encounter with Bill Doolin . . .

A few months after the cabin incident, Bill Doolin and his gang held up the express station at Woodward and made off with over ten thousand dollars. Will Dunn, who was being left free but kept on a short leash by the lawmen, informed Tilghman that Doolin and some of his men were supposed to meet up at his brother Bee's place in the next few days.

Tilghman, Heck Thomas, and a posse rode over to the Bee Dunn ranch. Tilghman dragged Bee out to stand in front of the posse.

"Dunn," Tilghman said, his face right up against Bee's, "you're gonna be arrested and tried as an accomplice if you don't help us capture Doolin and his men when they arrive."

"But they'll kill me, Deputy," Dunn protested.

Tilghman shrugged. "Better'n spending the next twenty years caged up like an animal," he replied.

Dunn finally nodded, broken.

Tilghman staked the posse out around the ranch, hidden and waiting for the outlaws to show up.

On the third night, Bitter Creek Newcombe and Charlie Pierce rode up to the corral.

When they got close enough, Heck Thomas stood up, his Winchester in his hands. "Hold on, boys. Put them hands up and give it up now, you hear?"

Newcombe and Pierce hesitated only a moment before they jumped from their horses to the ground. They pulled six-shooters and began to charge at the sound of Heck's voice, firing wildly into the darkness as they ran.

Heck and Bill calmly aimed and returned the fire, not bothering to duck. As lead slugs whistled around their heads, the two lawmen continued to pull triggers and fight the bucking of their rifles, trying to hit the crouching, running figures barely outlined against a night sky.

Newcombe was the first to fall, two slugs hitting him almost simultaneously, one in the face and the other in the chest. He was stopped in midstride as if he'd run into a brick wall, falling dead on the cold hard ground.

Pierce slowed when he saw his partner fall, and it got him killed. When he hesitated, both Tilghman and Thomas fired, killing him where he stood.

"Damn," Heck said, standing over the bodies. "Now Doolin will never come back to this place."

Tilghman nodded. "Yeah, but I'm gonna get him anyway. I heard he's got a hidin' place in the Osage Nation." He glanced at Heck. "You game to go up there after him with me?"

"Hell, yes," Heck replied.

They headed for the ranch in the Indian Nations a few days later, finding it just where they'd been told it would be. They rode quietly up to the wooden structure, their guns loose and ready for trouble.

As they approached the ranch house, a man walked

around the corner, his head down, not seeing the lawmen. Tilghman recognized him as Little Bill Raidler, a long-time member of the Doolin gang.

"Halt, Raidler. This is Bill Tilghman talkin'," Tilghman called out, jacking a shell into his Winchester.

When he heard the lawman's voice, Little Bill whirled around and drew, firing his gun. The slug passed within inches of Tilghman's head and he returned fire, striking Raidler in the right wrist and shattering the bone as the gun whirled away in the sunlight.

They doctored Raidler up as well as they could and took him to Guthrie, where he was placed under arrest. He would say nothing about the whereabouts of Bill Doolin.

After a few more unsuccessful attempts to locate Doolin, Tilghman was about to give up when he got word Doolin's wife was in Winfield. Tilghman went to the Winfield post office to see if there'd been any mail delivered to her from her husband. The postmaster told Tilghman that Mr. Doolin was in Eureka Springs, Arkansas. He said the outlaw had gone there to visit the hot springs to ease his rheumatism.

Tilghman was on a stage the next day, headed for Eureka Springs. The coach he was riding pulled into Eureka Springs on December 5th. Tilghman went directly to the Basin Hotel. He checked in and left his rifle and baggage there to go in search of Bill Doolin.

As he walked through the lobby, Tilghman saw Doolin calmly sitting on a couch, reading a newspaper. When Doolin glanced up to see who was walking by, Tilghman turned his head and moved away.

Then he stopped for a moment, wondering if he should approach the wanted man in the crowded lobby, fearing innocent people would get shot if there were gunplay.

What the hell, he finally thought, *I been chasin' him all over creation. Can't let him get outta my sight now.*

Tilghman pulled his Colt and walked back to stand directly in front of Bill Doolin.

"Bill Doolin, you are under arrest," Tilghman said.

Doolin assumed an innocent look, glancing around at the people in the lobby, who had stopped to see what was going on.

"What's the meaning of this?" he asked, spreading his hands as if he had nothing to hide.

"I'm Deputy Marshal Tilghman," Bill said.

Doolin stood on hearing Bill's name and reached into his coat, trying to get to one of the pistols he wore in shoulder holsters under his coat.

Tilghman grabbed his arms and the two began to wrestle in the lobby, Bill knowing if Doolin got a gun out, there would be lead flying everywhere.

One of the hotel clerks came running up.

"What's going on here?" he asked.

As they struggled, Tilghman gasped out, "Get his guns out from under his coat while I hold him. I'm a marshal."

The clerk stepped gingerly around the wrestling men, trying to get at the guns under Doolin's coat. He managed to get the coat open, but Doolin growled, "I'm gonna kill you, kid!"

The clerk turned and ran from the room without a backward glance.

This put Tilghman at a disadvantage. Now that Doolin's coat was open, he was more likely to get to his guns sooner or later.

Tilghman gritted his teeth, released Doolin, and stepped back, whipping his Colt out of his holster before Doolin could draw.

"I'll shoot you, Bill, if you go for that gun!" Tilghman said, his voice low and hard and mean.

Doolin hesitated, as if figuring out whether he had a chance or not, then finally relaxed. His shoulders slumped and he hung his head as Tilghman leaned forward and removed two pistols from shoulder holsters under his coat.

The next day, Tilghman and Doolin boarded a train headed back to Oklahoma Territory.

With the arrest of Doolin in his dreams, the images faded and Bill Tilghman finally sunk into a deep and dreamless sleep.

Twenty-nine

The next morning, after they all ate a breakfast of day-old biscuits and fried chicken, topped off with canned peaches that Sally had brought along on the train, the card game resumed among Louis, Cal, and Pearlie, while Monte joined Smoke and Sally and Bill Tilghman for another round of stories.

With the details fresh in his mind from his dreams of the night before, Bill was persuaded to tell the tale of his wrestling match with the famous outlaw Bill Doolin.

When he'd finished, he glanced at Smoke. "I hear tell you've had some righteous adventures yourself, Smoke. Ever wrestled a bad man to the end?"

Smoke smiled. "There were a few times," he said modestly.

"Tell him 'bout the time with the Sundance Kid an' his gang, up in the mountains," Monte urged, having been told the story by Smoke's old mountain man friend Puma Buck.

"Well . . ." Smoke hesitated, clearly embarrassed.

"Go on, dear," Sally said. "We'd all like to hear it to help pass the time away."

"The Sundance Kid was this young man who thought he was a bad hombre," Smoke started. "During a fight a year before, I'd cut his left ear off to make a point, hoping to save his life by getting him out of the gun-fighting business."

"I take it the lesson didn't work," Tilghman said, smiling.

Smoke shook his head. "No, in fact it just made matters worse. Humiliated by the experience, the young man went down to Mexico and recruited a gang of toughs to come back up to Colorado and teach me a lesson. One thing led to another, and before long we were all up in the High Lonesome in a fight to the death . . ."

Smoke was loaded for bear. He had his two Colt .44 pistols, a knife in his scabbard, a tomahawk in his belt against the small of his back, a Henry repeating rifle in one saddle boot, and a heavy Greener ten-gauge shotgun on a rawhide thong over his shoulder. He was ready to hunt, and to kill anything that got in his way.

He rode through thick ponderosa pines, making no sound that could be heard from more than a few feet away. By late afternoon he'd located the party of gunmen looking for him. Unused to traveling in the mountains, they were making so much noise they were easy to find.

Smoke stepped out of his saddle, leaving his horse ground-reined for a quick getaway should it be necessary, and slipped down a snowy slope toward a ribbon of trail the gang was following.

As the last man in line came abreast of his hiding place, Smoke took a running jump and leapt on the rider's horse behind him. Before the startled man could make a sound, Smoke slit his throat with his knife. Smoke pulled the dying man's gun from its holster and a knife hidden beneath the man's mackinaw as the outlaw slumped over his horse's withers.

He pushed the dead body out of the saddle, and threw

the knife at the next rider in line. The blade buried itself in the gunman's back, causing him to arch forward, screaming in pain.

Smoke thumbed back the Colt's hammer and began to fire. Two more of Sundance's hired killers were mortally wounded before any had time to clear leather.

Smoke whirled the dead man's horse in a tight circle and galloped into the brush, leaning over the saddle to avoid low-hanging branches and limbs.

Sundance's gang jerked their reins and tried to turn around to give chase, but the trail was narrow and all they managed to do was to get in each other's way. Two men were knocked from their mounts, one sustaining a broken arm in the process.

Only minutes after the attack began, Smoke had disappeared and the gunhawks counted four dead and one injured, while not a shot had been fired at the mountain man.

Sundance was furious as he rode among his followers. "Goddamnit! You worthless bastards didn't fire a single round!" He leaned to the side and spat on one of the bodies lying in the dirt. "Hell, I thought I was ridin' with some tough gunslicks." He shook his head in disgust. "I might as well have hired schoolmarms, for all the help you galoots have been."

"Fuck it!" yelled Curly Bill Cartwright. "I'm gonna kill that son of a bitch!" He filled his hand with iron and spurred his horse into the brush after Smoke.

Three other men pulled guns and started to follow Cartwright.

"Hold on there," yelled Sundance. "That's just what Jensen wants us to do." He waved the gang toward him. "Circle up and get ready in case he comes back. We'll stay here and see what happens. Maybe Cartwright'll get lucky."

Lightning Jack chuckled. "I doubt that, Boss. He's goin' into Jensen's territory now, an' I'll bet a double eagle he don't come out."

A loud double explosion came from the forest, startling the outlaws' mounts, causing one of the Mexicans to begin shooting wildly toward the noise while shouting curses in Spanish.

The gang waited expectantly, every gun trained on the spot where Smoke and then Cartwright had entered a stand of dense trees. After a few moments the sound of a horse moving through brush could be heard.

The men cocked pistols and rifles as a horse walked out of the trees onto the trail. In its saddle was the decapitated body of Curly Bill Cartwright. His head and upper shoulders had been blown off by a double load of ten-gauge buckshot. A tree branch had been stuck down the back of his shirt and his feet were tied together under the animal's belly to keep him upright in his saddle.

Lightning Jack spoke quietly. "You think maybe Jensen's sending us a message, Boss?"

Sundance said, "Shit! I want to kill that bastard so bad I can taste it!"

Perro Muerte walked his horse over to Sundance. "What now, jefe? We go into trees, or stay on trail?"

Sundance said, "Stay on the trail. If we can locate his camp we can keep him from gettin' to his supplies and ammunition. Sooner or later, he'll run low and then we can take him." He pointed to Jeremiah Gray Wolf. "Take the point, Gray Wolf, and see if'n you can find some tracks or sign showing which way his camp might be."

Moses Washburn spoke in a low voice to Bull. "I don't like this, Bull. I don't like it one bit."

Bull shook his head. "Me either, partner, me either."

Jeremiah Gray Wolf leaned over his saddle and began

to walk his pony up the trail, followed twenty yards back by the rest of the group.

After a quarter of a mile, he held up his hand and called over his shoulder, "I've found some tracks. Let's go."

The Indian straightened in his saddle and spurred his mount into a trot, disappearing around a bend in the trail. The others drew weapons and followed him from a distance.

Sundance rounded the bend and stopped short when he saw Gray Wolf's pony standing riderless by the side of the trail, grazing on the short grass partially hidden by melting snow. "Shit," he whispered under his breath. He hadn't heard a sound, not even a call for help.

When the rest of his men rode up to him, Sundance slowly urged his horse forward, scanning trees and brush on either side for a sign of Gray Wolf.

From behind him, Sundance heard a sharp intake of breath, and the words *"Madre de Dios,"* spoken in a hoarse whisper. He turned to see Perro Muerte crossing himself and staring up at a nearby tree.

He followed Perro Muerte's gaze, and found Jeremiah Gray Wolf hanging from a limb, a rope around his neck, his legs still kicking, quivering in death throes. The half-breed's bowels had let loose and the stench was overpowering.

Sundance held his bandanna across his nose and rode over to examine the area under the body. Horse tracks showed that Smoke had probably roped the man while hiding in the tree, then dropped to his horse, pulling Gray Wolf out of his saddle by a rope he'd looped over the branch.

Bull said, "He never knew what hit him."

"Shut up!" yelled Sundance. "Come on, Jensen can't be more'n a few hundred feet away. Let's go!"

The group cocked their weapons and started to follow

Sundance up a steep slope past the tree with the body hanging from it. It was a steep grade, covered with loose gravel and small stones, and they were only about halfway up the incline when a gunshot from above caught their attention.

They looked up to see Smoke standing next to a large pile of boulders, grinning, holding something in one hand and a smoking cigar in the other. He cried, "Howdy, gents," and put his cigar against the object in his other hand. As a fuse began to sputter and sparkle, he dropped the bundle amongst the rocks and ducked out of sight.

"Holy shit, it's dynamite," yelled Moses Washburn as he jerked his reins and tried to turn his horse around. The men all panicked and reined their horses to turn in different directions, running into each other, knocking men and animals to the ground.

The explosion was strangely muffled and it didn't sound very loud, yet the pile of boulders shifted. Slowly at first, then with gathering speed, huge rocks rolled and tumbled, racing down the slope, bounding as they descended toward the trapped riders milling about on the trail.

A huge dust cloud enveloped the area, covering screaming men and horses as rocks crushed bones and flattened bodies and ended lives.

When dust had settled, the only men left alive were Sundance, Lightning Jack, Bull, and Perro Muerte. The slide had killed four Texas gunfighters and Moses Washburn, who could only be identified by a black hand showing from beneath a huge boulder. Nothing but his hand was visible.

In the sudden quiet of dusk, the remaining men could hear the sounds of Jensen's horse in the distance galloping up the mountain.

"Moses," Bull said through gritted teeth, "I'm gonna kill him for you."

Sundance took a deep breath, looking around at all that was left of his band. "Okay, boys. He's headed straight up the mountain. There ain't much cover up there, an' there ain't nowhere to run to once he gits to the top."

He pulled his pistol and checked his loads. "Let's go git him!"

The moon had risen and, in a cloudless sky, it made the area as bright as day. Smoke was hidden in his natural fortress, leaning over the edge, peering below through his binoculars, waiting for Sundance and his men. It was time to end it, and he was ready.

There was movement below, and Smoke could see Bull and Perro Muerte crawling on hands and knees off to his right. They were going to try to inch up the slope, using small logs and rocks on that side for cover. Smoke grinned, remembering tricks Cal had devised for just that eventuality.

Smoke waited until they were halfway up the incline. Bull, panting heavily in thin air, motioned for Perro Muerte to stop so he could catch his breath.

Smoke worked the lever on his Henry and sighted down the barrel. "Hey, Bull!" he cried.

The big man squinted in semidarkness, trying to see where Jensen's voice was coming from, hoping to get off a lucky shot. "Yeah, whatta ya' want, Jensen? You wanna know how I'm gonna kill you?"

Smoke grinned. "No, I was just wondering if you'd noticed all those gourds and pumpkins down there."

Bull and Perro Muerte glanced around them, and saw for the first time a number of small squash and pumpkins resting on the ground. Bull looked up the slope. "Yeah, what about it? You hungry?"

Smoke laughed out loud, his voice echoing off surrounding ridges. "Did you ever wonder, you ignorant bastard, how gourds could grow on bare rock?"

Bull's eyes widened in horror and he opened his mouth to scream as he realized the trap they had fallen into.

Smoke squeezed his trigger, firing into the pumpkin directly in front of Bull and the Mexican. Molten lead entered the gourd, igniting black powder. The object exploded, blasting hundreds of small stones hurtling outward. Bull and Perro Muerte's bodies were riddled, shredded, blown to pieces. They died instantly.

Below, Sundance sleeved sweat off his forehead and turned to Lightning Jack. "Maybe we ought'a head down the mountain and come back later, with more men."

Lightning Jack looked at the gunfighter with disgust. "You low-down coward. You got over thirty good men killed lookin' fer yore vengeance. You ain't backin' out now."

Sundance dropped his hand to his Colt, but froze when a voice behind them said, "Hold it right there, gents."

Lightning Jack and Sundance turned to see a small, wiry man in buckskins pointing a shotgun at their heads. "Ease them irons outta those holsters and grab some sky."

As they dropped their pistols to the ground, Puma called out, "Hey, Smoke. I got me a couple of polecats in my sights. What do you want me to do with 'em?"

"Bring 'em up here."

Puma pointed up the hill with his scattergun. "Git."

As the outlaws struggled uphill, the mountain man, more than twice their age, walked nimbly up the slope with never a misstep, nor was he breathing hard when they reached the top.

Smoke stood there, hands on hips, shaking his head at

Puma. "It's easier to tree a grizzly than to keep you ornery old-timers out of a good fight."

Puma nodded. "Yeah, I'd rather bed down with a skunk than miss a good fracas." He cut his eyes over at Smoke. "You want me to dust 'em now, or just stake 'em out over an anthill?"

Sundance's eyes widened. "You wouldn't do that . . . would you, you son of a bitch?"

Smoke pursed his lips, rubbing his chin. "Well, I'm feelin' real generous tonight. How about you boys picking your own way to die? Guns, knives, fists, or boots, it makes no difference to me."

Lightning Jack grinned, flexing his muscles while clenching his fists. "You man enough to take me on hand to hand?" He inclined his head toward Puma. "Winner goes free?"

Smoke removed belt and holsters, took a pair of padded black gloves out of his pants, and began to pull them on. "Puma, if this loudmouth beats me, take his left ear as a souvenir and let him go."

Puma grunted and spat on the ground. "How 'bout I take his topknot instead?"

"Wait a minute . . ." began Lightning Jack, until Puma jacked back the hammers on his shotgun, shutting his mouth for now.

Smoke stepped into the middle of a level area at the top of the plateau. He bowed slightly and said, "Let's dance!"

Lightning Jack worked his shoulders, loosening up. "Any rules?"

Smoke grinned, but his eyes held no warmth. "Yeah, the man left alive at the end is the winner."

"Just the way I like it. Say good-bye to your friend, mountain man."

The two men circled slowly, bobbing and weaving and

throwing an occasional feint to test their opponent's reflexes. Lightning Jack suddenly rushed at Smoke swinging roundhouse blows with both arms. Smoke ducked his chin into his chest, hunched his shoulders, and took two heavy blows on his arms. He grunted with pain, and thought, *This man can hit like a mule!* As Jack drew back to swing again, Smoke unloaded two short, sharp left jabs, both landing on Jack's nose, flattening it, snapping his head back hard enough so that Puma could hear his neck crack.

Jack shook his head, flinging blood and snot in the air, a dazed look on his face. Smoke stood, spread-eagled, his fists in front of him, waiting patiently.

After a pause Jack sleeved blood off his lip and felt his flattened nose. He glared at Smoke, hate in his eyes. Growling like an animal, he advanced toward the mountain man, pumping his arms while swinging his fists.

Smoke stepped lightly to one side and swung a left cross against Jack's chin, stopping him in his tracks. Smoke followed with a straight right to the middle of his chest, knocking him backward, rocking him back on his heels. Another left jab to the forehead to straighten him up, and then a mighty uppercut to his solar plexus, just under his sternum, lifted him up on his toes before he fell to one knee. Jack remained there a few moments, catching his breath.

He looked up at Smoke, blood pouring from his ruined nose. He grinned wickedly, then snatched a slender knife from his boot and rushed at Smoke with the blade extended.

Smoke took the blade in the outer part of his left shoulder, bent to his right, and swung with all his might. His fist hit Jack in the throat, crushing his larynx with a sharp, crunching sound. The knife slipped from Jack's numb fingers and he fell to his knees, grabbing his neck with both hands. A loud, whistling wheeze came from his mouth as he tried to pull air in through his broken trachea, and his eyes widened, bugging out like a frightened frog. His skin turned dusky blue, then black as he ran out of air. His eyes glazed over and he died, falling on his face in the dirt.

Smoke took the knife handle in his right hand, closed his eyes and set his jaw, and yanked it free with a jerk. He staggered at the pain, then straightened, a steely glint in his eye as blood seeped from the wound to stain his shirt.

Puma started toward him, but Smoke waved him away. "Not yet, Puma. We got one more snake to stomp 'fore we're through."

Sundance stuttered, "But I'm not much good with my fists. I ain't no prizefighter."

"You fancy yourself a gunfighter?"

"Yeah, and I'm a hell of a lot better'n I was last time you bushwhacked me, Jensen. I been practicing for years."

Smoke, his left arm hanging limp at his side, bent down and picked up belt and holsters. "Buckle this on for me, would you, Puma?"

Puma placed the guns around Smoke's waist and snapped the buckle shut, then tied the right-hand holster down low on his thigh. Smoke slipped the hammer-thongs off both guns, using his right hand, stepping over to the center of the plateau. "Give the lowlife his pistols, Puma, then watch your back. Sundance is famous for shooting people from the north when they're facing south."

Sundance put his hand on the handle of his Colt. "You're gonna die for that, Jensen."

The two men squared off, thirty yards apart, hands hanging loose, fingers flexing in anticipation. "You called this play, Sundance. Now it's time for you to pay the band. Fill your damn hand!"

Sundance snarled and grabbed for his pistol, crouching and turning slightly sideways to give Smoke less of a target. Smoke waited a second, giving the gunfighter time to get his gun halfway out of his holster. In a move that was so fast Puma blinked and missed it, Smoke cleared leather and fired. His bullet took Sundance in the right wrist, snapping it, flinging his Colt into the dirt.

Sundance howled, cradling his right hand with his left, hunched over, tears running down his cheeks. "Okay, you bastard. You win," he sobbed.

Smoke shook his head. "No, I don't think so. You've got another gun and another hand. Use 'em."

Sundance looked up in astonishment. "My left hand against your right? That ain't fair!"

Smoke shook his head, twirled his right-hand Colt once, and then settled it in his holster. "I'll cross-draw my left gun, if that's more to your liking."

Sundance's lips curled in a tight smile. The cross-draw wasn't a speed draw. No one could beat him with a cross-draw, even left-handed, he thought. "Okay. It's your call, Jensen."

He stood up, threw his shoulders back, and went for his iron.

Smoke's right hand flashed across his belly, drawing and firing again before Sundance could fist his weapon. This time, Smoke's slug took the outlaw in his left shoulder, shattering it while spinning him around to land facedown on the ground.

Smoke looked at Puma. "Bring me a rope from that bag over yonder."

He took the rope from Puma, formed a large loop, and passed it over Sundance's arms to tie it around his chest. He dragged the sobbing, sniffling gunman across the plateau to the edge of the cliff on the east side of the clearing.

"Help me lower him down onto that ledge down there, Puma."

"What . . . what are you doing? No . . . no . . . please . . ."

The two mountain men lowered the crying outlaw twenty feet down the side of the sheer cliff, letting him down gently on a three-foot ledge that stuck out over a drop of two hundred feet.

Smoke leaned over the edge and called down. "I'm gonna do something for you that you never did for your victims, Sundance. I'm gonna give you a choice of the way you want to die. You can lay there on that ledge and slowly starve to death, or you can jump and fall two hundred feet so you'll die quick. It's all up to you."

"Wait, you can't do this to me. It ain't right . . ."

Smoke and Puma slowly walked away, ignoring cries from the coward below. Neither one much cared how he chose to die, just so long as he died, and that was a certainty.

"You want me to fix up that there shoulder?" Puma Buck asked as they reached the horses.

"Naw," Smoke replied. "Just get me home to Sally. She's a lot more gentle than you are, you old grizzly."

Puma smiled. "Yeah, Lord knows we don't want nobody to treat you rough, Smoke Jensen."*

Tilghman shook his head. "Smoke, that makes my little fracas seem like a Sunday School outin'."

Smoke shrugged. "Bill, things were a lot different back then, and especially up in the High Lonesome. The only rules were there were *no* rules."

Vengeance of the Mountain Man

Thirty

When the train pulled into the station at Houston, Smoke's group exited and got their baggage from the baggage car.

"What now?" Tilghman asked. "Do we head for Galveston right away?"

Smoke glanced at Sally, who was stretching and trying to get the kinks out caused by two days on a rough-riding railroad car.

"If it's all the same to you, Marshal, I think we could all do with some good cooking and a night in a fine hotel," he said.

Sally grinned in relief. "Yes, please. One with a hot bath and a soft feather mattress."

Tilghman grinned. "I guess another day won't make much difference. I hear it's almost fifty miles to Galveston, and to tell you the truth, I don't hanker to spend another couple of days in a stagecoach right now."

They went to the biggest hotel they could find, one called the Capitol Hotel. The proprietor told them the beautiful building had once been the capitol building of Texas, until the government was moved to Austin.

"All I want to know," Sally said, "is do you have a bath with hot water?"

The desk clerk looked offended. "But of course,

madam. The Capitol has all the modern conveniences, as well as a first-rate dining room."

Pearlie's ears picked up at the mention of a dining room. "Forget about the bath, just show me where the grub is," he said with relish.

Sally gave him a stern look. "Pearlie, if you plan to eat with us, you *will* take a bath first. After all," she said, a look of mock earnestness on her face, "cleanliness is next to godliness."

"Yeah, but starvation isn't," Pearlie moaned, picking his bags up and trudging up the stairs while the others laughed at his woebegone expression.

The next morning, after all were well rested and well fed, Smoke hired a special stage just for them for the two-day journey to Galveston.

As they boarded the stage, the station master warned, "Y'all be careful now. There's been reports of Mexican *bandidos* stoppin' some of the coaches."

"I don't believe we have to worry about that," Smoke said with a grin. "We have the famous U.S. Deputy Marshal Bill Tilghman with us."

The stationmaster frowned and leaned over to spit tobacco juice in the dirt. "Yeah, well, I'm sure the *mexicanos* will be impressed when they shoot you full of holes."

As they bounced and rumbled over the trail from Houston toward Galveston, Sally noticed the sparkling gold badge Tilghman had pinned on his shirt under his vest.

"That's a very interesting badge you have there, Mr. Tilghman," she said. "It looks almost as if it's made of gold."

"It is," Tilghman answered shortly.

"Man," Monte observed, "I've gotta get me a job with the U.S. Marshals Service if they're givin' out badges made of gold now."

Tilghman laughed. "No, Monte. It didn't come with the job. Back when I was first appointed, a group of my friends had a blacksmith hammer this one out of two twenty-dollar gold pieces. It's a bit gaudy for my taste, but"—he shrugged—"what could I do? I didn't want to insult my friends."

"They must've really appreciated what you were doin' for them," Cal said from the seat opposite.

Tilghman shook his head. "Let me tell you something about law enforcement, Cal. The average citizen appreciates what you're doin' for him only so long as it doesn't inconvenience him in any way. But as soon as you tell him he can't walk his horse on a boardwalk or carry a gun inside the town limits, suddenly you're not so popular anymore."

Smoke was about to add he'd lost a lot of so-called good friends when they found out he was a gunfighter, but he was interrupted by the sound of distant shots and the driver yelling "Whoa" to the horses pulling the stage.

Pearlie leaned his head out the window, his hand holding his hat to keep it from blowing off. He ducked back inside, his hand going for the butt of his pistol.

"Uh-oh," he said, looking from man to man in the coach, "looks like trouble up ahead."

"What is it?" Smoke asked, unhooking the rawhide thongs on his twin Colts as the other men did the same.

"Looks like about ten or fifteen men on horseback in the middle of the road ahead, just sittin' there with rifle butts restin' on their thighs."

Sally pulled her purse around, opened it, and withdrew her short-barreled .32 Smith and Wesson. She arranged her frock coat to cover it as she stuck it in the waistband of her dress.

When the stage ground to a halt, the brake making a high-pitched squealing sound as it slowed the steel-rimmed wheels to a stop, everyone piled out of the stage, looking ahead at the group of men sitting on their horses in front of the team pulling the stage.

The driver already had his hands above his head.

"We ain't carryin' no gold," he called to the man at the front of the pack, the evident leader.

He was a broad-shouldered Mexican, squat bordering on fat, Mexican with crossed bandoliers of shotgun shells on his chest and a sawed-off Greener in his hands.

"Buenos dias, señores e señoritas," he said, pulling his large Mexican sombrero off and sweeping it before him in an elaborate bow. "I am El Gato," he added, then said in English, "That means mountain cat."

"We understand Mex," Tilghman said, his voice hard and unfriendly. "What do you want?"

"Why, nothing much, *señor.* My *compadres* and me," he said, sweeping his arms out to point at the men riding with him, "are poor *vaqueros,* who want nothing more than a few *pesos* to feed our hungry children."

As he spoke, Monte, Louis, Smoke, Cal, and Pearlie slowly edged sideways to be away from Sally so when the shooting started, as they all knew it would, she wouldn't be in the direct line of fire.

"You men will get nothing from us," Tilghman said, letting his hands move closer to his pistols.

"Aw, *señor,* that is most unfriendly," El Gato said, opening his mouth in a wide grin, exposing blackened stubs of teeth.

"Where are you from, mister?" Tilghman asked.

"Just across the border, *señor,* a place called Piedras Negras. Why do you ask?"

"I just wondered if they didn't have dentists where you come from," Tilghman said, trying to goad the man into action.

The smile faded from El Gato's face. "As I said," he went on, twisting in his saddle to look around at his men, "the *señor* is not being friendly."

"You've got five seconds to get out of the way an' let this stage proceed," Tilghman said, moving his vest so El Gato could see the golden badge. "I'm a U.S. marshal, an' I'm orderin' you out of the way."

El Gato's voice became harsh and he frowned as he leaned over the saddle horn. "You do not order El Gato," he growled. "Can you not see I have fifteen men to your six?"

"I know the odds aren't fair," Tilghman replied scornfully, "but we just don't have time for you to go an' get more men."

El Gato's eyes widened in amazement and he started to lower the barrel of his shotgun.

Smoke's group all drew at one time, with Louis's and Tilghman's pistols firing a split second after Smoke's, and Cal and Pearlie's a split second after theirs.

Smoke and Tilghman both aimed for El Gato, figuring without their leader, the other *bandidos* wouldn't be as brave. El Gato took two slugs before he could aim his shotgun, one in the forehead and the other in the belly. He grunted as his head snapped back and he somersaulted over his horse's rump to land face-down in the dirt of the road.

His men managed to get off two wild shots before the fusillade from Smoke's friends tore into them, knocking them off their horses like a hurricane wind whipping through the coastal plains grasses.

Horses snorted and crow-hopped at the tremendous explosion of all the guns. Men yelled and screamed in pain, and still the guns kept firing.

Sally, only a second slower than the men, had her .32 in her hand and knocked two of the bandits out of their saddles before they could clear leather.

Monte got three men, Cal two, and Pearlie three within seconds of beginning the dance. Smoke and Tilghman whirled to the side and accounted for the rest.

As the giant cloud of gunsmoke and cordite slowly drifted away on the Texas breeze coming in from the Gulf of Mexico, bodies could be seen lying sprawled all over the landscape, some still moving in pain or trying to crawl away on hands and knees, dripping blood to mix with the dirt and form a scarlet mud that reeked of death.

"Should we finish them off, Marshal?" Pearlie asked.

Tilghman shook his head. "No, just take their weapons and scatter their horses. If the coyotes and wolves don't finish them, the buzzards will."

The stagecoach driver coughed and choked, and finally leaned over the side of the stage and vomited several times.

"What's the matter?" Tilghman asked him, walking to the side of the coach. "You hit?"

When the purple-faced man could finally speak, he said, "Hell, no! When all the shootin' started, I plumb swallowed my chaw of tobaccy. Damn near killed me!"

Tilghman laughed and walked over to Smoke, who was making sure Sally was all right.

"Yes, dear," she said, making a face. "But I ripped my dress pulling out my Smith and Wesson, and I didn't pack my sewing kit."

Smoke shook his head and turned to watch Cal and Pearlie and Monte move among the wounded men, picking up their guns and shooing their horses away.

Louis walked up to Smoke and Tilghman and grimaced. "Damn," he said, a disgusted look on his face.

"What is it, Louis?" Smoke asked as Tilghman looked on.

"Now there are two men who are *almost* as fast on the draw as I am."

Smoke chuckled, glancing at Tilghman. "Do you think we should just let him go on in his delusion?"

Tilghman smiled. "Sure, why not? I've always said, it's not who's the fastest on the draw that counts, it's who puts his lead where it needs to go that counts most in a gunfight."

"By the way, Marshal," Smoke asked, "you mind telling me why you shot El Gato in the stomach instead of the chest or head?"

"We have a sayin' in the Marshals Service, Smoke. Two in the belly an' one in the head sure makes a man dead."

He grinned. "I was just startin' on the belly when you beat me to the draw an' put one in his head."

Smoke and Louis laughed.

"That's pretty good, Marshal," Louis said.

"And true too," Smoke added. "I've seen men take so much lead they'd sink if they tried to swim, and still manage to get off a few rounds before they died."

Tilghman nodded. "I made a deal with myself the day I went into bein' a lawman. If I ever have to shoot, I'm gonna shoot till the job gets done. It's the only way to survive."

"Amen," Monte said from behind him.

Thirty-one

The stagecoach pulled up at a large dock, bustling with activity. Across the bay, dim outlines of Galveston Island could be seen through sea mist hanging low over the warm salt water. There were wagons lined up for the ferry carrying all manner of agricultural goods, but most prevalent were the many bales of cotton, stacked one or two to a wagon.

"My goodness," Sally observed. "This place looks busier than Dallas."

The stage driver leaned to the side and spat his ever-present tobacco juice onto the salt grass alongside the road. "It is, ma'am. Up north, all they talk about is cattle, but down here, 'cept for the King Ranch, of course, cotton is king."

After waiting in line for some time, the stage was finally allowed on the ferry and they made the short trip across the bay without incident, though Pearlie refused to get out of the coach and walk around the ferry as the others did.

"If God'd wanted man near this much water," the cowboy said from his seat inside the stage, "He'd've made us with webbed feet like ducks."

Finally, they made their way to downtown Galveston, which was just a few blocks from the beachfront, and Sally was amazed to see large, fine homes comparable to any she'd seen on her travels to visit her family in New York City.

The group disembarked at the stage depot, where there was another group of people waiting to make the trip back to Houston, it being a common destination for the well-to-do to travel to for both business and pleasure.

Smoke paid off the driver, and they proceeded to the Galvez Hotel, which was on a bluff overlooking the breaking waves of the Gulf of Mexico and the pure white beaches of the island.

"Let's get some grub and make some plans on how to find Gomez and Gatling," Smoke suggested.

"That sounds good to me," Pearlie piped up from the rear of the group.

Cal looked at him. "The mention of food always sounds good to you, Pearlie," he observed drily.

Down on the waterfront, Three-Fingers Gomez and Curly Bob Gatling, just awaking from a night of revelry in the red-light district of Galveston, gathered for breakfast at a small diner frequented by seamen.

The Albatross was a small, single-roomed shack made of what looked like driftwood and old lumber washed up on shore during storms, and was just up the beach above the high-water line of seaweed, set back in the sand dunes.

Its main attraction wasn't the cuisine, which was plain but adequate. It was the wide selection of liquors and beers that were served at all hours, breakfast being no exception.

As the two men leaned over their food in the dimly lit diner, Three-Fingers Gomez said, "When did they say that ship would be sailin'?"

"Tomorrow," Curly Bob Gatling answered as he shoveled runny scrambled eggs into his mouth, washing them down with coffee so black and strong he could almost chew it.

"Damn," Gomez said, glancing out the window at the many ships moored in Galveston Harbor. "With all them boats out there, you'd think they'd have some goin' our way 'fore then."

Gatling shrugged as he held up his cup to show the waiter he wanted a refill. "They do, but most of 'em are freighters, an' they don't carry but a couple'a passengers each. I got us in line to get the first places available."

When Gomez grunted gloomily and began to eat his food, Gatling asked, "Why are you so jumpy? Why not just sit back and enjoy the nightlife here? Hell, they got more good-lookin' women here than I ever seen before, an' we finally got some spendin' money in our pockets from sellin' those beeves."

"It's just that I got this here itch on the back of my neck, like somebody's on our back trail. I can't enjoy myself for lookin' back over my shoulder to see who might be there."

Gatling leaned back and lit a cigarette, blowing the smoke toward the ceiling, where it mingled with clouds of smoke from the other patrons in the place.

"One thing I've learned after all my years ridin' the owlhoot trail, podna, is that you can't think about what may be behind you. If you do, you soon go crazy in the head."

Gomez shook his head. "How do you stop?"

"You got to live one day at a time. . . . You got to figure you're gonna take a dirt nap soon enough, so worryin' about it don't do no good. When it happens, it happens."

Gomez finished his eggs and coffee and pushed the plate away from him on the table.

"That's easy for you to say, Curly Bob, but you didn't

put that bullet in the Kid, an' you don't have that Jensen feller on your trail."

"What do you mean by that?" Gatling asked hotly. "We're partners, ain't we? If they after you, that means they after me too. When it comes right down to it, if Jensen's still alive, which I doubt, he ain't gonna just come up to us an' say, 'Which one of you shot the Kid?' " He shook his head. "Nope. He's gonna just show up an' start blazin' away with those big Colts of his, so I got as much to lose as you, Three-Fingers."

Gomez glanced across the table and smiled. "I know, Curly Bob. You are a good friend, and I know I can count on you if push comes to shove."

"That's right!" Gatling said, nodding his head and grinning. "Now, we got twenty-four hours till we set sail for the East Coast, so let's see how many women we can bag, an' how much whiskey we can drink, between now and then."

After settling in at the Galvez and cleaning up from their dusty journey from Houston, the group met at the Galvez restaurant, where they dined on red snapper, speckled trout, fresh blue crabs, and oysters on the half-shell, along with fried potatoes, cole slaw, and corn bread.

Pearlie eyed the oysters skeptically. "I don't know 'bout eatin' those things," he drawled from the end of the long table in the dining room.

He picked up an oyster shell and held it under his nose, sniffing.

"Don't smell it, Pearlie," Sally said, "eat it." She took a shell in her hand, poured some red sauce on it, and tipped it up, letting it slide down her throat in one gulp.

Pearlie watched her through narrowed eyes. "What's it taste like?" he asked.

"Delicious," Sally said, a pleased expression on her face. "I haven't had food this good since New York."

Pearlie was thinking, but had the manners not to say, that he wasn't sure he wanted to eat food that looked like something he'd hawked up from the back of his throat.

"They say," Louis Longmont said as he tipped a shell and swallowed the shellfish, "that oysters are good for your nature."

"Nature?" Pearlie asked. "They ain't nothin' wrong with my nature."

"What's nature?" Cal asked innocently, his eyebrows raised.

As the men at the table laughed, and Sally blushed, Monte said, "It's something somebody your age don't have to worry none about, Cal."

"How about you, Monte?" Louis asked. "Are you going to partake of one of the sea's best delicacies?"

Monte shook his head. "No, Louis. My nature don't need no stirrin' up, not with Mary a thousand miles away." He smiled. "Though I might see if I can take some back to Big Rock with me."

As Smoke wolfed down a quick half-dozen of the oysters, Sally glanced at him and leaned over to whisper in his ear, "Go easy on those, big fellow. You don't need any help with your nature either. It's fine just as it is."

After they finished the meal, Sally went to browse the shops along the waterfront next to the hotel, and the men went to the shipping offices at the Port Authority.

While Tilghman and Smoke went in to talk to the clerk, Monte and Louis and Cal and Pearlie strolled along the beach, picking up shells and enjoying the balmy day.

A half hour later, Smoke and Tilghman emerged, smiles on their faces.

"What did you find out?" Louis asked.

"Yeah," Monte said. "We asked around out here an'

word is there's more'n a hundred bars and saloons and houses of ill repute along the wharf. Ain't no way we're gonna find two men among all those, not unless we get awful lucky."

"We got lucky," Tilghman said. "The clerk in there went through the records for us an' found a Juan Gomez an' Robert Gatling scheduled to sail out on the *Sea Sprite* tomorrow morning to Georgia."

"I can't believe they're still here," Pearlie said. "They had a two- or three-day start on us."

"There again, we got lucky," Smoke said. "The clerk told us the ships were backed up and running late due to some storms in the Gulf. There hasn't been a ship out of here for the past four days, or they'd probably be long gone."

"So what's the plan?" Monte asked.

Smoke shrugged. "I'm going to relax and spend the day with Sally, shopping and seeing the sights. It isn't often we get to make a trip like this together. Then tomorrow, at dawn, Marshal Tilghman and I are going to get on the ship early and be waiting for the two killers when they board."

"What about us?" Cal asked, a disappointed look on his face.

"You'll be our backup," Marshal Tilghman said. "You'll cover the roads to the ferry and the area around the ships' loading docks, just in case they decide to leave Galveston instead of boarding the ship, or in case they get by us."

Louis nodded and cracked his knuckles, stretching his fingers. "Well, while you play dutiful husband, Smoke, I'm going to check out the various gaming establishments along the shore here and see if Texicans can play poker any better than the men in Colorado."

Pearlie smiled. "You mind if Cal an' I tag along, Louis?

I want to try out what you taught us on the train, see if'n I can win some money."

Louis laughed. "Not at all, Pearlie. How about you, Monte?"

Monte shrugged. "Sure, why not? Beats hanging around the hotel missin' my wife."

Smoke nodded and left, going to look for Sally. He wanted to see if the oysters really *did* make a difference.

The next morning Smoke and Tilghman, followed by Louis, Monte, Cal, and Pearlie, walked through a fog so thick you could cut it with a knife. The sun wasn't quite up, but the eastern clouds were beginning to turn a brilliant orange and red and yellow on the horizon.

When they got to the dock where the *Sea Sprite* was moored, Tilghman stationed the other men around the area as a precaution, and he and Smoke walked up the gangplank.

A burly sailor, his massive arms covered with tattoos, started to stop them, but backed off when Tilghman pulled his vest back and showed him his gold badge.

They went to the quartermaster and asked him which cabin was assigned to Gomez and Gatling.

"Number three," he said, and led them down a long, dark, dank corridor to the room, which he opened for them.

The cabin was incredibly small, and both Tilghman and Smoke had to duck their heads, not being able to stand erect in the tiny enclosure.

"We can't wait for 'em here," Tilghman said. "No room to maneuver in case they resist."

"You're right," Smoke said. "Let's get settled up on deck. We can brace them there when they come aboard."

They searched the upper deck until they found the right

place to hide, just behind the opening to the belowdecks area. It was a small, raised wooden structure that would keep them concealed until the two men were well on board. Then they could step out and arrest them.

Smoke and Tilghman settled down, sitting on coils of rope as thick as Smoke's arm, and smoked and talked of Western things until it was almost eight o'clock.

Tilghman peeked over the wooden structure, and could see several people making their way toward the ship. "Time to get ready."

Smoke smiled. "Strike up the band?" he asked.

Tilghman grinned back. "Start the dance," he added.

Three-Fingers Gomez and Curly Bob Gatling strolled up the gangplank. Gomez was smiling and whistling, and Gatling laughed. "See, partner?" Gatling said, nudging Gomez with his elbow. "I told you we didn't have nothin' to worry about. Jensen's dead, an' we're on our way to Georgia."

Smoke and Bill Tilghman stepped out from behind the entranceway to the cabins, their hands hanging next to their pistol butts.

"The reports of my death have been greatly exaggerated," Smoke drawled, a grim smile on his face.

"Goddamn!" Gatling exclaimed, stopping dead in his tracks and dropping the duffel bag he had slung over his shoulder.

He glanced at Gomez, who shook his head.

"I knew it," he said morosely. "I told you I felt someone on our trail."

"Juan Gomez and Robert Gatling," Tilghman said in a formal tone of voice, "I'm a U.S. deputy marshal and I arrest you for the murder of Jim Slade, known as the Durango Kid."

Gatling held out his hands. "I didn't have nothin' to do with the Kid's murder," he said, a whining note in his voice.

"But you *did* conspire to have Smoke Jensen murdered by paying some *vaqueros* to kill him, didn't you?" Tilghman asked.

"Shit!" Gatling said.

"I think you boys have a date with George Maledon," Tilghman said grimly.

"Who's this Maledon feller?" Gomez asked. "I don't know no Maledon."

"He's known as the prince of hangmen," Tilghman said. "He is the chief executioner for Judge Isaac Parker, the man who's gonna judge you boys."

Gomez began backing away, his hands near his pistol. "I ain't gonna get my neck stretched for killin' a snake like the Durango Kid. It ain't fair," he said, sweat breaking out on his forehead.

"It ain't fair to be shot in the back either," Smoke said, "but the Kid didn't have any choice in the matter, and neither do you, Gomez."

"Yes, I do!" Gomez said, going for his gun.

Gatling did the same, crouching and slapping at his holster.

Smoke and Tilghman drew in the same instant, guns coming up and firing almost simultaneously, twin explosions that shattered the peaceful morning and caused seagulls to wheel away from the ship, keening and screeching in fear.

Gomez flung his arms backward, his pistol still in its holster, as the molten lead from Smoke's Colt punched a hole in his chest and exploded his heart. He whirled around and fell facedown on the deck of the ship, smashing his nose and breaking three of his front teeth. . . . But he felt no pain. He was dead before he hit the deck.

Tilghman's slug took Gatling in the gut, his gun also still in its holster, and doubled him over, so that Tilghman's next shot entered the top of his head and drove him to his knees. He stayed in the bent-over position for a few seconds, as if giving up a prayer for his sins, before he toppled over to sprawl on the deck, leaking blood and brains over the hardwood planks.

Smoke took a deep breath and sighed as he put his Colt back in its holster.

Tilghman just let his hand drop to his side, shaking his head at the waste of human life he'd seen.

Tilghman turned his head and stared at Smoke. "I'd always heard you were fast enough to snatch a quarter off a snake's head and leave change 'fore he could strike. I guess I heard right."

Smoke laughed. "I think you beat me by a split second, Marshal."

Tilghman shook his head. "No way, Smoke. It was a dead heat."

"Remind me never to draw against you, Bill," Smoke said.

"Don't worry, mountain man, I will!"

Thirty-two

Smoke and everyone said their good-byes to Marshal Bill Tilghman at the ferry on the mainland side of the Bay of Galveston. He was heading back north to Arkansas to file his report on the murder of the Durango Kid, while Smoke and his friends were heading south to Corpus Christi and the King Ranch.

Smoke stuck out his hand. "Marshal, it's been a pleasure knowing you."

Tilghman took his hand and shook it. "Same here, Smoke. I'll be sure and clear your name with Judge Parker an' let him know it was all a mistake."

"So, I don't need to stop by there on my way back to Colorado?"

Tilghman smiled and glanced at Sally. "No, I don't think so. Besides, from what I hear, the judge would just as soon not have to face Mrs. Jensen again. It seems she made quite an impression on him at their last meetin'."

Smoke raised his eyebrows. "Oh, is that so?"

"Yeah," Tilghman said, laughing. "He said something about how he'd rather face a mad dog than another woman like her takin' up for her man in his court."

Smoke smiled at Sally. "She does have a rather . . . forceful way about her when her dander's up," he said.

"I resent that," Sally said, her face reddening. "I just

told him the truth, that Smoke Jensen would never shoot anyone in the back."

"Oh, it's not what you said, Miss Sally," Tilghman said, "it's how you said it. You see, the judge, he kind'a feels like he's the king of his courtroom, an' he's not used to someone gettin' in his face like you did. It upsets his equilibrium somehow."

"Well," Sally said, standing up straight, "the only king in my world is Smoke, and the judge will just have to accept that fact."

Smoke and his group of friends spent an enjoyable week at the King Ranch near Corpus Christi. Sally was much impressed by the modern way Richard King and his foreman used new scientific methods to improve the breed of cattle known as Santa Gertrudis. She hounded the poor foreman for several days, inquiring about bloodlines and breeding methods and feed and the amount of meat they could expect from their shorthorn crosses with the Gertrudis bulls, until by the time they'd taken the bulls to the train yards for shipment to Colorado, he was glad to see her go.

While Sally was inquiring into the breeding and care of the new breed, Richard King took Smoke, Cal, Pearlie, Monte, and Louis hunting on his thousands of acres of prime land.

Smoke, after killing a Texas mule deer, allowed as how he'd never seen a deer so big.

Pearlie and Cal were more impressed by the number of quail and doves they killed. Especially Pearlie, who said he'd never tasted anything so good as quail barbecued over a mesquite fire.

"So, you like them better than the oysters?" Louis

asked as he gnawed meat off one of the small birds next to the campfire.

King glanced at Pearlie. "You didn't care for our oysters?"

Pearlie shook his head. "Not enough so's you could tell," he answered.

"That's the first thing I ever saw ole' Pearlie wouldn't eat," Cal said.

"I done tole you, ain't nothin' wrong with my nature," Pearlie said defensively.

King laughed. "Well, out here on the ranch, we have another kind of oyster you might like better."

Pearlie gave him a funny look. "If you're talkin' 'bout mountain oysters, we got those up in Colorado too, an' they're not too high on my list of things I like to eat either."

Smoke looked at him. "But, Pearlie, you always said you liked the stew that Puma Buck made for us when we stayed up in the High Lonesome with him that winter."

Pearlie turned his head to stare at Smoke. "You don't mean . . ."

"Yep," Smoke said. "One of the prime ingredients was deer testicles, or mountain oysters as you call it. Where do you think they got the name?"

Pearlie made a face and got up from the campfire. "Excuse me, gentlemen," he said. "I think I'll go wash out my mouth."

As the men all laughed, Cal said, "Pass me another one of them quail quick, 'fore Pearlie comes back an' eats 'em all up."

Thirty-three

Back at the Sugarloaf, Smoke and Sally leaned on a fence, watching the Santa Gertrudis bulls as they discovered the delights of Smoke's shorthorn cows in a large pasture out behind their cabin.

Sally smiled. "Well, I can see the Santa Gertrudis bulls seem to take to our shorthorn cows just as well as the ones back on their home range."

"Sally," Smoke said, "bulls are just like men. They don't much care who the filly is when they get in the mood, just as long as she's ready and willing."

Sally cut her eyes at Smoke, giving him a look. "Are you speaking from experience, Mr. Jensen, sir?"

"Uh . . ." Smoke stuttered, knowing he'd made a tactical mistake of major proportions.

"Go on, answer me," Sally said, turning to stare at him with her hands on her hips.

"Uh . . . why, no, Sally," he answered weakly. "Just commenting on most men . . . in general, I mean. Of course, I only have eyes for you, dear."

She nodded, not smiling. "Uh-huh."

"By the way," Smoke said, taking her by the arm and leading her toward their cabin, "I want to talk to you about those oysters we had. They had the strangest effect on me."

She smiled up at him, putting her arm around his waist and her head on his shoulder. "I noticed, dear. I noticed."

William W. Johnstone
The *Mountain Man* Series